It's the vampire weddii empire.

PALADIN'S KISS

Invited to the marriage ceremony of two old friends, Carwyn ap Bryn and Brigid Connor venture south, ready to relax in the company of Marie-Hélène Charmont, the vampire queen of the Delta, and four hundred of her esteemed immortal guests.

The upper echelons of vampire society have gathered in New Orleans, curious to witness the joining of Gavin Wallace, the immortal business mogul, to the human woman who captured his heart.

But when Gavin asks Brigid and Carwyn to look into a mysterious man stalking his human employees, they're unprepared for the tangled web of deception they uncover. Tug on the wrong string and centuries-old alliances might fall apart.

In a tenuously balanced society full of apex predators; even one slip can prove disastrous.

Paladin's Kiss is a supernatural mystery in the Elemental Covenant series by Elizabeth Hunter, nine-time USA Today bestselling author of *A Hidden Fire*, the *Irin Chronicles*, and over forty other works of fantasy fiction.

I think this one was my favorite of Carwyn and Brigid's adventures. A definite must-read for fans of Hunter's elemental world stories. I'm really looking forward to the next one next summer!

This book is an absolute mind-shock, and it's going to leave the readers completely stunned!

PALADIN'S KISS

AN ELEMENTAL COVENANT NOVEL

ELIZABETH HUNTER

Paladin's Kiss
Copyright © 2022
Elizabeth Hunter
ISBN: 978-1-941674-97-0

Cover: Damonza
Content Editor: Amy Cissell, Cissell Ink
Beta reader: Bee M. Whelan
Line Editor: Anne Victory, Victory Editing
Proofreader: Linda, Victory Editing

Recurve Press LLC
PO Box 4034
Visalia, California 93278
USA

ONE

Brigid saw the flashing blue lights in the side mirror, and her fangs dropped. She turned to her husband, who was driving the van. "I told ya it was a speed trap."

Carwyn glanced to the side, then at the rearview mirror. "I was barely over the limit." He pulled over onto the rough gravel shoulder. "I'll do the talking, wife. You have a habit of rankling law enforcement."

Brigid glanced at the three unconscious humans in the back of their converted Volkswagen van. "Can't imagine why."

The back of her throat burned when she smelled the humans behind their vehicle. The men passed out behind her stank of alcohol, methamphetamines, and sour sweat. It was easy to ignore their scent, but the officers behind them?

They smelled like dinner.

"He's sitting on the hood of his car," Carwyn muttered. "No respect for the schedule of others."

"It's a tactic to make us nervous." Brigid narrowed her eyes as she watched her side mirror. "They definitely think we're carrying drugs. Second one out of the car."

"A camper van with California plates driving through rural

Louisiana in the middle of the night?" Carwyn smiled as the man who'd been perched on the hood of the cruiser started to walk toward them. "I can't imagine why they'd think drugs were an issue."

She cranked down the van window and saw the outline of a second officer eyeing her window with interest in the flashing lights from the other side of the police cruiser.

"Tá dhá cheann acu." *There are two of them.* She spoke in Irish, unwilling to give any information to the humans. "Second one is staying back."

Carwyn glanced in the mirror. "Noted."

"Má chuardaíonn said an carr..." *If they search the car...*

"They won't." He was wearing a black button-down shirt dotted with bloodstains. He carefully buttoned it up to the neck.

Brigid frowned. "What are you doing?"

He quickly folded a receipt and stuck it in a cup holder, then fiddled with his collar. "Keeping us from having to incapacitate any more humans tonight."

She rolled her eyes and sat back, her eyes continuing to flick to the side mirror where it looked like the second officer had lit a cigarette.

Gimme.

Brigid stared at the glowing tip of the cigarette, the fire that lived under her skin pricking her to act; she pushed it back with practiced resolve.

Not tonight. Not here.

The human officer approached Carwyn's window, and the scent of his blood made Brigid's mouth water. She needed to feed, and not the blood in the drug-laced veins of the humans in the back of the van. This one smelled like he believed in clean living, mother's cooking, and wild game.

Delicious.

The police officer finally sauntered to the window. He was a human in his early forties if Brigid was guessing correctly. He looked tired and a little worn-out.

Putting in the hours. Brigid recognized the expression. Punching the clock. This officer was sick of night shifts and bored to tears.

He cleared his throat and spoke in a broad Southern accent. "Evening, sir. Do you happen to know how fast you were going?"

It was as if her husband turned into a pile of friendly Jell-O instead of the mountain of muscle he was. "Oh, I'm so sorry, Officer!" The Welsh vampire laid on a thick Irish accent.

Brigid snorted and covered her mouth, turning it into a cough.

Carwyn continued, "I do believe I was going eighty kilometers an hour, was I not?"

The officer frowned. "'Scuse me? Where y'all from?"

"Oh shur, we're from a humble Catholic mission in Ireland. I'm Father Cormac, and this is Sister Mary Clarence from the Sisterhood of the First Miracle in Kerry." He motioned toward her. "Sister Mary Clarence, wave hello to the nice Garda." Carwyn turned back to the officer. "She can't speak, sir, as she's recently taken a vow of *complete silence.*"

Jesus, Mary, Joseph, and the wee donkey, she was going to kill him when this was over. Brigid leaned forward and waved.

The human frowned. "From... Did you say Ireland?"

"We're borrowing a vehicle from the parish in Los *Angeleez,* where we flew in from our last mission in..." He glanced at Brigid.

She smiled and pointed to her mouth.

"Fiji," Carwyn blurted. "We were on a mission to Fiji."

The police officer was already turned in circles from the accent. "I... I don't know where that is."

"Beautiful place." Carwyn nodded solemnly, his accent

growing broader by the moment. "A beautiful part of the Lord's creation and full of heathen... cats."

She snorted again and covered it with another cough.

"Cats?" the officer asked.

"Yes, that's where we work, you see. In animal evangelism." A beatific smile spread over his face. "Working among the world's most vulnerable creatures to show the love of God to the voiceless." He nodded toward Brigid. "That's why my dear sister doesn't speak."

"Because of the cats?"

"Exactly. You don't eat the flesh of God's created animals, do you, young man? Ours is a strictly vegetarian mission."

The officer rallied. "Sir, can I see your driver's license? You were speeding."

"Was I? Surely not." Carwyn fumbled for his wallet. "The sign said fifty-five miles an hour there, and that's nearly ninety kilometers and I was doing only eighty."

The officer frowned. "Right. You were doing eighty in a fifty-five."

"But eighty is below ninety, so I don't see how I could be speeding."

Brigid could see the police officer doing the math in his head.

"I don't... I'm not sure what you're used to—"

"I'm a law-abiding man, sir. A servant of God and the church."

Brigid's skin prickled when one of the humans in the back shifted his arm. The windows might be curtained, but all the officer would have to do was look back and the three bloody and crumpled men would be visible.

Carwyn said, "We're trying to reach our new mission in New Orleans, you see. There's a pack of feral dogs roaming the city that needs to know the Lord. Are you a Christian man, Officer?"

The man stammered. "Of course I am. I mean... I guess it's been a while—"

"Perhaps the Lord brought you to me and my dear Sister Mary Clarence tonight. Do you need to unburden your heart? Perhaps call your mother or grandmother? I have a mobile phone here and we can do that. Can I pray for you, Officer...? I'm sorry, what is your name, sir? We could say a prayer right now. Together."

"Okay, just slow down." The police officer let out a nervous laugh and patted the side of the vehicle. "There's your... blessing. Okay?" He stepped away. "Y'all keep it below fifty-five, you'll make it to New Orleans nice and safe. Take the warning; keep it slow."

Go. Just go now. Brigid braced for another round of blarney from her mate. Carwyn had a tendency to push a bit too far, which often caused more problems than it solved.

"Oh bless you, young man." Carwyn made his voice creak just a little even though the officer looked older than the vampire did. "Bless you and your cats, sir."

"Right. Y'all have a good night and keep it slow."

Carwyn started the van and pulled onto the road, leaving the still-flashing blue lights in the distance behind them.

"Can we turn back to the interstate now?" Brigid asked.

"As soon as we drop off our young friends here." Carwyn glanced across to her. "I see that you've chosen to break your vow of silence."

"Mary Clarence? We're making *Sister Act* jokes to the humans now?"

"Sister Mary Clarence had the voice of an angel; it was a compliment."

"Evangelizing feral cats in Fiji," she muttered. "I can't believe that worked."

"It wasn't the feral cats, darling girl. I threatened to call his

5

mother and pray with him. I could see the Catholic guilt radiating from him as soon as I called myself Father Cormac."

"Never underestimate Catholic guilt." She saw a sign flash by. "Take the next right." She glanced at the human who'd moved before. "They're starting to wake up."

———

ALL VAMPIRES HAD an element given to them by their amnis, the immortal energy that lived within them like a current beneath their skin. Her husband was animated by the earth, the foundation of his energy, his immortality, and his massive strength. He stood over six feet with shoulders the size of a minor mountain range, a shock of dark red hair on his head, and a short beard he'd been growing for over a year.

So it came as no surprise to her that in addition to the handcuffs she'd used to secure the men to the railing, Carwyn had also buried them up to their waists in front of the sheriff's substation in Lafayette Parish.

They were definitely not wiggling out of that restraint.

The men all had signs around their necks that advertised their crimes. One read: ASK ME ABOUT THE STOLEN PROPERTY IN MY GARAGE! Another read: I STOLE THE BENSONS' CAR AND BEAT UP AN OLD MAN. And the last one had a sign that read: I DEAL DRUGS TO HIGH SCHOOL STUDENTS.

Carwyn clapped his hands together. "And that's what happens when you try to carjack a couple of vampires."

Brigid saw the moment the humans began to wake.

They were bruised and had to be aching, but she didn't have any sympathy. They'd attempted to disarm her husband with friendly banter and a false welcome at their local pub before sticking a gun to his back in the hallway, forcing him to their van, and trying to rob him.

"Hello, boys." Brigid crouched down in front of the three men. "Remember what happened?"

What happened had been Brigid. The men didn't know that she'd followed them out and saw them pull the firearm. Unlike most vampires, Brigid knew what kind of damage a gun could cause to their kind if used in the right way.

No gun was going to end a vampire's life unless it completely severed their spine at the base of their neck, but a bullet wound anywhere along their nervous system could be catastrophic, if not life-threatening. As best as Brigid could figure, amnis worked with the nervous system, so any major damage to the spine or a primary nerve could produce severe consequences.

She looked at the men. "You put a gun to my husband; that wasn't wise."

The ringleader of the group blinked slowly. "You have fangs."

"I do, but don't flatter yourself. I'd sooner drink from a sewer than your neck. I understand addiction—heroine was my candy —but that doesn't excuse the violence. Get help before you end up dead." She stuffed the number of a local rehab place in the pocket of one of the men. "You don't want to meet me again."

He was still staring. "You have fangs."

"Jaysus." She stood and sighed. "What else should we do? Just leave them here?"

Carwyn was squinting at the darkness. "I think that's our only option. Do you think the alligators leave the bayou and go roaming?"

"Carwyn, if I have to deal with you chasing any more wildlife—"

"They wouldn't come and take a bite out of one of these two, would they?"

Brigid started to protest the men were fine, but she had to admit Carwyn might have a point. She crouched down in front of another of the men. "Wake up." She patted his cheek, giving him a slight shock from her amnis when he was slow to rouse.

"Fuck." The man jerked awake. "Where the hell am I?"

"How far can an alligator travel from water?" Brigid asked. "We're not from around here, so I don't know."

The man looked around himself in a panic. "George? Buddy?"

"Answer the question." She patted his cheek. "Alligators. Are you in danger from them if we leave you here?"

The man they called Buddy appeared to still be sleeping, but he spoke slowly and in an accent that Brigid barely understood.

"Yeah, gators gonna be a problem all right," he muttered quietly.

Did she care?

Not really, but Carwyn might.

Brigid stood and walked back to the van. "He said the alligators wouldn't be a problem."

Her husband frowned. "Are you sure?"

"Very sure. Come on now; we need to get to New Orleans before sunrise." She walked quickly to the van.

Carwyn started to follow her. "We'll call and report them from the highway."

"Excellent idea." That should get the men arrested before the creatures ate them.

The last thing Brigid needed was another black mark against her soul. She might be immortal, but eventually she'd be judged.

And if it wasn't Saint Peter, she'd have to face Carwyn.

They were heading back toward the highway within minutes, and Brigid sighed in relief. No more local police officers. No more shady characters at darkened petrol stations. They were back in the world of the American interstate system, replete with garish neon signs, brightly lit parking lots the size of football fields, and plastic-packaged food that smelled of chemicals.

"I need to feed." She'd been half hoping the police officer wouldn't fall for Carwyn's friendly-Irish-priest bit and would cause them problems.

No.

He hadn't agreed to be her dinner.

"We'll be at a safe club in two and a half hours. Can you make it that long?"

She cracked open a bottle of blood-wine and drank. "This should keep me from any road rage incidents."

"Good, but crawl in back to drink that unless you want another encounter with law enforcement."

"Fine." She crawled in the back of the van and kicked her feet up on the bench. "Onward then."

"To the wedding!" Carwyn grinned as he took the on-ramp.

"To the wedding." Brigid took an extra gulp of blood-wine.

To the wedding.

The *wedding.*

On second thought, maybe she should have stayed behind with the alligators.

TWO

"Welcome to Revel." The slow slide of a steel guitar was audible from behind the velvet curtain the hostess drew back, and the press of heat and humanity surged toward Carwyn as he ushered his mate into the vampire club.

There were gold and red lanterns hanging from the ceiling and deep purple velvet lining the walls. The whole place had an air of burlesque, and the DJ was a woman wearing feathers and lace. It was a twenty-first-century bacchanal; the aura of vampire amnis was everywhere.

He felt Brigid vibrating next to him and knew her bloodlust was surging. "Easy, darling girl." He scanned the club and immediately noted the discreet red earrings that approximately half the servers wore. "Donors spotted."

"Rooms?" The touch of her palm on his sparked.

Oh, she was uncomfortably close. He'd be speaking to her about leaving for road trips without a set feeding plan for dry areas.

"I see them; follow me." Carwyn linked their hands, tucked Brigid behind his left shoulder, and strode through the crowd, letting his millennia-old amnis announce his presence. Humans and vampires alike stepped back, suddenly aware of the massive creature among them. Carwyn kept his guard up what with his mate teetering on the edge of violence behind him.

He nodded at the vampire hostess guarding a curtained hallway on the far side of the club next to the stairs to the VIP room. "Carwyn ap Bryn and Brigid Connor, guests of Gavin Wallace. Need a room and a donor."

Brigid was pressed against his back, and he could feel the heat of her fingers curled into his abdomen. She wasn't speaking anymore, but he could feel her focus pushed entirely inward. Without blood, she'd explode within the hour, the fire that lived in her body bursting out and engulfing any human or vampire in her vicinity.

The vampire took one glance at Brigid and raised a perfectly arched eyebrow. "I see. Male or female?"

"Don't care, but pick someone who likes a hard bite if you catch my meaning." Carwyn winked at her, and the corner of the woman's lip curved.

"We have a few of those." She drew the curtain back. "Room 3. Welcome to Revel, Carwyn ap Bryn and Brigid Connor. I am Minerva. You are under the aegis of Gavin Wallace until you leave the premises; accorded to you are all the rights and responsibilities of his aegis. Do you understand?"

"I understand." It was the standard disclaimer for feeding at Gavin's clubs. "The donor if you please. Thank you, Minerva."

The hostess nodded and slipped into the crowd as Carwyn walked past the curtain and into a hallway where sound sank into the walls and the only thing to be heard was his mate's low growl.

He opened the second door on the left and walked inside. The light was dimmed for vampire eyes. Music from the club was pumped into the room with invisible speakers, but the volume was set low for preternatural hearing.

Carwyn kept the door cracked open and gently drew Brigid from behind him. "Darling girl, you need to drink from me. Just a little."

"I already—"

"Had a bit to keep you from tearing the heads off those three thieves. Yes, but now you're going to get a nice fresh human, and I don't want you tearing their throat out." He rolled his right sleeve up. "Come now, are you going to deny your man? All I'm asking for is a bit of— *Fuck*." He grunted when her fangs hit.

Carwyn hadn't even seen her move, but Brigid was clamped onto his wrist, and her fangs were deep in his flesh. She pulled hard, and he was doubly glad he'd made her take a nip from him before the human came; otherwise, he'd be explaining to Gavin why his voluntary donor wasn't volunteering anymore.

A few minutes later, she pulled away, her lips glossy red from his blood and her color a little better. "Sorry."

"We'll talk about it later." He led her to the low couch that wrapped around the room just as a discreet knock came at the door. Carwyn walked toward the door and opened it to find a young man in his early twenties who was only a little smaller than Carwyn.

"Excellent." Carwyn clamped his hand on the young man's shoulder. "Sturdy. You'll do."

The man smiled. "I'm Jordan. Are you my client tonight?"

"No indeed." Carwyn opened the door wider and let the young man in the room. "My lovely wife, Brigid."

Brigid was still twitchy and there was a smear of red on her lip from Carwyn's arm. Her eyes stalked Jordan as he approached the couch. She looked like a tiny, angry fae creature with black-lined eyes, bloody lips, and a ragged pixie cut who would kill you for crossing her garden gate.

Jordan turned to Carwyn when he caught the look in her eye. "You're... going to—?"

"Stay? Absolutely." He sat on Brigid's right as Jordan sat to her left. "Normally she'd prefer the wrist but— Oh, there you are."

Brigid had pulled the man's head down, her mouth hovering over his neck. Still she waited, drawing ragged breaths against his skin.

Jordan must be an experienced donor because he was completely calm. "Go ahead, Brigid." The young man caught Carwyn's eye. "So are you in New Orleans to visit or—? Hot damn, she's real hungry, isn't she?"

Brigid struck hard, her fangs sinking into the human's neck. The pain was brief, but from the flush on Jordan's lips, not unwelcome. Then Brigid's manners took over, she flooded his skin with amnis, and a dreamy, floating expression overtook the human's face.

Carwyn kicked his feet up on the tufted ottoman and threw his left arm around Brigid, keeping his hand around her neck, his thumb stroking up and down her nape. Normally his wife was the epitome of control. As a fire vampire, she had to be.

The amnis that rooted him to the earth, to creation and humanity, had lashed her to the burning, clawing element of fire, which meant the same energy that had given her eternity could destroy her if she ever lost control.

He murmured to her in Irish as she drank, silly endearments and sweet stories. He could feel the donor's inevitable arousal from Brigid's bite; it was a common by-product of amnis, and Carwyn tamped down his territorial instincts.

He could sense the turn, sense when her amnis was satisfied. "Brigid."

She pulled away, blood still shining on her lips as the red gashes in the donor's neck began to close.

Good. She hadn't been too far gone to seal the wounds properly.

Jordan was splayed on the couch, his erection evident in his trousers. He turned to Brigid. "I don't suppose you want to—"

"Fuck off." Her voice was raspy. "Sorry. Go find another partner, I mean." Her eyes turned to Carwyn, and he could see her desire.

For him. Only for him.

"Right." Jordan stood and adjusted his pants. "Room's yours of course. Blah blah blah, you probably know the drill. Nice to meet you and all that. Have a great time in New Orleans."

Carwyn's eyes didn't move from Brigid's feral gaze. "We'll leave a tip with the hostess."

"Thanks." He sounded more chipper. "Think I might go find Minerva right now."

Carwyn followed the human out the door; then he closed it, dead bolted it, and turned back to Brigid. "Hello, love."

What was the phrase? Undressing him with her eyes.

Carwyn smiled and started unbuttoning his shirt. "I feel like you want something, but I'm going to ask you to use your words."

"You. Now. Couch."

He didn't have to be told twice. He dropped his shirt to the floor, then sat in his previous position, his legs splayed out as she crawled over him.

"Ah." The muscles in his chest jerked at the red-hot feel of her fingertips on his skin. Brigid straddled his hips and peeled her black tank top off, leaving nothing but a scrappy bit of lace covering her breasts and black leggings he wanted to rip.

"Don't." She could read his mind. "I'll take them off."

"Be quick." He was the predator now. "I wanted to rip his head off."

"You always want to rip their heads off if they're men."

"You're too rough for most female donors. I know it's not rational." He leaned forward, grabbing her by her bare hips.

Then he lifted her up until she was standing over him on the sofa, straddling his face. "Exactly where I want you."

He didn't wait but put his mouth directly on her sex, her flesh already swollen with desire and her scent nearly driving him to use fangs on delicate skin. He wanted to devour her. He wanted to be inside her, but he needed her to come first.

She braced herself as he pleasured her, one hand on the wall and the other clutching his thick hair as his lips and tongue wrung the first climax from her. Her skin was on fire, and he could feel a blister forming at his neck where she pressed her fingers when she came.

The physical pleasure threw a little water on the flames, but she was still aching for him.

"Bite me." Her voice was raspy. "Carwyn."

He turned his mouth from its leisurely exploration to trace his tongue up her inner thigh. "Here?"

"Yes."

He played with the soft skin, sucking and scraping his teeth over the place where he could feel her pulse beating beneath the skin.

"Please." The plea came in a whisper.

He bit.

She screamed and nearly fell, but Carwyn held her up, his massive arms bracing her body until he'd finished drinking the sweet blood from her inner thigh. Then he lowered her slowly, unbuckling his trousers with one hand, releasing his erection so she could slowly sink to the hilt.

She laid her head on his shoulder, and her satisfied sigh was the sweetest music. "My fine man."

"You're sweet tonight." He turned his face and captured her lips, tasting the lingering blood from the human. "Sweet and a little salty." He smiled and thrust his hips up.

"Fuck me." She groaned. "And you said *I* was holding back."

He put his hands on her hips and helped her as she rode him. He had no words when they were joined this way. It was too much of a miracle. Too precious. The mystery of their union still bent his mind even after a decade together.

"Are you mine?" He put his hand on her cheek, forcing her gaze to his own. "Are you mine, Brigid?"

"I gcóna." *Always*. She wrapped her arms around his neck and pressed her lips to his neck, but instead of the bite he was expecting, she pressed a single kiss behind his ear.

It was enough to make him fly.

———

SHE LAY OVER HIS CHEST, her body exhausted and her bloodlust sated. Carwyn held her, Brigid still straddling his hips, her breasts pressed against his chest as her body slowly cooled. The room felt like an oven, but neither of them was sweating.

"You're pushing yourself too hard." He kept his voice soft.

"I know."

"You should have fed from one of those thieves tonight even if they tasted like piss."

"They were criminals; they didn't consent to be my dinner."

He angled his head so he could meet her eyes. "It's not the same."

She stared at him. "For me it is."

Brigid had been violated as a child, abused by those who should have protected her. It had led her to a life of medicating her trauma with drugs that had eventually taken her human life.

It hadn't been the end for Brigid, but the scars of her human life still lingered, and in the past year, she'd become more and more conflicted about feeding from anyone or anything that couldn't consent to give blood.

"We're going to have to talk about this." He took a deep

breath and let it out slowly. "It's not the same for me. I'm so much older than you. You still need to feed every few days."

"I probably need to commit to hunting with you more."

"You don't like animal blood."

"In a situation like tonight, I'd much rather feed from a deer than lose control like that."

"You didn't lose control; you kept it together." He sighed and stroked a hand over her velvet cap of dark brown hair. "But you were on the edge. This is partly my fault. There are vampire clubs between here and Houston, just not ones I like."

"Because?"

"Not to Gavin's standard, put it that way." Gavin Wallace was an old friend and the reason they were in New Orleans. He was a wind vampire who ran his clubs with strict rules. No violence. No nonconsensual biting. No making a spectacle of yourself in front of the humans.

In Gavin's clubs, all the human donors knew about the vampire world and immortal needs. They were all healthy; none of them gave more blood than was safe, they all volunteered, and it was not a condition of their employment.

Gavin's clubs never had problems finding amenable donors. They were paid handsomely for their blood, and most vampires knew how to make the experience highly pleasurable for the human even if—like Brigid—they didn't set out to arouse.

"So there were clubs out in the country?" Brigid shook her head. "I probably wouldn't have felt safe any place like that. I should have fed in Houston. This is on me."

"Either way, lesson learned." He stroked her neck. "But hunting would be good too. For emergencies."

"Agreed." She shifted on his lap. "Is there a washroom attached to this room?"

"There is." He stood, Brigid carried in his arms, and walked them to the half bath attached to the feeding room. "I believe there's even a shower."

She reached down and wrapped her fingers around his growing erection. "Is that so?" She ran her fangs along his neck. "These clubs really do think of everything, don't they?"

THREE

"I'm so excited you're here." Chloe Reardon was Gavin Wallace's human companion and soon-to-be wife. The vibrant human woman was a dancer in her professional life, a trained ballerina who had unwittingly grown up surrounded by vampires. She couldn't have been older than thirty, but her eyes revealed a wise soul.

"We were flattered to receive an invitation." Brigid stood on the front porch of the graceful house in the Garden District and looked at her husband. "Carwyn tells me this is a big event."

"In the next two weeks, roughly four hundred vampires will be flooding into New Orleans along with their entourages. Trust me..." Chloe let out a breath. "It's a lot."

The wedding of Gavin Wallace, vampire entrepreneur and owner of Wallace Enterprises, to Chloe Reardon, a human ballet dancer formerly under the aegis of legendary fire vampire Giovanni Vecchio, had quickly turned into the vampire social event of the year. Chloe, through her relationship with the Vecchios, was also connected to the vampire lord of Los Angeles. Gavin had connections and business partners all over the globe and was the protégé of Marie-Hélène Charmont, immortal queen of New Orleans and one of its most prominent business owners.

"Four hundred?" Brigid didn't even want to think of that many vampires in one city. The human population was going to take a hit.

"And their entourages," Carwyn added. "That's what I call a party. And Chloe, you're looking radiant. The city suits you."

Chloe's light brown skin glowed with health. Her hair was threaded into long braids that were bundled on her head in a regal up-do, and her cheeks showed the flush of healthy living. Most of all, she looked happy.

"I really love New Orleans," Chloe said. "I've made some wonderful friends, and I'm definitely looking forward to spending more time here. I told Gavin that from now on, once the snow hits New York, he can call me a Southern girl."

"Can't blame you for that," Brigid said.

"It's quite a friendly place, I think." Carwyn looked out the window and saw the shadow of live oaks and magnolias in the yard. "Lived here for a short time nearly a hundred years ago. Love the feel of it. This house is beautiful. It's light safe?"

Chloe nodded. "Marie-Hélène owns the property and loaned it to us for our guests. You'll be here with Giovanni and Beatrice, some vampire from Chicago, and Ben and Tenzin when they show up."

Brigid smiled. "*If* Tenzin shows up. This might be too many people for her."

"Oh, Tenzin will show up." Chloe's smile was wicked. "I made her part of the bridal party."

The skies parted, the moon shone brighter, and everything in Brigid's world suddenly glowed golden. "Are you telling me that you made Tenzin—a...many-thousands-year-old vampire assassin—a bridesmaid for your posh wedding?"

That was possibly the best thing that Brigid had heard in her entire life.

"Better." Chloe's eyes were dancing. "I made her the maid of honor."

Carwyn was clearly horrified. "This will end... *very* badly. I cannot express to you how badly this will go wrong."

Chloe quickly raised a hand. "I gave her backup of course. Audra is also in the bridal party for security reasons. And Arthur. Dema and Therese, who's a friend from the Dancing Bear in New York, and three of Marie-Hélène's daughters to make for seven attendants, which is good luck or something."

"Jaysus," Brigid muttered. "How many people are attending this thing?"

"I honestly have no idea." Chloe shrugged. "Months ago this became way more about Gavin and Marie-Hélène's business network than a wedding, so I stopped trying to wrap my brain around it."

Brigid felt her lip curl. "Are you okay with that?" She hadn't known the young woman for very long, but she was a dear friend of Ben Vecchio, whom Brigid felt quite protective toward. Any friend of Ben's was a friend of Brigid's.

"I'm *fine* with it," Chloe said. "I knew as soon as Marie-Hélène asked to host it that it was going to become a huge production. She's doing all the planning, and all I have to do is point at what I like and she arranges everything, so I can deal. As long as Gavin and I end up married by the end of the ceremony, I'll be happy."

"Good." Brigid admired the woman's flexible attitude. She was marrying a relatively public type of vampire, which was Brigid's worst nightmare. Carwyn was the head of a large clan, and that was more than enough people for her. Christmas dinners alone were enough to make Brigid want to run.

"So there will be seven vampires in this house?" Brigid

turned to the massive white structure. "Including Giovanni Vecchio?"

Chloe nodded. "Will that be a problem?"

"Eh..." Carwyn frowned. "Is there another place you might be able to put them?"

"Or put us," Brigid added quickly. "Giovanni and I are both fire vampires. If we spend too much time in enclosed spaces together, we'll want to rip each other's heads off."

Chloe's eyes went wide. "So that's why Gavin nixed the Russian, huh?"

"Probably?" Brigid shrugged. "Two fire vampires at a large event are probably the maximum number if you're trying to avoid bloodshed, and it helps if they're not the same sex. We're like feral dogs—no idea why."

"Good to know." Chloe frowned. "I can swing it. I'll put them in our guesthouse. They're kind of... parental. Gavin won't mind."

Oh yes, he will. Brigid smiled because Gavin would mind having a territorial fire vampire in his territory, but he'd shut his mouth because he adored Chloe.

"So I'm going to get you settled and then head to sleep, 'cause I do not sleep well in daylight," Chloe said. "But I know Gavin wanted to meet with you as soon as you're unpacked if you have time. Something to do with work, I think?"

Brigid and Carwyn exchanged a look.

"We were wondering why he invited us down for three full weeks," she said.

"Give us an hour or so," Carwyn said. "He can meet us here."

———

"YOUR ROOMS ARE COMFORTABLE?" Gavin held the door for them, ushering them into a library where a young woman in

22

black jeans and a T-shirt was waving a device over the walls and bookcases.

"Very comfortable," Brigid said. "Very secure. We appreciate the hospitality, thank you."

Gavin watched the young woman for a few moments; then the technician gave him a thumbs-up and left the room.

"Searching for listening devices," Gavin said. "This house isn't mine."

Brigid said, "I thought it belonged to your business partner."

"As I said." Gavin settled on a sofa in front of the fireplace and motioned for them to join him. "Not my house."

Carwyn and Brigid exchanged a look. Cautious or suspicious? They joined Gavin near the fireplace, Brigid sitting closest to the flames out of habit.

Gavin made a note of it but didn't remark. "I knew the ground floor would be the best option for both of you," their host said. "You found the access point?"

There was a hidden door in the room that led under the house and directly to the earth, which had made Carwyn feel much more secure.

"We did," Brigid said. "Thank you."

"And Tenzin and Ben's rooms have balconies," Carwyn said. "Handy for wind vampires."

"Indeed."

Gavin Wallace was a Scottish vampire who'd been turned in the 1800s and had steadily built himself up from human poverty to being one of the wealthiest vampires in the United States and probably the world.

Though he didn't flaunt his wealth, Brigid knew that Wallace's clubs were located all over the globe, catering to humans and vampires, and beyond offering safe and consensual vampire sustenance, those clubs and bars served another specific and important purpose in vampire society.

Neutral ground.

Gavin Wallace wasn't political in the worldly sense; he had no thirst for power or influence. He collected no tribute or taxes but paid many of them. Most especially, he took no sides in vampire disputes, at least not publicly. Because of that, his clubs and quiet diplomacy had probably prevented more bloodshed than any number of human treaties.

"Chloe said that you had a question for us," Brigid said. "I'm not sure how we can help you, but we're willing to listen."

Gavin had no alliances, which could be dangerous for ordinary vampires, but in his circumstances, it worked well. Because he cultivated a strictly neutral organization and always asked permission to set up businesses, vampires in authority welcomed his investments. A Wallace club or bar was an asset to any city, providing a safe place for vampires to meet, though at the first hint of interference or attempt to politicize him, Gavin would politely remove himself and his organization from a territory.

He did not offer second chances. He was cautious, suspicious, and kept his cards close to his chest.

"I don't *know* that I have a problem, but I may," Gavin began. "Before we begin, Brigid, are you still working for Murphy?"

Patrick Murphy was the vampire lord of Dublin, Ireland, and her former employer. "No. I may still be perceived as his employee, but it's been a few years since I've been on his books. We parted on good terms, but my only aegis is to my sire."

"Who falls within the aegis of your mate." Gavin nodded. "Which is why I am approaching you." Gavin turned his attention to Carwyn. "You're an unusual figure, Father."

Carwyn smiled. "I haven't been a priest for many years." Carwyn had spent the majority of his eternity in the quiet embrace of the Catholic Church. He'd been a married priest in his lifetime, and while he'd lost his mortal family, he'd kept his spiritual one until he left service to marry Brigid.

"You're not an ancient," Gavin continued, "but you are an elder. Your family is vastly influential but surprisingly nonpolitical. Your children have never sought power."

"Gemma." Brigid coughed. "I'm just saying Gemma is functionally a coregent in London."

"Functionally is the key." Gavin folded his hands. "More importantly, I trust you, and I don't trust many." He looked at Brigid. "Marie-Hélène and I are developing a Nocht competitor."

"Good." Carwyn grunted. "About time."

Brigid glanced at her husband with a wry smile. "You *would* say that." She turned to Gavin. "No love lost there. I understand the motivation, and I'm surprised that you're the first."

"I'm not the first, and you know it." Gavin smiled. "Your old boss doesn't take out his competition violently, but he does take them out."

"I don't think mergers and acquisitions could be considered 'taking someone out,' but I see your point." Brigid shrugged. "He's successful and rich for a reason."

"My motivations are both financial and—to quote my wife-to-be—paranoid. I don't like anyone having that much knowledge of my operations. My business group has avoided technology or used workarounds with Nocht for years now in an attempt to preserve our privacy, but I'd like to have something more reliable."

"You'd certainly have an edge marketing it," Carwyn said. "You're seen as more independent than Patrick Murphy." He glanced at Brigid. "So what's the problem?"

"A few months ago, Chloe was kidnapped from her mother's home in Los Angeles."

"What?" The fire leaped near Brigid. "Sorry, I didn't hear a word about that."

"What happened?" Carwyn asked. "Who on earth would tempt your wrath by targeting someone in your organization?"

"We'd been *too* discreet about her role in my life at that point. She was taken by Rens Anker's daughter, who tried to hire her." Gavin's mouth twisted. "Mila thought Chloe was a biomechanics specialist. A new employee. I had approached Mila Anker months before Marie-Hélène and I partnered to create Paladin Ventures. I determined that she wasn't trustworthy enough; I was proven correct."

"But Chloe was taken in the process."

"She wasn't harmed and Mila was dealt with by Alvarez in Los Angeles."

"Paladin Ventures," Carwyn said. "Great name."

"The Paladins were the most trusted knights in French legend. The name is a nod to Marie-Hélène's heritage, but I do like it. The system will operate on three levels. Hardware, software, and security."

Brigid raised her eyebrows. "You're creating a vampire communications suite."

"I'm creating an upgrade. One that's not subject to the whim of Patrick Murphy's alliances."

"No," Brigid said. "It's subject to yours."

"But I have no alliances." Gavin spread his hands. "Neither does Marie-Hélène. That is why Paladin will be successful."

"So what do you need us for?" Brigid asked. "Clearly you got Chloe back, and your explanation explains why Mila Anker is suddenly very quiet these days."

"Mila was always a problem," Carwyn muttered. "I'd like to regret that she's gone, but I can't."

"There is someone else targeting my employees now." Gavin leaned forward. "There have been attempted hacks into our security. Numerous employees feel they've been followed. It's possible that they're imagining things, but it's also possible they're not. We've had break-ins that have been made to look like they're random or petty theft. Employees have reported hang-ups and calls where no one speaks to them. Blocked numbers of course. Numerous strange emails. Several weeks ago, I had a programmer quit abruptly only to find out he's taken a job writing code for an agricultural technology firm in Oklahoma where he's making half the salary he was here." Gavin lifted his hands, palms up. "And he won't take my calls."

"You think someone is trying to derail Paladin," Brigid said.

"I don't think." Gavin raised one eyebrow. "I know."

"You know more than what you're telling us," Carwyn said. "That's the reason you want to hire Brigid and me."

Brigid turned to him. "What are you talking about?"

Carwyn's eyes never left Gavin. "He doesn't think it's an upstart like Mila this time. He thinks it's a competitor."

Brigid turned back to Gavin, her mouth dropping open. "You think it's Murphy."

FOUR

"Is it possible?" Carwyn asked. "You know him better than almost anyone else. He trusts you."

"Is it possible?" Brigid thought about her former employer. Patrick Murphy was one of the richest men in the vampire world because of his ruthless ambition, business savvy, and keen intelligence. "Stalking a business rival? Yes. But kidnapping Chloe? No."

"He might consider it the price of competition."

"Not kidnapping." Brigid sighed. "I can't see any of his people agreeing to it."

They were tucked in their day chambers, and she could feel the day coming on her. The wild swing of events that night had taken its toll on her mind. They'd started from Giovanni's old home in Houston and driven out of the city in a rush to make it to New Orleans with enough time before dawn.

They'd taken a detour that should only have taken an extra hour but had led to an attempted mugging, a retaliatory fistfight her husband had enjoyed far too much, another detour to put the men in the jurisdiction where they'd committed their previous crimes, a traffic stop, and then another rush to the city where she'd nearly ripped out the neck of a nice young man named Jordan.

"I thought the pace of life in the American South was reported to be slower than California." Brigid frowned. "Don't they call New Orleans 'the Big Easy'?"

Carwyn slipped an arm around her. "Maybe it's easier for humans."

"Feckin' hell, I hope so." Brigid took a deep breath, inhaling the scent of Carwyn and absorbing the feeling that came with the smell of her mate, enjoying the feel of his solid arm around her and his amnis humming beside her.

It seemed obvious, but he grounded her as no other person in the world did. Her relationship with her sire was fraught, to put it mildly, and her relationship with her human family was tenuous.

Carwyn, the incongruous giant beside her, was her anchor in the world.

"Why have you been pushing yourself?" he asked quietly. "We need to talk about it."

Annoying man.

"I don't know what to tell you," she said. "When I woke at dusk, I honestly thought I was fine. I didn't expect the detour or the three humans. Don't make a singular event a pattern."

"It's not just tonight." He rolled to his side. "It's last month in Portland. It's Montana in May. It's every time we travel to the East Coast, and there's no excuse for it there, Brigid. There are clubs everywhere. It's—"

"I get the picture. Can we talk about this after we decide if my boss and former mentor is sabotaging a new rival and possibly messing with humans in unethical ways?"

"Don't tie this and Murphy together. This is your own stubborn—"

"I hate it," she snapped. "I never wanted this, remember?"

Feck, that came out wrong. Brigid closed her eyes and sighed as Carwyn sat up abruptly.

"You didn't want what?" Hurt and anger simmered in his voice.

"Not you. I'm not talking about you or our life together." She rose and immediately wrapped her arms around him, waiting for Carwyn to return the gesture. "You and me? Our life together? That's the only thing that makes this bearable, do you understand me?"

"I thought you were happy, Brigid." His arms came around her, but his voice was still stiff. "I thought this new direction, working for yourself, was better for you."

"It is. I promise it is." She closed her eyes and pressed her face into his neck. "It's not you. It's not the work. It's me."

"Tell me."

"I don't... There's no helping what I feel, Carwyn. It's useless to dwell on it when there's nothing to be done."

"We're not helpless, Brigid." He took her by the shoulders and shook her a little. "Whatever is bothering you, we can conquer it together. I am your husband. Your mate. Don't tell me there's nothing to be—"

"I'm a heroin addict." Brigid's voice was matter-of-fact.

Carwyn froze. "And?"

"It didn't go away when I turned. I wish it had. I thought it would have to because I can't get high anymore, but it's not..." She swallowed the lump in her throat. "Being immortal was never the plan. And to top it off, I became a *fire* vampire. So now I live with another addiction, because it feels good." She closed her eyes. "God help me, when I release my control, it feels so damn good. It's better than getting high, but I can't. I can't... I fecking destroy the world when I use my element, and part of me is dying inside."

She opened her eyes, and his gaze was everything that kept

her sane. There was no judgment. No anger. Just love. Such profound love she felt like shrinking under his examination because she could never be worthy of it.

Never.

"I don't understand the addiction." He kept his voice soft. "If I could take it from you, I would."

She closed her eyes. "Pushing myself... I suppose it breaks up the monotony. Makes me feel stronger. I don't know. Ten years I've been immortal, and there is no end to it. Don't misunderstand me; I have no death wish. But the idea of grinding on, forever craving a high that's completely out of my reach, is..."

"Maddening."

"It's maddening." Her stomach dropped. "And the hunger for fire—"

"*That* is not an addiction," Carwyn said. "And you need to stop thinking of it that way. Your fire is beautiful, Brigid. It's gorgeous and brilliant and it's a part of who you are."

"Destructive."

"Transformative." He shook her shoulders. "Fire creates life. It's not a simple thing; it's a gift, not a curse."

"But the control—"

"You need to be able to release it in a safe space. That's not indulgent—that's healthy. You've bound yourself to these rules and you don't need them. Your element is not a danger to you, and it never has been."

She closed her eyes, released a long breath, and pressed her forehead to his chest. "I don't deserve you."

"I know." He took a deep breath. "I am *extraordinary*."

Brigid snorted.

"You managed to secure the most coveted bachelor in the vampire world," he continued. "Do you practice gratitude? Because they say that you should make gratitude a daily practice, and I'm not sure what that means, but I think it has to do with admiring your husband."

Her shoulders were shaking. God, she adored him.

"I think that, generally, all vampires—and humans, shouldn't leave them out—should admire me more, but as my wife, *your* admiration... Worship seems excessive, but I don't know, maybe it's not. In a secular sense—"

Brigid kissed him to shut him up. She could feel the day coming, a long, slow pull that would drag her inexorably toward a solid, blissful darkness unbroken until dusk. Vampire sleep was profound.

"I'm going to sleep, my most admired husband." She lay down in their bed and pulled up a single cotton sheet. Anything else was nearly oppressive in the humid heat. "When I wake up, we'll talk about how we find out if my old boss is crossing ethical lines here in Louisiana."

"If your old boss is in Louisiana, he's crossing ethical lines. That's one of Patrick Murphy's hallmarks." Carwyn lay down beside her.

"Fine, we'll find out if it's more lines than usual. Tracking employees? That wouldn't surprise me, but the one who quit and won't return Gavin's calls is worth exploring." She closed her eyes.

"Brigid?"

"Hmm?"

"I love you."

She turned toward him and smiled. "More admiration, you were saying?"

"Worship maybe. Worship might be the better term."

———

CARWYN STOOD over the human employees lounging around Paladin's corporate office in the Central Business District and tried to look intimidating, but none of the humans seemed the least bit impressed. There were five of them, all clearly wishing they were somewhere else.

Traffic buzzed outside the windows in the early-evening darkness, and a light rain spattered against the six-paned windows in the conference room.

The human who spoke first was a young woman with a crop of dark curls, pale skin that looked a stranger to the sun, and dark, horn-rimmed glasses. "Gavin said you wanted to talk to us about the creep."

Brigid had a notebook out. "Your name?"

"Bex." She rolled her eyes. "Rebecca Romero." She was wearing a bright pink tank top, baggy cargo pants, and a polka-dotted headband. Dark tattoos covered both her shoulders. "I'm from Southern California. Moved here two months ago. This place is hot as balls."

"And you've been followed?" Brigid asked. "Can you give me more details? Describe the man or woman who followed you?"

"The first time I saw him was in the Quarter." She pursed her lips. "I don't know, I just thought he was a weirdo, you know? It's not like Bourbon Street doesn't attract its fair share of creeps."

"It was the same guy that followed me." Another voice popped up from the corner of the room. It belonged to a lanky young man with red hair that nearly matched Carwyn's. "I wasn't in the Quarter. I'm Nic. Nicolas Cooper. I'm the only one from the city, so it's a little easier for me to spot a tail. I gave Gavin a sketch." The young man rubbed the back of his neck and spoke mostly to the floor. He wore a pair of jeans and a plain white T-shirt along with black Converse shoes.

Brigid handed Carwyn the sketch. "That's what he gave Gavin."

Carwyn's eyes went wide. "This is excellent."

"But not particularly helpful," Brigid said. "I'm sorry, Nic, but it's too stylized for us to match with law enforcement databases."

The young man shrugged and looked out the dark window. "That's how I draw."

The sketch Brigid had handed Carwyn showed clear artistic merit, but it was in a Japanese animation style.

"It's excellent." Carwyn examined not just the face but the surroundings the young man had drawn, a lively street scene with a jazz band playing on a corner and bright neon signs hanging from windows. "Where was he?"

"I saw him on Frenchman Street, and he followed me down Chartres when I was walking home from the Marigny. There's a jazz club there I like. It's not too crowded. I live in the lofts." Nic continued talking to the wall. "We all do. I tried to lose him by walking up to Royal and ducking into a warehouse party—it was really loud and crowded—but I don't know if he just hid himself better, you know? He probably knows we all live in the lofts."

Carwyn asked, "The lofts?"

Bex spoke up again. "Paladin bought an old rice mill over in the Bywater and fixed it up. The ground floor is where our offices are, and the top floors they turned into a coliving space for employees. They call them the lofts." She looked around the conference room. "We only come here for department-head meetings."

Carwyn frowned. "Wait, do you five run the whole company?" The lot of them barely looked out of short pants. "How old are you?"

Brigid held up a hand. "That's not important. This man who looked similar to all of you, did he follow you at night or during the day?"

"Day." Nic looked around the room, checking with his four peers, who all nodded at him. He had a quiet manner, but he was clearly a leader. "I think we were all followed during the day." He glanced at Brigid and Carwyn. "We all know about the vampires."

"Now." Another young woman spoke. "*Now* we know."

Her accent marked her from South Asia, but Carwyn couldn't be sure where.

The young lady smiled a little and raised her hand. "I'm Savi Gamage. Hi. I'm from Sri Lanka, and I'm the clueless one in the group because my parents worked for vampires for years and didn't tell me. Gavin offered me the job last year, and I received a very fast education." She was the only one of the group wearing what Carwyn would consider professional clothing. Her neat collar was buttoned to the top, and her pants were pressed with a crisp line down the front.

"The man that Nic described?" Savi continued. "I think he followed all of us at different times and in different places. He was White, medium height, brown hair, and very ordinary-looking. He was trying to look like a tourist, I think. A polo shirt, jeans, and tennis shoes. A very plain man. He followed me when Kit and I were attending a gallery show in the warehouse district."

"I was visiting the botanical gardens in City Park." Another young man with dark brown skin and locs to his shoulders spoke. He was wearing a concert T-shirt, a pair of knit joggers, and bright yellow-and-green sneakers. "I think it was the same guy, and it was definitely during the day. We tend to stay close to the lofts at night. And I'm Miguel Wallace from Savannah. No relation to Gavin. Kit, Savi, and I share a living unit in the lofts, and we compared our memories this afternoon when we got the message that y'all wanted to talk."

"Yeah, we all remember basically the same person, but he

changed his hat and his glasses a lot." The last employee smiled, revealing clear braces on their teeth. "I'm Kit and I'm from Colorado. They, them please. I just took over Lee Whitehorn's department, so I'm kind of playing catch-up." They sat up straight and adjusted the knit cap covering a crop of bright green hair. "There are probably a hundred people working in our building now, but only forty of us live in the lofts, so we're pretty tight."

Nic spoke again. "I asked around. It's just the five of us who have been followed. And then I'm guessing Lee was followed too. Maybe that's why he left."

Brigid nodded. "It's possible."

Bex smiled and looked around the room. "Dude, I feel like we're in a department meeting right now at the big office. Where are the donuts?"

Carwyn frowned. "So you're *all* the heads of your different departments?"

The five humans nodded.

Brigid's eyes swept the room. "I'd ask what departments you're head of, but I probably wouldn't understand a word."

Carwyn could see the wheels in her head turning. His wife was a keen detective, and while he could offer insight and assistance, he was definitely the Watson to her Sherlock.

He kept the question in Irish. "What are you thinking, my girl?"

"Why these five only?" She answered in the same language. "There are forty people in the Paladin building, not to mention a hundred employees, but these are the only ones who reported being followed?"

"What language is that?" Bex asked. "It's kind of rude to talk about us in front of us."

"I'm thinking aloud," Brigid said in English. "You're all heads of different departments, so I'm assuming you all have specific expertise."

"Of course." Bex rolled her eyes again. "That's kind of the point of having... you know, departments?"

"If someone wanted to sabotage Paladin, taking one of you out or hiring you away might be the way to do it." Brigid looked at Bex. "If you took another job, who could step into your position?"

Bex frowned. "He'd bitch about it, but Josh. He hates meetings, and he's not as good with people, but he could run things."

Brigid turned to Kit. "And you?"

Kit blew out a slow breath. "Um... harder because we just transitioned from Lee to me, but probably Ashanti. She doesn't have as much experience in project management, but she's my second-in-command and supersmart. We work in the software-development department." Kit caught Carwyn's confused expression. "Specifically voice command, which is unique to vampires but not nearly the most difficult. We have a lot of existing software to reference, including Nocht, but we're trying to improve accent recognition; that's a big problem with vampires."

"It definitely is," Carwyn said. "The voice control only works for me half the time."

"You have an unusual accent, but we're working on improving that function in Paladin's voice assistant."

"Huh." If the children could improve his ability to use the infernal devices, he had to admire that.

Kit pointed at Miguel. "If we're talking about specialties, you're probably the most novel."

The young man smiled. "I don't know about that. I'm the gadget guy, but I also have the biggest department and we collaborate. I think I know what Brigid is getting at. If I disappeared, there'd be like... three people jumping to take my job. They'd barely notice I was gone."

Carwyn looked at Nic. "You?"

"I'm working on the payment platform and financial integration." He shrugged and kept his eyes on Bex's shoes. "I'm boring, and there are like five people who could take my place."

Miguel huffed. "Hardly."

Bex rolled her eyes. "That's very not true, but Nic does have two assistants; either of them could step in if he needed them."

Carwyn nodded. "So the better question for the five of you is who is irreplaceable in this crew?"

Nearly as one, everyone in the room pointed to Savi, whose friendly smile disappeared.

"Me?"

"Security," Nic said. "No one here is even close to your firewalls; you're a genius."

"Yay for me?" Savi lifted both her hands and waved them, but she looked as thrilled as she sounded. "I'm going to get locked in my office, aren't I?" She deflated. "I was supposed to go to a concert with Bex on Friday."

Carwyn felt for her. "Bad luck, my girl. I promise we'll work as fast as we can."

"Sadly, until we find the ordinary man," Brigid said, "consider yourself grounded."

FIVE

"A reception?"

Carwyn smiled. "We're out-of-town guests."

"Two of four hundred," Brigid countered. "Why do the two of us warrant a reception?"

"Marie-Hélène will have a reception nearly every night for the next two weeks, welcoming every immortal guest to her territory. We're not the only new arrivals, so it's not just about us, but we do need to make an appearance."

"How many—?" She stopped herself because any number over ten would just make her want to light something on fire. "I don't have anything to wear. I was going to shop later this week."

Carwyn smiled and smoothed a hand along Brigid's nape. "Just throw on something black and dangerous. You'll look amazing."

"Black and dangerous?" She looked at him sideways. "I suppose I can manage that."

Black and dangerous she could do.

Two hours later, Carwyn had a hand on the small of her back as he led her toward a palatial glowing house in another part of the city. Someone watching them might see the hand as a sweet gesture of support.

Only Brigid knew it was purely to keep her from running away.

The sign on the gate read BONNEVUE, and it was guarded by four humans in actual footmen's uniforms. They walked through the gates leading to a wide alley of oaks on the expansive grounds of the lavish estate where Marie-Hélène Charmont, vampire regent of New Orleans, doyenne of hospitality, and Chloe's wedding planner made her home when she wasn't visiting one of her other historic properties.

"I'm underdressed." Brigid glanced at a flock of women standing near a blooming magnolia tree, wearing brilliant pinks, yellows, and creams.

"You're perfect." Carwyn squeezed her hand. "You look like a vampire."

It was late fall in New Orleans, and the weather during the day was pleasant, but the night brought cooler winds off the river. Brigid wasn't wearing a jacket, but she wished she had one if for no other reason than to have a shield.

She'd kept her wardrobe that night simple—long black pants, a black vest, and a stunning Victorian necklace made of cut steel that Carwyn had found for her in an antique shop in Dublin. The center drop looked like a decorated sword hilt.

It was one of Brigid's favorite pieces of jewelry because at first glance, she hadn't known if it was a bauble or a weapon. She wore blood-red rubies in her ears and no other adornment. With her hair as short as it was, Brigid knew it was best to keep things simple.

While she had committed to black, her husband let his personality fly in a robin's-egg-blue shirt, cream pants, and blue suede shoes. In London or Dublin, he would have stood out, but in New Orleans?

Brigid had already spotted at least three other men in bright floral ensembles.

"We're in your city." She nodded toward the dandies. "At least when it comes to clothing."

"One of my favorite things about the South is that it's socially acceptable for men to wear color."

Brigid saw vampires and humans dressed in everything from pressed linen suits to seersucker overalls to carnival head-dresses. The theme of the evening seemed to be more eccentric than formal, and she felt Carwyn's amnis jump with excitement as they approached the front door.

"You're loving this." Brigid smiled.

He smiled. "I do enjoy a good party."

"We need to have more of a social life in California."

"We live in the middle of nowhere," he said. "Hardly the place for parties, my love."

"Or maybe exactly the right place." She slid her hand into his and gripped hard as the door opened into the grand entryway of the main house. "No neighbors to complain."

A butler bowed and took the invitation card that Carwyn handed him. He glanced at it, then motioned them toward a pair of tall wooden doors. Candles lit the overhead chandelier, and a jazz band played from the landing of the double staircase in the foyer.

Despite the press of people, Brigid couldn't deny her wonder. She felt like she'd stepped into a fairy tale, only the very adult variety.

There were beautiful men and women everywhere in sparkling costumes. There were discreet donors drifting through the room, their status marked by red crystal chokers. Uniformed waiters with crystal glasses of champagne and blood-wine wound through the crowds.

Carwyn squeezed Brigid's hand as they followed the butler. "How are you doing?"

I'm overdosing on amnis and humanity. "I'll be fine." She caught the butler handing their card to a towering Black vampire in a feathered headdress.

"They're not going to... Fuck me, they are, aren't they?" Brigid abhorred the formality of European courts, and Marie-Hélène appeared to have replicated it in her own unique way.

Carwyn had a massive grin on his face. "Just wait. It's not what you think." He reached for the woman's hand and bowed over it, kissing her fingertips. "Miss Arabella, you haven't aged a day."

"And you haven't lost a bit of your charm." She winked at him and smiled, revealing delicate white fangs. "Long time, no see, baby."

What was this? Carwyn had spent more time in Marie-Hélène Charmont's court than Brigid realized. She nudged him. "You've been holding out on me."

"I can't tell you all my stories at once. Where would be the fun in that?"

"And what a treat." Arabella's eyes turned to Brigid. "Your necklace, Miss Connor." The woman called Miss Arabella touched her bare neck where Brigid could see multiple discreet feeding scars. "Absolutely stunning. Victorian?"

"Good eye," she said.

She raised an eyebrow accented with swirls of purple rhinestones. "Oh honey, I have good *everything*."

That made Brigid smile. "It was a gift from my husband. Thank you."

"If you'll give me a moment to announce you..." She craned her neck over the crowd, waiting for the proper moment. There was a pause in the hubbub; then the woman sang out, "Madame Charmont, your gue-ests have arrived."

There was a whoop and a floating wave of laughter. The band did a drumroll as eyes turned toward Arabella.

An unseen voice dripping with Southern charm replied, "Miss Arabella, whoever has come to visit me?" The voice was coy, as if its owner wasn't already surrounded by a raucous party. Every eye in the room turned toward them.

Arabella parted the crowd with a sweep of one graceful arm, and Brigid could see a regal Black woman in a purple satin dress holding court on a velvet chaise at the far end of the room. Two uniformed stewards stood behind her, a beautiful young man in a red suit lounged next to her in a wingback chair, and a whisper-thin woman in a gold bodysuit was perched on a gold-tufted ottoman in a contortionist's pose.

Miss Arabella sang, "Carwyn ap Bryn and Brigid Connor of Dublin, Ireland, have come to call."

"Well, send them in to see me." Marie-Hélène raised a gold fan and fluttered it. "Tell my friends they are welcome at Bonnevue."

The crowd cheered, and the band struck up a new jazz tune heavy on the brass.

Brigid knew when she'd been announced. It was unconventional but highly choreographed. Carwyn's amnis was practically jumping up and down with glee. He pressed his and Brigid's folded hands to his abdomen as he led them through the crowd and toward Marie-Hélène.

She glanced up at him. "I cannot believe how much you're loving this."

"Yes, you can." He was like a little boy at a birthday party.

The vampire in front of them looked like the portraits of European royalty in museums, only this woman was even more stunning with an air of unmistakable power emanating from her.

Decorative fountains trickled in four corners of the room,

leading Brigid to the belief that Marie-Hélène drew her power from water, not a leap when her territory was at the mouth of the mightiest river in North America.

The woman at the center of attention sat up straight and held out her hands. "And there he is. Le renard sacré."

Did the queen of New Orleans just call her husband a holy fox?

Wait, was that a come-on?

Marie-Hélène was still talking. "You must introduce me to the singular woman who tempted the most charming man of the collar away from the church."

Carwyn bent down and kissed their hostess on both her cheeks. "Stunning as always, ma reine."

Brigid couldn't be mad because it was true. Marie-Hélène Charmont was a regent in all ways, her amnis matched by her sheer personal magnetism. She'd been turned in her late forties or early fifties, just enough time for mortality to sculpt her face into a masterpiece. Silver hair was piled on her head in intricate braids, and her light brown skin appeared sun-kissed even though—according to Brigid's sources—she hadn't seen daylight in well over three centuries.

Brigid spoke just enough French to be dangerous. She bowed slightly. "Enchanté, madame."

"Enchanté, mon amie." Marie-Hélène put her hand to her breast. "Carwyn, you have found a deadly flower, have you not? She intrigues me, and I want to know *everything*."

No. Brigid plastered a smile on her face. *No, you do not.*

Carwyn grinned. "We might need more whiskey for that story."

Brigid's smile remained fixed. "I'm flattered, Madame Charmont. It's a true pleasure to meet you."

Marie-Hélène flicked the contortionist away with a flip of her fingers. Then she motioned to the two attendants behind her who brought upholstered chairs and set them on her left. "Sit." She waved at Brigid and Carwyn. "I want to know about your wife because let me tell you." She leaned toward Brigid. "I tried many times to seduce this man, and I was unsuccessful."

What the hell was she about? And how was Brigid supposed to respond to that?

Carwyn burst into laughter, shattering the tension. "Marie, you did not. If you had, I would have been helpless to your charm."

Wait, was that better? That wasn't much better.

"I find that it's best if you knock him unconscious a few times before you decide to seduce him," Brigid said. "Two or three well-timed explosions probably would have done the trick."

Marie-Hélène's smile was sly. "I like you already."

Carwyn winked at Brigid. "I like you more."

"Chantelle!" Marie-Hélène waved at someone on the other side of the room. "Viens me voir, mon trésor. Come meet my friends."

A tall woman with a short cap of black hair walked through the crowd in an elegant green pantsuit, her vivid blue eyes fixed on Marie-Hélène. She glanced at Carwyn, then at Brigid.

"Hey." She held out her hand. "I'm Chance."

"Carwyn." He stood and shook it. Brigid did the same. "And this is my wife, Brigid; we're from Dublin via California."

"It's nice to meet you." Her skin had the pallor of a vampire, and her amnis felt ephemeral and glancing, unusual for a water vampire.

"Carwyn and I are friends of Gavin and Chloe," Brigid started.

Carwyn jumped in. "Though I've known your sire for many years."

"Oh, she's..." Chance smiled. "Marie-Hélène is not my sire. We're just very close."

"Well, it's nice to meet you." Brigid focused on the newcomer. "You said your name was Chance? I don't think I've ever heard that name before."

"Technically it's Chantelle, but I haven't gone by that in years," she said. "Only Marie calls me that; everyone else calls me Chance."

"I love that," Brigid said. "It's very cool."

"Chantelle is the most gifted woman with animals you have ever met," Marie-Hélène said. "She has a farm north of the city. She is a horse whisperer." She waved a hand. "You have never seen anything like it, I promise."

"Thank you." Chance's eyes were warm when they touched Marie-Hélène's. "I take great pride in my warmblood breeding program, but my farm is also a sanctuary for horse rescues."

"Fair play to ya. I don't know anything about horses, but my sire loves hers more than me, I think." Brigid smiled.

"Horses are wonderful creatures and good judges of character." Chance looked at Marie-Hélène. "I'm going to keep introducing Chloe to your friends, all right?"

"Of course!" Marie-Hélène waved her off, and Chance melted back into the crowd. "Chantelle loves her farm and her animals more than attending parties." The elegant woman shrugged. "Whatever makes her happy."

"I like shooting guns more than going to parties." Brigid said. "Raising horses is probably a better hobby."

Marie-Hélène let out a tinkling laugh. "Such a warrior, Carwyn! She is not at all what I imagined for you, my friend. She is so much more fascinating."

"So you're saying that you thought I'd marry someone boring?"

Marie-Hélène gave him a playful gasp. "Don't get me into trouble with your darling wife, cher. Do you want her to think I'm so gauche?"

Carwyn's warm eyes landed on her, steadying Brigid from the urge to squirm. "Don't worry yourself. She knows who's the source of the trouble."

"This one." Brigid kept her eyes locked with his. "Every time."

Carwyn winked at her. "Aren't you the lucky wife?"

Brigid turned to Marie-Hélène. "Enough chitchat. I have a feeling you know all the dirt on the troublemaker I married, and for the right price, you'll share it."

Marie-Hélène leaned toward Brigid and pitched her voice low. "For you, Miss Brigid, I will offer it up for free."

SIX

Carwyn chose to speak with his second-oldest daughter via video the following night, which was necessary with Deirdre. Too much was lost to sarcasm via text or phone call.

"We're following a number of leads here, but as you can imagine, we can't ignore Murphy's obvious motive to interfere with Gavin's operation. It would be helpful if we had an inside perspective from Dublin."

"Are you asking me to go spy for you?" Deirdre was wearing a barn coat, and her hair was tied into a bun that still had some straw tangled in it. She appeared to have been checking her animals in the barn. "That's not my department; that's yours and Brigid's."

"Brigid can't contact any of her people there. They're all loyal to Murphy. But we need to know how threatened he is by Gavin's project."

"Lord save me from grown men playing with the world like it's their toy box." Deirdre growled. "Why the hell should any of us care if Gavin and Murphy get into a pissing match? They'll play their games and make god-awful amounts of money in the process. What does any of that have to do with the rest of us?"

"You don't have to care about Gavin and Murphy's rivalry, but you should care about young people trying to live their lives and getting tangled up in vampire power plays."

"Don't work for vampires then." She blew a strand of bright auburn hair from her forehead. "Or work for different vampires."

"Not everyone likes cows as much as you do."

Deirdre muttered, "They should."

"I agree the world would be a better place." Carwyn tried to placate her. "How are the dogs?"

"Mad ruffians, just like their breeder." Deirdre cracked a smile. "I'm not giving them back, you know."

"I didn't think you would." He'd seen his daughter and his wolfhounds at Christmas, and it had done his heart good. The old farm in Wicklow was where Deirdre and his oldest son, Ioan, made their home, and even though Ioan had been killed years before, Deirdre remained, surrounded by the vampire-and-human family they had created there.

The corner of Deirdre's mouth turned up. "So Gavin Wallace is marrying a human, is he?"

"You were involved with him," Carwyn said. "Are you feeling any sort of way about it?"

A soft smile crossed her lips. "Gavin was... uncharacteristically kind to me at a time in my life when I needed kindness. I'll always be grateful for that. I'm glad he's found someone lovely to share his life. Please give him my best."

"I will." Carwyn leaned toward the protected screen. "And you're going to Dublin to spy for us."

"Ugh." Deirdre rolled her eyes. "Fine. You're a terror. I'll go and spy for you. What do you want to know?"

"Mostly if anyone from his organization has actually come to the States and how threatened he is by this new company."

"Didn't Gavin start this project a few months ago?"

"He did."

Deirdre frowned. "Carwyn, I'm as big a Luddite as any vampire, but even I know that these types of things take years to develop. Murphy spent ten years developing Nocht. Gavin will be able to go faster because of Murphy's work, but he's nowhere near a competitor yet."

"What are you saying?"

"I think anyone targeting one of Gavin's companies this early is far more likely to have a personal grudge against Gavin than view him as a competitor."

Carwyn sat back. "You're probably right. I'll pass that along to Brigid."

Deirdre's lip twitched. "How is she?"

"In her element." Carwyn smiled. "Literally."

"What are you talking about?" Deirdre's eyes went wide. "She's a *fire* vampire."

"Exactly."

———

THEY HEADED INTO THE DARKNESS, the blasting vibration of the motor behind them and the Gulf of Mexico in the distance. They were headed to one of the barrier islands owned by one of Marie-Hélène's charter companies.

Brigid sat next to Gavin, who'd politely chosen to join her on the boat instead of flying. He held a hand out, calmly creating a bubble of cool air that barely stirred Brigid's short hair.

"When Carwyn asked if there was any place suitable for you to let your guard down, I immediately thought of this place." Gavin craned his neck to see past the human standing in the bow. "I don't even know if the place has a name, but she uses it as a picnicking spot when her charter company takes passengers out. There are some rudimentary facilities, picnic tables, and shade covers. That sort of thing. But it's mostly dry brush and beach."

"Brush that needs burning?"

"Indeed it does." Gavin nodded at the bow. "There's been a burn prohibition for a good long while now and the island is overgrown. Normally she'd have burned it ages ago, so you came at the right time."

"And there's no one on the island?"

"Not a soul, Miss Connor." Gavin smirked. "If you'd like, we can drop you off and come back in an hour or two."

"That would be grand."

Gavin looked at her. "We brought a water vampire just in case. Our pilot."

"I'm not really spilling secrets to tell you that my fire has never harmed me."

"Not once?"

"Not once." She smiled. "It turns away from me. Almost like I've trained it. I have no idea why. It's a quirk of my amnis, but the fire always spreads out. I've lost hair, but that's it."

"Fascinating." Gavin nodded. "Very well, but if anything happens to you, you know you're condemning me to a violent and horrible death."

She smiled. "Carwyn would know who's to blame."

"I'm not talking about Carwyn; I'm talking about my wife."

Brigid laughed. "She and Ben are good friends."

"They are that." Gavin leaned back and peered into the darkness. "Was it an odd thing for you? To marry someone so much older? I've recently been reminded that I belong to the virtual Stone Age."

"Had a meeting with your department heads, did you?"

"Fuck me, they make me feel ancient." Gavin shook his head. "I think the average age of Paladin employees is twenty-three. Can you imagine?"

"Sounds like you're on the cutting edge, Wallace." Something occurred to Brigid. "You approached Mila Anker about collaborating on the project before Marie-Hélène, correct?"

"Correct."

"Did you consider anyone else?"

"Not even for a moment. I only considered Mila because I knew her pockets were deep and she was looking to spend money. She was smart but not smart enough considering she made an enemy of me, Giovanni Vecchio, and Ernesto Alvarez all in the space of an hour when her men shot Chloe's guard and took her."

"You must have been mad with worry."

Gavin didn't say a word, but she could read the silent fury the vampire still projected.

"She's safe now," Brigid said. "That's the important thing."

"And with very public status and mounds of security. I brought my head of security from Los Angeles with me. Raj. You'll meet him tomorrow night; he's coordinating with Marie-Hélène's man Alonzo on all the guests' security needs."

"I look forward to meeting him. Why did you decide to collaborate with Marie-Hélène?"

"I trust her."

"You sweep her house for bugs," Brigid said.

"I don't trust her blindly." Gavin smiled. "Neither does she with me. It's a form of respect."

"So you say."

"Marie-Hélène is like me. She's loyal until you give her a reason not to be. I don't give her a reason to doubt me."

"What about romantic partners?" Brigid said. "Any old girl-friends who might see you as a target?"

The corner of his mouth turned up. "Other than your sire?"

"Fuck me, yer takin the piss!" Brigid blinked. "You and Deirdre?"

"I'm speaking out of turn." He crossed his arms over his chest. "She wasn't a girlfriend. I cared for her dearly, but it was not long after her mate died. She was in no place for anything serious." He shrugged. "And it all worked out for the best in the end. I cannot imagine my life without Chloe."

"I can't imagine you and *Deirdre*." Brigid was still trying to wrap her mind around the suave millionaire beside her and the immortal farmer who'd sired her. "She would have hated your life."

"Thoroughly and completely." Gavin grinned. "Not unlike Marie-Hélène's late mate."

"Oh?"

Gavin nodded. "They made it work until Gerard died, but she was very much the public face of the company and he was very private."

"What happened to him?"

Gavin's expression turned wistful. "A bout of melancholy. That's what Marie-Hélène calls it. 'Gerard's melancholy.' He'd lost the last of his human family the year before and he was depressed. She woke one night and he'd walked into the sun."

"That's terrible."

"They had one hundred and twenty years together, but it still seems tragic, doesn't it?" Gavin shook his head. "She has her daughter Chance and her friends. And me. I don't think Marie-Hélène has ever experienced melancholy. Not once in her very long life." Gavin nodded toward the bow. "I see the island coming up."

Brigid tucked Gavin's nuggets of information away and turned her attention toward the island ahead. "Lots of dry brush, you said?"

"Gobs of it." He waved an arm. "Wipe it all out; you'll be doing her a favor."

———

GAVIN and the boat crew left the island, and Brigid immediately stripped. She doused her clothes in seawater and secured them under a rock before she flicked open her lighter and poured the flame into her hand.

Fire vampires couldn't *create* fire, but she could manipulate it, and in dry air, any spark of static would do. The warm, humid air on the surface of the gulf was anything but dry, and the liquid breeze wrapped around her like a soft blanket. The air was redolent with moisture, so she used a brass lighter to set one of the dry bushes on fire.

Brigid stood back and let the energy build in her chest.

The fire called her, fed her, and laughed as it grew. She stepped forward, feeling the heat against her bare skin. The ground beneath her vibrated with energy, the sand shifting and heating with the growing flames.

Brigid opened her chest and swung her arms toward the pile of brush, lifting the flames into a massive column that grew and grew until it resembled a pulsing wall of fire.

She held the fire, releasing her tension, anger, and frustration into the flames. As she held it, she felt a soothing shudder run down her spine and her mind flipped into a kind of waking trance.

Who would be targeting Gavin so early in his venture? She'd done some reading and the statistics for technology companies were not good, particularly when those companies had to cater to such a small market. For an immortal population already resistant to change, Gavin's new company was going to have an uphill journey. It could very easily die on the vine.

Brigid knew Patrick Murphy in and out, which was one of the perks of being somebody's chief of security. Secrets could kill you, so even the most paranoid immortal tended to be forthcoming when it came to their safety.

She spoke into the fire. "Why wouldn't he wait? He's not impatient."

Patrick Murphy was cautious, deliberate, and loved making money. He had a healthy ego but wasn't a narcissist. He knew exactly how big a target he was but managed to be a decent politician when the occasion called; many might even describe him as gracious.

Stalking Gavin Wallace's young employees was just... beneath him. He'd consider it an amateur play. If Murphy had inclinations to poach talent, he'd do it the traditional way with gobs of money and flattery.

Brigid couldn't dismiss Murphy completely, but she found herself focusing on the ordinary man following Gavin's kids. A single individual, likely to be spotted by five bright young people? It was clumsy. Amateur. She kept coming back to that word. Following human employees was an amateur move, particularly when dealing with someone like Gavin Wallace.

It wasn't that Wallace was a power unto himself, but he was ruthless when it came to protecting his people and he didn't give second chances to those who crossed him. If you or anyone in your organization became banned in Wallace establishments, you lost an important negotiating tool.

"Who wants Gavin to fail?" The massive piles of brush were slowly curling into themselves as they turned glowing red, then black, then grey.

The night wind licked along the sand, teasing her toes and caressing her bare skin. She was heated to the touch, and the damp wind clung to her mere seconds before it turned to steam and drifted away.

"Who wants to freak out those kids?" Brigid asked the fire.

The fire was predictably silent.

Brigid called the fire to her, gathering it with her hands before she started to run across the sand, her arms spread and fire trailing behind her. In her wake, flames started to eat the dry periphery of the island.

Visceral joy pulsed through her body.

Who was following those kids?

The Ankers sprang to mind, but what had once been an influential network of information merchants was now, with the loss of Mila Anker, hardly more than a memory. Mila's sire had built the Anker Company into a clearinghouse for immortal information, but first Rens was killed, then Mila. The clan was leaderless now. Would someone be searching for revenge?

Then there was the matter of the employee in Oklahoma who had left. *Why* had he left? What had driven a successful employee from such a lucrative position? And why wouldn't he answer Gavin's calls?

Brigid ran the circumference of the island in one burst, turned to watch the growing inferno, and took a deep, satisfied breath.

"I need to go to Oklahoma, don't I?" She sighed as she watched the flames grow. "Dammit."

SEVEN

"Oklahoma?" Carwyn tried to ignore the sinking feeling in his chest. "But there are jazz clubs and crawfish boils and oysters in New Orleans. We've been invited to a crawfish boil tomorrow night."

"What's a crawfish boil?" Brigid had just walked into the room. "It's not for long, and Gavin promised we could take his plane so we won't have to spend two full nights driving. We agreed to help, Carwyn."

It was not the news he wanted to hear. Well, the plane bit was nice.

Carwyn narrowed his eyes. "What does Oklahoma have?"

"The employee who won't take Gavin's calls."

"Besides that."

Brigid racked her brain. "Cowboys?"

"Do these cowboys host crawfish boils?"

She sat next to him. "Probably not." They were in the library, the very comfortable library where Carwyn was reading a book and drinking a whiskey concoction made for him by the very attentive butler in the house who was also an excellent bartender and cook.

Carwyn looked at his drink. "Will we have a butler in Oklahoma?"

"We will not, but we'll have our own plane so we can go, question the man, then come back, probably in the same night."

He felt a small, petty whine building at the back of his throat. "Will there be fisticuffs? I can't lie; I enjoyed the scuffle the other night. It was good to stretch my shoulders a bit."

Was provoking fights godly? No, but it could be an amusing way to pass the time. Carwyn had never been a brawler, but there was just something about a good round of physical violence that satisfied the old Celtic warrior that lived in his blood.

Brigid couldn't stop her smile. She sat on the sofa next to him and leaned against his arm. "Did you just say fisticuffs?"

Carwyn spread his arm and put it around her. "I'm sitting in my library and my butler just served me a drink. I could get used to being a rich gentleman."

"You know you have a very large amount of money, don't you? We could hire a butler if you wanted."

Carwyn sipped his drink. "Ridiculous thing to spend money on; don't be daft."

She rolled her eyes. "Okay, Oklahoma. I say we leave tonight, find a safe house there, then question the man at dusk. No calls. No warnings. Surprise him and maybe we'll get more information."

"We can't go tonight; we have plans." He brushed his lips across her forehead.

"I thought you said the crawfish boil was tomorrow night?"

"We are here for a wedding." He was smiling. "You do remember that, correct? This is primarily a social visit."

Brigid griped. "I can choose to focus on what I want, and industrial espionage and harassment are far more intriguing."

"We have another reception; this one includes some dignitaries from Rome, so Marie-Hélène asked me especially to attend."

Brigid tried not to curl her lip. "Church people?"

"No, just Emil Conti's people. And I believe Beatrice and Giovanni will be arriving tonight too. I don't know if they'll be there, but it's possible."

That would assuage her. Brigid and Beatrice got along well.

"Fine," Brigid said. "But I'm going to have to wear the same basic outfit that I wore to the last party. I still haven't gone shopping. And we can't get out of going to Oklahoma. We need to question Lee Whitehorn about why he left."

"Tomorrow night," Carwyn said. "That's soon enough. Gavin has put more guards on the Paladin employees, especially that darling little security consultant."

"If anything happens to that little girl—"

"It won't." He kissed her temple. "How was your own personal Burning Man last night?"

"It felt amazing."

He could tell. Her energy had calmed and her eyes were clear and focused.

"Did I singe?" She touched the edge of her hair. "I didn't think I did."

"You didn't. You look more balanced. There's that look in your eye."

"What look?"

It wasn't unlike the look she had after a particularly strong orgasm, but he didn't mention that part. "You seem less tense."

"I am." She snuggled into him. "I feel like I cleared my head a bit. Gavin was lovely to show me the island, and apparently there's another just as overgrown should the need arise."

"How convenient. I had a chat with Deirdre while you were gone. She's going to look into things in Dublin. See if any of Murphy's employees have recently traveled to America."

Brigid snorted. "Are you serious?"

"She can spy when she needs to."

"Ha!" She sat up straight. "Deirdre has got to be one of the bluntest people in the entire world. You think she's going to sneak information out of Murphy or Anne?"

"No. But she might unearth some useful information while she's stumbling about, don't you think?"

"Purely by accident?"

"Tell the truth: you don't think Murphy did this."

Brigid opened her mouth, then closed it.

Carwyn frowned. "Brigid?"

"I don't want you to think I'm influenced by Murphy's and my relationship. He was the first one to give me a chance after... everything."

A former heroin addict turned volatile fire vampire wouldn't have been at the top of many hiring lists—despite the power position fire vampires had—but Murphy had given her a chance and had earned a fierce ally in the process. Everyone knew that the immortal leader of Dublin had Brigid Connor in his pocket; pissing her off wasn't worth the pain.

"You don't think Murphy's involved?"

"It's not his style, is it?" She shook her head. "None of it. He wouldn't target humans. And he wouldn't try to disrupt anything this early in the process. If anything, he'd let Gavin pay for the new research and development and then try to rip him off *after* Paladin had made progress."

"That does sound far more likely." Carwyn rubbed a thumb along his chin. "I don't see him setting a tail on human employees either. Or trying to scare them off."

"He'd try to lure them to Nocht; hire them for his own company. I know it's a gut feeling, but this doesn't feel like his kind of move."

"I know what you're saying." He took a deep breath. "But we

have to keep an open mind right now. Gavin needs our help, and he doesn't have many people he can trust."

———

THEY WERE WALKING across the lawn when Carwyn felt the cold water sliding under his collar and down his spine.

He turned and looked for the culprit, but he could only feel her amnis, he couldn't see her face. "Oh, you brat."

Brigid frowned at him. "What are you about?"

"Beatrice is here."

The splash of water came again, this time when he turned his face. It was as if he'd run into a wall of water in the middle of Marie-Hélène's Bonnevue estate.

"De Novo, I know it's you," he yelled. "Show yourself, fiend!"

Brigid rolled her eyes. "Do you have to make it so dramatic?"

He felt a cold rush of air a moment before the spatters of icy rain pelted him in the chest.

Carwyn crouched down and put his hands into the lawn. "Now it's war."

He sent out his amnis, searching for her familiar energy. She wasn't a wind vampire; if she were, he'd be out of luck.

There. The shadows on the far edge of the property. He punched down and pulled a vein of earth toward him, yanking the ground from beneath her feet.

Carwyn heard a yelp in the distance.

"If you break my ankle—"

"You're a vampire—you'll be fine!" He ran toward the sound of her voice, more pelting rain battering his face and neck. His heart leaped with joy; he kicked off his shoes and dug in, feeling the surging energy of the earth beneath his toes. He spotted his quarry in the distance, a shadow leaning against an ancient oak.

The man's eyes widened a moment before Carwyn tackled

him to the ground, rolling across the lawn as Carwyn's amnis dug a car-size divot in the rolling lawn.

Giovanni Vecchio spat grass out of his mouth. "I will never understand why you tackle *me* when my wife is the one who taunts you."

Carwyn brushed the dirt from his forehead. "I can't go tackling a girl, can I?"

"That *girl* is more likely to draw a sword on you than wrestle you, and then where would you be?"

"Exactly." He stood and dusted off his clothes. "That's why I tackle you." He offered Giovanni a hand.

The fire vampire rose and flicked off the dirt with an imperious hand. "The Royal Rumble isn't for months."

Carwyn grinned. "Look at you, making jokes about your embarrassing hobby." He rubbed a grubby hand over Giovanni's curls, scattering more dirt in his dark hair. "Someday I'm going to drag you to a live event."

Giovanni shook his head. "Highly unlikely."

From the first time he'd seen professional wrestling in a roadside arena in the 1960s, Carwyn had been fascinated by the confluence of carnival spectacle, athleticism, and storytelling. Wrestling was a drama, a Greek play of human gods complete with boasting, betrayal, and bone-crushing violence.

Absolute delight.

"Carwyn!" Brigid was standing at the top of the hole in the ground. "I think security is coming."

He pointed at Beatrice, who was next to her. "This is your fault."

"Me?" The water vampire put a hand on her chest. "How?"

Carwyn hopped to the top of the hole and spread his arms, sending his amnis into the earth to repair the dirt. "You threw water at me."

Giovanni, Beatrice De Novo's husband, vampire mate, and

scapegoat, climbed out with the help of Carwyn lifting the earth beneath him to the edge where his wife was perched.

"Water?" Beatrice could barely keep from laughing. "I tossed a little water at you, so you decided to excavate your old friend's lawn?"

"Threats like that cannot be ignored." There were few people in the world who understood Carwyn's humor the way that Beatrice De Novo did. She was older than his wife, but not by much, and she'd been sired to water, the perfect balance of amnis with his old friend Giovanni Vecchio. And when Giovanni had disappeared from Beatrice's life, Carwyn had been faithful, knowing that his friend was an idiot and would eventually come running back to the only woman he'd ever loved.

Beatrice was the sister eternity had given him, Carwyn's personal object of torment, and a dear friend.

Brigid was nudging Carwyn in the ribs.

"What is it?"

She kept her voice low. "I need to answer my phone."

He frowned. "So answer your phone. It's Giovanni and Beatrice. They won't be offended if you take a call."

"Don't even think of it." Giovanni walked over and gave Brigid a kiss on each cheek, his lips sparking against her skin. "I see you haven't had any luck with the obedience classes."

"Did you really think I would?" She put a hand under her bust. "And answering might not be as simple as you're guessing. I wrapped the damn thing in a leather case to protect it and tucked it under my tits."

Giovanni laughed.

Carwyn raised an eyebrow. "Not that I'm jealous of your phone—which I definitely am—but that sounds uncomfortable." He looked at the sleek black pants she was wearing. "What's wrong with your pockets?"

"Do these trousers look like they have pockets?" She shifted a little. "It keeps buzzing over and over again. Someone is not taking my voice mail for an answer."

"I'm getting you a purse to wear to fancy things. Not a backpack, a purse. I'm warning you, it will have sparkly or shiny things on it."

Beatrice curled her lip. "Purses are annoying."

"Tell that to the one who wears pants with no pockets. Go on then." He reached down, pinched Brigid's bottom, and motioned toward the house. "Giovanni, Beatrice, and I will go be entertaining at the party. Don't be long."

Brigid gave them all a wave and walked away, her hand already reaching into her blouse.

Beatrice walked to his side and watched Brigid walk toward the trees. "You realize she's going to use whoever is on that phone to avoid socializing, don't you?"

"I expect nothing less."

EIGHT

"Bex, slow down." Brigid walked to an isolated part of the garden. "Who is Roland?"

"Oh fuck." She sniffed. "It's... it's an inside joke, okay? The development team for Paladin, right? We all gave ourselves knight names because... Well, we didn't give them to ourselves, not all of us. Nic thought it was stupid because he's very literal and that's the way his brain works, but he was so completely Roland with the sense of honor and—"

"Bex, focus." Brigid could hear the woman's nerves. "Is something wrong with Savi?"

"Savi is fine. I just told you it was Roland. Nic. It's Nic."

"Nic is Roland?"

"And I'm Berenger and Savi is Oliver, and we all have nicknames, okay? But that's not important. They took Nic!"

Brigid's heart dropped. "Nic is gone?"

"I'm telling you someone took him."

"Did someone break into the house?" She was moments away from calling the guards on the house and reading them the riot act.

"Not exactly." The girl seemed to waver. "Nic left earlier

today, saying he was going to go visit his cousin about something later this week, but then he disappeared."

None of this was making sense. "So Nic left, or Nic was taken?"

"Someone took him! He never came home. Aren't you like, private detectives or what?"

Security consultants. Brigid bristled at the detective label. Detectives had overcoats, silly hats, and a cynical secretary named Flo.

Brigid had fangs, black leather, a buzz cut, and a small mountain of a husband who collected Hawaiian shirts and was horrible about remembering any kind of paperwork.

Bex was panicking. "Hello? I feel like I'm going crazy. Why won't anyone—?"

"When did Nic leave? From where? Was he at work?"

"He got off work at six today. We were working together on the applications interface between the—"

"Not going to make any sense to me, Bex."

"Fine." She huffed. "We were working on a joint project and we hit a wall, so he said he was going out for a drink to clear his head. He does that sometimes, but then he never came back."

"Did a guard go with him?"

"Yes."

"And when was that?"

"About..." Bex sighed. "Maybe five hours ago?"

"Five hours?" Brigid gripped her phone and resisted the urge to scream. "Bex, he's a grown man. He went out for a drink. Maybe he ran into a friend. Maybe he *made* a friend if you know what I mean."

"I know what you mean, but Nic doesn't, okay?" She was nearly yelling over the phone. "You don't understand Nic. He will sit in the corner of a jazz club for exactly one hour, then wait for the band to finish whatever song they're on because he thinks it's rude to leave a club in the middle of a song. He thanks bouncers. He tips in exact change. He does *not* understand when women flirt with him. And he definitely does not spontaneously disappear for over five hours when we're in the middle of a project!"

Brigid glanced at the clock on her device. "It's after midnight."

"So? We work better at night."

Brigid knew the feeling. She glanced at the glowing windows and heard the faint sound of jazz drifting across the grounds. She hadn't met any of the people she was probably supposed to meet that night. She should calm Bex down, call Gavin's security team to deal with this, then meet the girl at dusk the following night when Nic would undoubtedly be back at the lofts in the Bywater and everything would be calm.

She glanced back at the lit windows of Marie-Hélène's mansion. A giant whoop rose from the midst of the jazz band.

On the other hand...

Brigid saw their driver standing near the gate, guarding the car that held her favorite 9mm and her leather jacket. He watched as she drifted toward the exit.

"Bex?"

"Yeah?"

"I'm going to swing by the lofts just to be cautious. Can you gather the other kids who've been followed? Grab whichever guard seems to be coordinating the others too, okay?"

"Okay." The girl seemed relieved. "Okay, I can do that. I think Oli, Samson, and Gerard are playing pool."

Brigid frowned. "Who?"

"Savi, Kit, and Miguel! I told you we had nicknames."

"Right." Brigid would send a message to Carwyn, but there was no reason he needed to spoil his night by checking out something that was probably nothing.

But one of them should check it out. Better safe than sorry.

———

THE LOFTS in the Bywater were the oddest combination of working and living space Brigid had ever seen. The whole bottom floor was taken up with workstations that were clearly technologically driven with computers, printers, and various other gadgets—there was not a surface that didn't look like Brigid could short it out if she came too close—but there was also a pool table, several lounge areas with giant cushions the size of couches, and what looked like a full bar at the end of the room.

Brigid chatted with the guard at the front door, getting a rundown of the overall security before she went inside. The head of security had received a file on her and Carwyn, so he verified her identity, then gave her a summary of their procedures.

She was impressed with Paladin's team. Gavin hadn't slouched on personnel or equipment, and they weren't idiots, which made the idea of one of their charges disappearing even more remote. If something had happened to Nic, it was likely of his own doing.

A Black man of medium height with a barrel chest and closely cropped hair met her at the foot of the stairs. He looked to be in his early forties, and a sprinkling of silver hair marked his temples. "You must be Brigid Connor." He held out his hand. "I'm Gaines. It's good to meet you. Raj is on his way."

She took his hand in a quick shake. "Pleasure. I got a call from Bex."

Gaines offered a rueful smile. "Yeah, she's been giving us hell too."

Brigid raised both eyebrows. "With good reason?"

"Hard to tell because it's Nic." They started up the stairs. "Nic Cooper's primary guard is Charles Daxon—we call him Chuck. Nic has always been uncooperative, and this isn't the first time we've lost track of him. We tripled the guards on Savi when Gavin clarified that she was probably the main target the other day, but we kept at least one guard on each of the kids at all times."

Through her conversation with Bex and her memories of the young man, Brigid had started to get a feel for Nic Cooper's personality, and she suspected having constant supervision would grate on the young man. "Have you been able to reach Chuck yet?"

"We haven't, but sometimes the clubs are real loud so..." Gaines sighed. "It's a problem. We try to stay inconspicuous and not wear earpieces, but then we miss a lot of calls."

Brigid looked around the first floor of the loft where at least a half dozen young employees still buzzed around, many of them talking into what looked like thin air. All of them had a white earpiece in at least one ear.

"Gaines, I'm afraid you're showing your age." She pursed her lips. "Every blessed human in the city is wearing an earpiece connected to their bloody phone. Get your people earbuds; it's the twenty-first century."

"Right." Gaines looked a little embarrassed. "Nic's a smart kid. Honestly, he knows the city really well. He's probably the one we worry about the least. He's got street smarts."

"Street smarts have limited value if a vampire is hunting you."

Gaines frowned. "But the guy following them is human."

Brigid stared at him. "And we all know that vampires never hire humans, don't we?"

He had the smarts to look abashed. "Right."

"I'm going to talk to the kids." Brigid was trying not to be annoyed, but it was looking like Bex might have good reason for concern. "Make it your priority to find Chuck. Right now. Send people out and find him and Nic."

"Yes, ma'am."

She took her phone out and punched in a code through the thick plastic cover. "Message Carwyn and Gavin."

A polite computer voice answered her. "What would you like to say?"

"Don't overreact. I'm at the lofts. Bex called me when she couldn't find Nic. It's probably nothing, but I wanted to check it out." *And avoid a party with so many people I didn't know.* She put her phone in her jacket pocket and forgot about it for a time as she surveyed the lofts where Paladin's employees lived and worked.

Cameras, guards, and clearly defined boundaries with limited entry and exit points. There was one long roof garden that would be accessible to wind vampires, but according to Gavin, he and Gaines had a vampire guard patrolling the skies around the loft at night.

Inside the lofts, security appeared to be ironclad. Outside was another picture. There were too many dark alleys and hidden corners in New Orleans for Brigid's liking.

It was picturesque as hell and just as dangerous.

Brigid reached the top of the open-concept staircase made of glass and wondered what architect hated women who wore skirts. She'd have to talk to Gavin about that. She looked around at the wide-open windows of the old factory, the reclaimed brick interior, and the modern furnishings.

Gavin was a club and bar owner by profession, and the attention to detail wasn't lost on Brigid. The space was undeniably comfortable, a large common area that would be full of light in the mornings. A central kitchen and dining area filled the space with a mix of counter seating near the cooking areas, cozy booths for more private dining, and long friendly tables for group meals. That dining area bled into a large living space at the end of the floor with a collection of seating in front of a movie screen dotted by small, enclosed seating areas for more private space.

The generous use of houseplants gave the space verdant life and calm at the same time, a neat trick for a group of residents who likely lived in their own heads much of the time.

Along the east side of the loft were two stories of rooms, some larger, more like double or triple suites, and some small and private. It seemed that Gavin had accounted for every type of personality in the house, those who craved company and others who liked solitude.

"It's the best place I've ever lived."

Brigid turned and saw Kit behind her. They were looking toward the living area where three other people sat, surrounded by five large security guards.

Kit continued toward the group, and Brigid fell into step beside them.

"Is it like a dormitory?" Brigid asked. "I lived in one of those for a year."

"More like a grown-up dorm." Kit shrugged. "But like, a lot more luxurious. We have cleaners and our own contractor who can make stuff for us or help us put furniture together. We all signed leases for the space we have, so we can customize it however we want."

"And did I catch that you and Miguel and Savi live together?"

Kit nodded. "We have, like, really complementary personalities. Pretty sure Miguel is half in love with Savi, so he's superprotective but not in a gross way. She just lives in her head a lot so she misses stuff. She's hilarious though. Like, seriously one of the kindest and funniest people I've ever met in my life."

"Had you met anyone here before you came?"

"Miguel. He's my best friend. We've known each other since college; he's the one who recommended me for this position. I was working in Lee's department but got promoted when he went back to Oklahoma."

"Lee Whitehorn, correct?"

"Yeah, Nic probably knew Lee better than anyone else here. And I know operating systems." Kit smiled. "That's why I'm here."

"My husband and I are planning to visit Lee in Oklahoma City tomorrow night. Have you spoken to him since he left the company?"

"No, he wouldn't answer any of our calls. It made the transition pretty difficult." Kit shook their head as they approached the group. "Nic might have had better luck; he and Lee were pretty friendly. I think Lee respected Nic more than the rest of us."

"Are you worried about him?"

"Nic?" Kit shook their head even more vehemently. "Nic's one of the smartest people I know. He's like MacGyver, only less friendly. Not that he's *un*friendly or anything. He's just particular. He's got, like, a set amount of social interaction time."

"Bex called him Roland." Brigid watched Kit's face for their reaction.

Kit smiled, their face only showing a hint of embarrassment. "It may seem like a silly nickname, but he *is* Roland. He's... honorable and brave." Kit sat down next to Savi. "Right, Oliver?"

Savi smiled at Kit. "Nic is... Well, he's Nic." She turned to Bex. "I know you're worried about him, but it's not like he hasn't done this before."

"Done what?" Brigid turned to Bex. "You said this wasn't like him."

"It's not." Bex looked irritated. "Before when he went off on his own, he told me he was doing it."

"Maybe he just didn't this time," Miguel said. "I heard the two of you fighting."

"We weren't fighting!" Bex covered her eyes. "Oh my God, you guys, we weren't fighting. We were talking about the guards. He was trying to ditch his and I told him not to. That it was dangerous, and he said no one cared about the fintech guy because there're a million other programmers who can do what he does—"

Bex was interrupted by a general murmur of disagreement.

"What?" Brigid scanned their faces. "Is that true or not? You tell me."

"It's *very* untrue." Savi spoke directly to Brigid. "I may have the most specialized skills, but Nic is a key member of the team, and he's the one almost everyone here at the loft would go to if they ran into a problem."

Miguel nodded. "Nic's not wrong when he said there're a lot of people who understand fintech—financial technology—but that hardly touches on what Nic really does around here. He was one of the first people Gavin hired, and he understands Paladin's vision."

Savi added, "He's a very creative thinker and a surprisingly good communicator."

Brigid frowned. "He struck me as the quiet type."

"He is," Bex said. "When it comes to work though, he's good. He can talk about that stuff easily."

Savi smiled. "This is true. Personally? He can be a bit awkward."

"And yeah, we were arguing about work, but that's why I don't think he went off on his own by choice," Bex said. "He left to refocus, but he would have come back to finish arguing with me. You guys need to go look for him."

"I've already sent Gaines to look for Chuck and Nic." Brigid kept her voice even. She needed to keep all of them calm. "They have GPS locations on their phones, so let's give them a little time." Brigid decided that as long as she had the group to herself, she'd ask a few more questions. "What can you tell me about Lee Whitehorn?"

"He was the previous operating systems head, then he like, left really abruptly." Bex frowned. "I mean, Miguel knew him a little. And Nic knew him."

"Lee got along with Nic and me, but I wouldn't call us friends," Miguel said. "Lee was a pro, but like, real independent too. He didn't want to live at the lofts. He didn't really hang out with any of the rest of us. Not socially anyway."

Savi looked apologetic. "We did not give him a Paladin nickname."

Miguel put a hand on Savi's shoulder. "I don't think that's why he left."

"But we left him out, and I feel very bad about that," Savi said.

"Lee is a very polite person," Kit said. "And honestly, really great to work with. I just think he liked to draw more lines between work and personal if that makes sense."

"Absolutely." It made sense to Brigid, but unfortunately it might make her job harder. She needed information from Lee Whitehorn, and she wouldn't be able to use attachments to former workmates as a motivator.

She'd need to take the direct approach.

Gaines came jogging toward her. "Raj found Chuck." His face was grim. "Knocked out by a sedative behind the Spotted Cat on Frenchman Street. Nic's phone was in his pocket."

"Call Gavin." Brigid wasn't fooling around anymore. "He either drugged his guard and scarpered or someone took him. Either way, finding him is first priority."

NIC 1

Nic sat against a wall in a bare room on a dirty floor. He'd done his best to clean the area before he sat down, but there was nothing more than his shoe to clean with. He'd spent roughly an hour in the trunk of a car after a vampire had knocked him out with amnis. He'd woken up in what seemed like the broken-down remains of an old farmhouse.

He didn't hear the sounds of the city around him. He didn't hear anything familiar.

There were tall windows with the shutters nailed shut. The air smelled of green living things, water, and decay. The floorboards had been painted once, but the paint was chipped and flaking away. There was an old mattress, a bucket, and nothing else.

He'd trusted the wrong person. Again.

He was irritated at himself for not being able to read their intentions. He'd been studying the science of human expression, but he still got it wrong more often than he got it right.

Like with Bex earlier.

Bex would be worried about him, which would make her not think straight and possibly trigger her anxiety disorder. Nic hated to think he would be the reason Bex might have a panic attack, especially when he wasn't there to count for her.

He looked up when he heard someone in the hallway, but they didn't come in. Instead, they went to the room next to his and dropped something heavy on the ground.

More sounds in the hall.

Shouting in a language that reminded him of French but wasn't quite the same. His mother was French, and he'd grown up hearing her and his grandmother argue in the language. He wasn't fluent, but he could understand most native French speakers in Louisiana.

These vampires were not from Louisiana.

Someone jiggled the doorknob; then he heard the latch give way and they cracked the door open.

"'Allo!" A vampire with dark hair, a scruffy beard, and sickly, pale skin poked his head through the door. "My friend, how are you? All awake now?"

Nic glanced at him, then stared at the wall across from the dirty mattress.

"We will get you sheets for your bed, non? We don't want you uncomfortable when you are our guest here."

"I'm not a guest; you kidnapped me."

"Ehhh, I suppose that depends on your perspective, Mr. Cooper." The vampire walked over and crouched down in front of Nic, trying to make him meet his eyes. "You are not afraid, yet you will not look at me."

"Sensory input is valuable, and you are not." Also, Nic didn't want to recognize these people. The fact that they were willing to let him see their faces meant that his chances of being released were extremely low. "What do you want?"

"All in good time. Our friend needs some time to set up his equipment before he is ready for your expertise."

"My expertise?" This wasn't good.

"We know who you work for, Mr. Cooper. Paladin has something we want, and you are going to help us get it. The quicker that happens, the quicker you can go home."

Lie. Nic didn't need to look at the vampire's face to know that was a lie.

"Cool." He rested his head against the wall. "Until then, I want something to eat."

The vampire chuckled. "Smart boy."

"Rice and gumbo should do it," he said. "Can you get that around here?" The contents of the gumbo might clue him in to how far he was from the ocean.

"I think we can accommodate that," the vampire said. "Thank you for being so cooperative."

No use trying to escape until I know what I'm dealing with.

He could pick that lock easily. He could break through the nailed shutters. But Nic was biding his time. He'd already misjudged someone he thought he could trust, and he didn't want to do it again.

The vampire stood. "Very well, Mr. Cooper. We shall see that you get your... gumbo."

He left and the hall beyond the locked door grew quiet again. Five minutes later, it was as if Nic was the only person in the lonely old house.

That was until he heard a low sound from the room next to him.

A moan, then a soft cry.

Muffled crying had him pressing his ear to the wall; his heart began to race.

They hadn't dumped something in the room next to him. They had dumped some*one.*

NINE

There wasn't anything Carwyn and Brigid could do to find Nic that Gavin's security team wasn't already doing, so the following night, they borrowed a plane and flew to Oklahoma City at dusk to find Lee Whitehorn.

"Do you think the young man took off on his own?" Carwyn asked.

"Nic?" Brigid stared ahead from her seat in the center of the cargo hold. "The impression I get from friends is that he's stubborn, inventive, and independent. A subject like that is bound to chafe at having a guard on him twenty-four seven. So for sure, it's possible he ditched his guard and his phone. It's equally possible he was taken."

Carwyn smiled. "Hmm. Stubborn, inventive, and independent..." He stretched his arms out across the back of the seats. "Who does that remind me of?"

Brigid gave him a look that almost managed to be apologetic. "I had to go calm the humans."

"You had to ditch the party." He wasn't angry. In fact, Marie-Hélène had been amused when Carwyn told her he'd lost his wife. It had given the woman more than a few new avenues to prod him. "I had to make excuses for you."

"You love making shagging excuses for me," Brigid said. "What was it this time?"

"Relationship counseling with your hamster. The pet psychiatrist flew in from Los Angeles for the session and you couldn't miss it."

"It would have been horribly rude." The corner of her mouth turned up. "What did she say?"

"She expressed surprise that you would want any furry pets other than me."

Brigid barked a laugh, and Carwyn saw her relax a little.

"She's not a monster." Carwyn shifted in his seat and yawned to pop the pressure in his ears as the plane ascended. "Marie-Hélène is selfish and impulsive, but she's also generous to those she loves and endlessly amused by novelty."

"So I'm a novelty?"

"A fire vampire married to a former priest? Of course you are."

She nodded. "What did Gavin say about Nic?"

"He was annoyed the girl didn't call him first, but he's confident his men will find him. I believe he is also in the 'Nic is having a tantrum and running away' camp. According to Marie-Hélène's man Alonzo, it's not an unknown occurrence for Nic to give security the slip."

Brigid narrowed her eyes. "Bex was certain, and there's something between them. I'm not sure if it's romantic, but there is a tie. I noticed it the first day. I tend to trust her instincts."

"They're searching the city, my girl. And Marie-Hélène's people have very big ears." Carwyn didn't particularly enjoy flying even if he recognized the utility of it. "Distract me."

"Are you feeling anxiety again?"

He scoffed. "Of course not." *It's just a great metal tube hurtling through the sky for no apparent reason.* "You were at the lofts last night. Spill the tea, as the children say."

"The tea?" Her lips twitched, trying to keep from laughing at him. "I found out that Miguel, Savi, and Kit are not a throuple. I assumed they were, but Kit and Miguel are platonic."

Carwyn blinked. "A throuple?"

"Yes, when three people are in a relationship. Instead of a couple, you say it's a—"

"Throuple." Carwyn sighed. "There has to be a better name for it. Throuple sounds like the name of a small furry animal in a science fiction movie."

Brigid raised an eyebrow. "No condemnation from the former priest?"

"It's not my place to judge the private relationships of people, wife." He let out a small smile. "The old man in me does want to say 'Kids these days.'"

Being married to one person was complicated enough. Carwyn had no idea how polygamists kept their sanity intact.

Of course, none of them were married to Brigid Connor.

Carwyn watched the indicators above his head, and as soon as the captain turned off the seat belt light, he released Brigid's belt, pulled her into his lap, and ran his hands over her pert bum. "You should distract me from my horrible flying anxiety."

She turned to him and nuzzled his neck. "But how could I do that?"

"I have an idea or two. Or three."

"Do any of these ideas involve forming a throuple?"

"God help me, wife. One of you is more than enough for any man, living or dead."

———

THE LIGHTS of Oklahoma City sprawled on their descent into the city. Brigid and Carwyn were ready to depart the plane as soon as the captain unlocked the door. Gavin had arranged a car for them along with a driver who knew the city and had already been briefed on their assignment.

The friendly young woman held the door for them on the tarmac of the small private airport. "Mr. Bryn and Ms. Connor?"

Carwyn reached out his hand. "Carwyn and Brigid please."

He noticed when she shook his hand that she wore gloves, the better to prevent unwanted influence on her human mind. "I'm Leanne, and I'll be your driver tonight." She had long dark hair, a clear, light brown complexion, and striking green eyes. "I understand you wanted to surprise Mr. Whitehorn at his home, is that correct?"

"We really just need to talk to him," Carwyn said. "He hasn't returned our calls."

Leanne nodded briskly. "I understand. Mr. Wallace knows that I'm not willing to do anything illegal in the course of my employment, but I can drive you to his house. If he asks us to leave, however—"

"We'll leave." Brigid raised her hands. "But it's very important we get some information from him. There's now a young man who's missing, a man who works for Paladin."

Leanne motioned to the low-slung black sedan. "Then we don't have any time to waste. I have Mr. Whitehorn's address programed in the GPS."

They sat in the back seat, and she walked around to open the driver's side door. Within moments they were exiting the airport and sliding through the silent streets of Oklahoma City.

Carwyn broke the silence. "Not a city known for its nightlife, I think."

Leanne smiled. "That depends on if you like cowboy bars."

Brigid asked, "Do the cowboy bars have real cowboys? Or only the rhinestone variety?"

"They're as real as it gets, ma'am."

Brigid turned to him. "We may need to investigate the cowboys."

"What are you on about?" Carwyn feigned outrage. "Are you attempting to form a throuple with a sexy cowboy, wife?"

Leanne tried to hide her snort, but she couldn't.

"I've been living in America for over a year now, and I have not seen enough cowboy hats, Carwyn. Or fancy boots."

"Work first. Cowboy hats second."

She pretended to pout. "Fine."

"Ridiculous woman."

Leanne caught his eye in the rearview mirror, and Carwyn winked at her.

Brigid was checking her phone. "No word on Nic."

"Surely there must be street surveillance," he said. "In the French Quarter? There has to be security everywhere."

"He wasn't in the Quarter though. He disappeared from a club in the Marigny, and they found his guard in the alley. He grew up in that city, Carwyn. He likely knows how to stay hidden if he wants to."

"Or whoever took him knows how to keep him hidden."

"But we still don't have any evidence he was taken."

"I'll be very curious to see what Mr. Whitehorn has to say," Carwyn said. "I have a feeling he may be able to shed some light on the Nic situation."

———

THE DOOR SLAMMED in their faces faster than it had opened.

"Don't talk to vampires anymore." The man's low voice

carried through the door. "Don't work for 'em. Don't socialize with 'em. Don't date 'em."

Don't date them? Carwyn raised an eyebrow. Interesting.

Brigid was the one who spoke. "Mr. Whitehorn, we're here because Nic Cooper is missing, and we're hoping you might be able to help us find who's responsible."

There was silence on the other side of the door; then they heard the man speaking quietly. "I don't want to talk about work or why I left. There are two of your kind here, asking me questions about Paladin. Did you send them?"

It sounded like one side of a phone call. Carwyn guessed the man had called Gavin. Smart.

Another long silence ended with "I haven't decided yet."

There was another silence; then Whitehorn said, "You can talk to Oukonunaka about that." The door cracked open a few seconds later and a suspicious dark eye peered out. "They took Nic?"

Carwyn asked, "Who's they?"

He looked at Brigid, then at Carwyn. "You working for Gavin?"

"We work for ourselves," Carwyn said. "But we're helping Gavin. Is he the one who hired you?"

"Yeah, came on real slick. My dad warned me that the East Coast kind aren't like the ones round here, but I'm such a smart-ass, aren't I?" The door opened a little more. "Gavin isn't that bad, I guess, but that whole scene..." Lee Whitehorn shook his head. "Not my thing."

The man who stood before them was in his early thirties, bronze-skinned with long black hair and a sharply planed face that spoke of Native ancestry.

"We spoke to Miguel and the other team leaders," Brigid said. "They spoke very highly of you but said that you kept to yourself."

"I have friends," Lee said. "I have my people. I have work. That company wanted to blur the lines." He shrugged. "Some people are into that; I'm not. The work I'm doing now? I leave it at home the end of the day. Suits me better."

Carwyn watched the man's guarded eyes. "The work environment wasn't why you left Paladin though."

Lee turned his eyes to Carwyn. "You're an old one."

"I am. I was a priest for most of my life. I value honesty, and you have a forthright face, Mr. Whitehorn. Yet when you left Mr. Wallace's employ, you gave no warning and no explanation. That doesn't seem like something a forthright person would do."

Whitehorn visibly shifted a shotgun from his right hand to his left, propping it next to the door as he opened it wider. "I'll talk to you, but if you even try to touch me, you'll only do it once."

Brigid looked him straight in the eye. "You have my word that neither of us will touch you in any way."

Someone had used amnis on this man without his permission. To a straightforward man like Lee Whitehorn, it was a grave violation. No wonder he left Gavin's employ so abruptly.

But who?

Whitehorn examined Brigid carefully, then gave a sharp nod and opened the door wide. Carwyn and Brigid stepped carefully inside. The man's illusion of security was just that, an illusion, but that didn't mean that he or Brigid wanted to violate that. They wanted Lee Whitehorn to give them information, not start a fight.

"To be clear about who we are," Carwyn started. "I am the oldest of my line, so I owe allegiance to no one. Before I met my wife, I was a priest in the Catholic Church and those vows are eternal, so I do owe them spiritual loyalty, but I do not work for them."

Whitehorn nodded. "I can respect that kind of loyalty."

"We try to help people when they need help," Brigid said. "That's all. My background is in security work. When we know a friend is having an issue, we try to help."

Whitehorn led them into a kitchen area with a small table off to the side and motioned them to the chairs. "So Gavin Wallace is a friend of yours?"

"We're actually closer to his wife-to-be, Chloe," Brigid said. "But we're friendly with Gavin as well."

"You're Irish." Whitehorn sat across from Brigid. "You work for Murphy?"

She smiled a little. "I used to."

"You know what Wallace is trying to do, right?"

"I have friends and family in Ireland, Mr. Whitehorn. That doesn't mean I'm invested in Patrick Murphy remaining unchallenged in the business arena."

"Hear, hear," Carwyn said. "Bring on the competition."

The corner of Whitehorn's mouth turned up, but the wariness never left his eyes. "What happened to Nic? He'll take off sometimes—you know that, right? He's kind of different, but he's cool."

Carwyn leaned his elbows on the table, ignoring the slight creak from his weight. "Gavin's people are looking for him right now. The guard he had on him was drugged, but we don't know if that was from a kidnapper or Nic's doing."

"Heh." Whitehorn smiled a little. "It could be either. There's definitely someone coming for Wallace's people though, so don't count out a kidnapping."

Carwyn asked, "Why did you leave Paladin?"

Lee Whitehorn leaned back, crossed his arms over his barrel chest, and took a deep breath before he let it out slowly. "I didn't like the work environment over there. That was one strike, for sure. The pay was..." He shook his head and looked at the table. "More money than I'd ever been offered for a job." He turned to

Brigid. "I'm thirty-two. In that environment, I was creeping into old age. Didn't love that part, but I'd have been able to put up with it for the money if other stuff hadn't happened."

"Understood," Brigid said. "We need to know the other stuff. Five Paladin employees reported being followed by the same ordinary-looking man in different caps and sunglasses. That sort of thing. Were you followed as well?"

"That's how it started, yeah." He nodded. "But then I started having gaps."

"Gaps?" Carwyn frowned. "What kind of gaps?"

"The kind that told me one of your kind was messing with my head." Whitehorn swallowed hard. "I didn't think that was it at first. I don't drink, so I went to the doctor, thought I was stressed out maybe. The pace of work at Paladin is pretty intense because Gavin wants to launch in eighteen months. That might seem like a lot of time, but trust me, for a new device with a new operating system, eighteen months is nothing."

Brigid gently prodded. "But it wasn't work stress?"

"Causing gaps like that?" He shook his head. "The doctor couldn't find anything wrong with me, but he put me on antianxiety meds just in case." Whitehorn curled his lip. "They messed with my thinking, my concentration. Plus the gaps didn't stop, so I stopped the meds."

"You're sure it was someone using amnis on you?"

"Pretty damn sure, yeah." He pulled his T-shirt collar to the side. "Can you see it?"

Human eyes wouldn't have picked it up, but there was a faint feeding scar on Lee Whitehorn's shoulder.

"One of our tribal elders is a real elder, if you know what I mean. I was..." The man's gaze turned inward. "I was messed up when I came back from New Orleans. Was going through a healing ceremony a couple of weeks ago and he spotted it."

Carwyn understood the dark anger in the man's eyes. "Your elder, did he—?"

"It took a lot of convincing on my part to keep him from going down there, but I didn't want anyone innocent getting hurt, and I had no idea who it was. I'd been having the gaps for like, three months at that point, and I had no idea. Plus there were the letters."

Brigid frowned. "What letters?"

"I left New Orleans fast, okay? I don't normally treat jobs that way, but I was messed up, and I needed to get home. I got back here" —he looked around— "this was my granddad's house. He left it to me when he passed, so it's always been a safe place. I settled in, started looking for a place to work—I hate not working and I wanted to distract myself—but I got a few letters. The first one was just... vague. Weird. 'Keep your mouth closed about New Orleans.' Something like that. I tossed it because I was fucked up and I didn't want to talk to anyone about it anyway, right?"

"I understand that," Carwyn said. "But if you're under someone's aegis, they would need to know about a threat like that for your own protection."

"Aegis doesn't work that way for us. It's not like a top-down authoritarian kind of thing." He shook his head. "I wanted to forget about it." He stood and walked to the kitchen, opening a drawer next to an old green refrigerator. "I saved the other two."

He took two white envelopes from the drawer and put them on the table.

Brigid didn't hesitate to open the first. "What are these houses?"

The paper held no threat, but there were pictures of houses along with addresses typed out beneath them.

"My mom and dad's house." Whitehorn pointed to one. "My

sister and her husband." He pointed to another. "My baby cousin and her boyfriend. My uncle's place."

"He was showing you that he knew where your family lived." Carwyn abhorred those who used the bonds of family as a threat.

"My family is under protection now." He glanced at Brigid. "So am I. You're being watched."

Carwyn planted his feet on the floor and sent his amnis out, sniffing for other vampires. Just as Lee Whitehorn indicated, he sensed three immortals on the periphery of the house, two belonged to the earth. He kept his energy on a tight leash, pulling back so he wouldn't alarm the man's guards.

"We're not a threat to you," Brigid said. "We're not like the man who sent these letters."

"Or woman," Whitehorn said. "I wouldn't put it past her."

"What woman?" Brigid asked. "Who are you talking about?"

"That lady Gavin works with," Whitehorn said. "The other owner. Marie something? It could be her or one of her people. Maybe they got to them, or they were having second thoughts about making an enemy out of Nocht. Or maybe they got paid off. Who knows?"

Carwyn was intrigued. "Why do you suspect Marie-Hélène?"

Whitehorn shrugged. "All I know is the first time I had a gap was right after I was at her place." He unfolded the other letter. "First time I remember missing time was the morning after a party she hosted with a bunch of fancy people at her mansion. We were all invited. 'Perks of the job,' Gavin said." Whitehorn shook his head. "I remember that tall lady yelling out my name, meeting all kinds of people. The next morning I woke up and I couldn't remember half the night."

"It happened there," Carwyn said. "That's when they targeted you."

"Yeah." He showed Carwyn the last letter. "Find out who did

this, and I'll be able to tell my elder that this problem has been dealt with. I don't like violence, but putting up with threats like this?" Whitehorn shook his head. "Whoever this is? They don't know who I am or what kind of people I come from. If they try anything, they'll die."

The last letter contained a half dozen photographs of Lee Whitehorn lying unconscious on dirty floors, surrounded by what looked like drug paraphernalia, liquor bottles, and pornography. To anyone who didn't know the man, they were the pictures of an addict at rock bottom.

On the bottom of the page, there was a single line of text.

I HAVE MORE. KEEP YOUR MOUTH SHUT.

TEN

Brigid was still mulling over Lee Whitehorn's statement when they landed back in New Orleans later that night. "Do you think Marie-Hélène would have introduced the Paladin employees to vampires she didn't trust?"

"I don't know." Carwyn looked out the window as the plane taxied to the private hangar Gavin was using. "She's a hostess, Brigid. People drift in and out of her orbit all the time. Do you think Gavin knows all the people who come to his clubs?"

"Does Gavin invite bar patrons to his home?" Brigid asked. "I think we have to strongly consider this as an inside job. Do you think Gavin's prepared for that?"

Carwyn's lips were a firm line. "He's a man who vets his associates carefully and trusts very few. This won't sit well with him."

"So we brief Gavin first and let him decide how much to reveal to his partner."

He nodded. "We also need to find out who hired the security team locally. I know Gavin has some people in town for the wedding, but for Paladin security he may have depended on

Marie-Hélène since she has more people in her organization and knows the area."

"Good point."

It wasn't sitting well with Brigid. None of it was. She found the posed pictures of Lee Whitehorn most disturbing. It was one thing to violate another's mind with amnis and make them forget, but to use amnis to trap them in acts they abhorred was evidence of a twisted psyche.

A realization hit her. "Paladin wouldn't have hired White-horn without knowing his vampire connections."

"Of course not. From what I can tell, they targeted hiring to humans who already had vampire connections, so I'd say that's accurate."

"Do you think whoever used amnis on Lee Whitehorn and took those pictures knows that he's under immortal aegis?" Brigid sat back in her seat.

"If they're close to Marie-Hélène or Gavin, it's likely."

Brigid was interrupted by the voice of the pilot telling them they were cleared to leave the plane. Carwyn gathered the backpack he'd brought and put his hand on the small of Brigid's back as she walked to the front and down the stairs.

She waited until they were both seated in the waiting car. "This was a reckless act. A desperate one."

"Why do you think that?" Carwyn said. "The threats, the gaps in memory. That all seems very calculated to me."

"Gavin is hiring humans already under vampire aegis." Brigid kept her voice low. "Think about it. Nondisclosure agreements and professional courtesy would have kept the workings of the company safe, but by using employees under aegis, you're adding another layer of security to your staff. Your own security and the attention and threat of whichever vampire owns their loyalty."

"So whoever is targeting Paladin's employees—"

"They're playing with fire, Carwyn. This has the potential of spoiling Gavin's reputation, Marie-Hélène's, and starting a fucking vampire war if we don't find out who's targeting these young people."

He frowned. "We need to be looking at vampires with nothing to lose."

"Or everything."

"What do you mean?"

"I mean that to violate Lee Whitehorn like that—using aegis, taking those pictures, threats in an entirely different immortal territory—they're desperate. And I'd also say..." There was something else. Something she wasn't putting her finger on. "It's... insecure."

"Insecure?"

Shite! Of course it was. Brigid turned to Carwyn. "If you used amnis on a human against their will to erase their memory of an event, would you threaten them later?"

Carwyn shrugged. "I wouldn't need to."

"Why not?"

"Because the whole point is that they wouldn't remember. If I used amnis on a human against their will—which I *wouldn't*—they wouldn't even know I'd done it. They might have a gap like Whitehorn did but..." His mouth dropped open. "Oh right. Obviously."

"They're young. Or younger. You probably haven't questioned your amnis in hundreds of years."

Carwyn shook his head. "Humans have varying resistance to amnis, but none are completely immune and these were repeated uses, repeated incidents. The first few were probably trials to see what Whitehorn would remember."

"He remembered nothing, so it continued, but this vampire is still threatening him. Whoever did this wanted insurance. This is a younger immortal who is reckless and either has nothing to lose or everything, and they're desperate. Whoever did this to Lee was *not* a professional."

"And they might be in Marie-Hélène Charmont's organization," Carwyn said. "Or maybe a good friend."

Brigid sighed as the sedan slid through the streets of New Orleans, deeper into the night city. "This has big, giant mess written all over it, Carwyn."

"And it's in the middle of an immortal society wedding too." He glanced at his phone. "There's another reception tomorrow. The guests are starting to arrive."

God help her.

———

GAVIN SAT across from them in the library of their guesthouse, a trim dark-haired vampire with a neat beard standing behind his left shoulder. It was Raj, his security chief from Los Angeles, who happened to be the vampire who'd discovered Nic's guard.

"Please tell me Lee Whitehorn told you why he left the company," Gavin said. "He's under the aegis of one of the oldest vampires in North America, and this doesn't sit well with me. Plus I liked the man. His leaving felt very out of character."

"Someone was using amnis on him." Brigid leaned forward and didn't mince words. "He had gaps in memory. At least a half dozen that he could identify, but there could have been more. He has no idea what he revealed during that time."

Raj let out a long breath. "Fucking hell. He didn't tell Gaines any of this. He would have told me."

Brigid continued. "Whitehorn left because of the violation, but now he's being threatened, and he has no idea by who."

Gavin's jaw grew tight. "Has he told—?"

"The man told his elder, but he agreed to keep it contained

for now," Carwyn said. "If the threats continue, it won't remain that way."

Gavin's mouth was set in an angry line as he stared at a spot on the library wall. "He could have revealed anything under amnis. Using human employees who were already under aegis was supposed to prevent this kind of meddling." He looked up and saw Brigid's face. "And yes, I know that sounds like I don't care about the violation against Lee, but I do care. I won't be able to hire good people if I can't guarantee they'll be protected."

"And it's *wrong* to violate a human's mind," Brigid said.

Raj remained silent, staring at the wall behind Brigid's head.

Gavin frowned. "Of course it's wrong, but vampires do wrong things fairly regularly, Ms. Connor. This act was stupid and intended to embarrass me, make my employees doubt my protection." He drummed his fingers on the table. "It worked with Lee, and now they've taken Nic."

"Are we sure about that?" Brigid asked. "We're positive he didn't just go off on his own for a while? Drugging his guard like that..."

"Come with me." Gavin stood and walked toward the door with Raj walking before him. "I'll fill you in."

"Where are we going?" Carwyn asked.

Brigid rose and grabbed her jacket, then put it down. "I'll stand out more with it, won't I?"

The corner of Carwyn's mouth turned up. "It's warm in New Orleans even at night. You might look conspicuous with a heavy leather jacket."

"Where am I supposed to keep my guns?"

Raj laughed a little. "This isn't California, Miss Connor. As long as you're not going into a bar, you can carry your gun anywhere you want."

———

"NIC'S MOTHER was one of Marie-Hélène's debutantes." Gavin opened up in the car as soon as the divider was raised, which cut off sound from their driver and Raj, who was sitting in front. "She married someone that her patroness did not approve of. For good reason, as it turns out, because Nic's father left when he was three and hasn't been seen since."

Brigid began painting a mental picture of a proud young woman raising a headstrong little boy on her own.

"Marie-Hélène did relent when it came to schooling. Nic attended a very exclusive private school. It likely wasn't the most comfortable for him socially, but his grades and academic achievements were exceptional. He graduated from the Georgia Institute of Technology when he was only twenty."

Brigid watched as the newly refurbished waterfront in the Bywater slipped away and the neighborhood flashed between industrial buildings, old shotgun houses, and brightly painted fixer-uppers as they made their way away from the river up Poland Street. Graffiti littered her eyes, painted over utility boxes, old trailers, corner stores, and warehouses.

"Nic grew up here and went to an elite prep school?" Brigid asked. It was no wonder he didn't feel comfortable socially.

"He did." Gavin glanced at her. "Marie-Hélène did offer to help, but Nic's mother—"

"Too proud to take it?"

"Yes."

Brigid nodded. She didn't judge the woman; she knew how hard it could be to break away from family, especially when you'd been wrong.

"For the record, according to Nic's mother, his father left because Marie-Hélène made his life miserable," Gavin said. "Which is... possible."

"Really?" Carwyn asked. "She'd interfere in a young woman's marriage like that?"

"If she thought the man unsuitable? Yes. I'm sure she thought as soon as Nic's father left, his mother would return to the fold and Marie-Hélène would have a brilliant, charming little boy she could raise to her liking."

"Well, that's..." Carwyn shook his head.

Gavin caught Brigid's look. "She's overbearing. Absolutely. She's also loyal and smart. I don't interfere with her humans."

"Someone interfered with Nic." Brigid was getting more and more worried. "If whoever was threatening Lee Whitehorn is behind Nic's disappearance, they're very dangerous."

"The security camera behind the Spotted Cat revealed nothing, unfortunately. It was not working that night."

"How goes the hunt for the ordinary man?" Carwyn asked. "The fella who was following the others."

Gavin nodded at his driver. "Better than you might have suspected."

Brigid looked around as the car turned again. "Where are we going?"

"To find one Auguste Peregrine, or as you know him, Ordinary Man." Gavin kept his eyes forward. "My men are already in the neighborhood. Raj found him by following surveillance footage in the area." He looked at Brigid. "We learned in Los Angeles about the useful features of doorbell cameras. It's amazing how vulnerable their security firewalls are."

Brigid felt her fangs drop as the car slowed. "We're hunting?"

"Mr. Peregrine proved surprisingly wily, but we finally discovered a particular sex worker he seems to frequent regularly, and Gaines has been waiting with his men. Mostly human, but we're hunting a human, so it shouldn't matter." Gavin glanced at the old-fashioned pocket watch in his hand. "We shouldn't have to wait much longer."

The car came to a stop on a residential street, and someone tapped on the window a moment before Gavin opened it. They exited the car to find Gaines and two other security guards, a man and a woman, waiting for them.

Brigid smelled the adrenaline and her amnis roused. She hadn't had a proper hunt in months, and she was looking forward to it.

The target Gaines pointed out was a neat two-story house at the end of a street that dead-ended into another industrial park. There was a long chain-link fence with vines growing up and over the barrier, giving the street a hidden quality. The houses on the street were all older, but most of them looked to have been refurbished. There were white picket fences on a few and a wrought iron railing around the two-story they watched.

"How long has he been in there?" Raj asked Gaines.

"Since I texted you."

"Half an hour?"

"Maybe a little more." Gaines plucked at the long-sleeved black shirt he wore. "I think he might have spotted me, but he went inside. Apparently he didn't want to miss an appointment with his girl."

Brigid frowned. "He clocked you?"

"What?"

"Clocked." She shook her head. "*Spotted*. He spotted you?"

"Maybe."

"So you have people watching the back?"

"Absolutely."

Brigid looked at the tall chain-link fence separating the warehouse from the neighborhood. "What about that exit?"

Gaines looked at the end of the street. "The old loading docks?"

"He could climb the fence."

"This guy isn't the fittest if you get my meaning." Gaines put a hand on his belly. "He's a good tail, but he's not exactly in commando shape."

Brigid said, "One of the most effective humans I had on staff in Dublin looked like he carried a keg of Guinness under his shirt, but he could outrun a slow vampire if he got his adrenaline going. Physique can be deceiving; put a man on the factory."

"I'll go myself." Gavin took to the air. "Brigid, if you'd—"

"I'll follow you." She looked at Carwyn. "Stay with this lot?"

"Your wish, my queen." Carwyn bowed dramatically, and when he smiled, his fangs were showing. "Enjoy the hunt."

Enjoy the hunt.

Brigid snorted as she jogged around the block to the street parallel to the one Gaines was watching. With a human, it wasn't likely to be much of a challenge. She ran down the road at just barely over human speed, leaping over the vine-covered chain link just in time to see the Ordinary Man duck under a semitrailer.

"Gavin!" She knew he'd hear her even from the sky. "He's out."

Of course the man was escaping via the loading yard. Of course he was. He wasn't an idiot, and he'd been eluding Paladin's security for days.

She froze, listening for his footsteps, but she heard none.

Interesting.

Brigid approached the trailer where she'd first seen the man duck from sight. The ground was pocked with footprints made from rain that had drenched the city earlier that night.

Damn.

The ground was soft, meaning the damp earth would swallow the sound of his footsteps if the man knew how to run.

"Anything?" Gavin called down. He was perched on top of a trailer. "I can't see him."

"He knows you're up there." She raised a hand to quiet Gavin and scanned the alley of metal boxes surrounding her. "He's smart."

She heard the crunch of gravel in the distance. "There." Brigid spun and ran toward the sound, only to arrive at the source and find a brick thrown into a pile of loose pea gravel used to absorb the mud beneath truck tires.

Clever, clever human.

She heard a whisper in the wind and ran toward it, leaping over trailer tongues and dodging stacks of massive tires.

"He's heading toward the street," Gavin said. "Streetlights and people. Damn."

The Ordinary Man was smart. He knew Gavin wouldn't fly after him into a street where he might expose himself in front of humans.

"I've got him." Raj had appeared at her side and sped away.

"Humans," Brigid warned.

She broke through the forest of semitrailers just in time to see the backside of the man in a dark tracksuit jump into the back seat of a black sedan.

"Damn it," Raj fumed. "I had to slow down once I got near the streetlights."

She was tempted to race after the car, but there was a crowd of people who'd gathered in front of a corner store and spilled into the street. There was music, laughter, and plenty of mobile phones visible to catch her taking off running at vampire speed.

Damn, damn, damn. *Damnaigh.*

The Ordinary Man was clever.

Then again, so was Brigid, and she had a good memory. She walked back to the truckyard and looked for Gavin, who was glaring at the disappearing sedan.

"Let's get back to Gaines," Brigid said. "I have a license plate for him to run."

ELEVEN

"Meet Auguste Peregrine." Gaines pointed a remote at the screen and a picture popped up. "The Ordinary Man."

"Ordinary indeed." Carwyn examined the picture and saw a thousand men of no particular interest looking back at him. A father of three trudging through an amusement park. A bank manager on a break from a staff meeting. A high school gym teacher or a chef. The man was utterly average.

Carwyn glanced at the paper Brigid handed him—it was a collection of information Gaines had gathered about Peregrine during the day while they rested.

"He's forty-two, five foot nine inches tall with brown eyes, according to the DMV. A little under two hundred pounds, but that's likely an underestimate." Gaines flipped through more pictures on the screen. "Here he is following Savi and Kit in the Quarter." Another picture popped up—all were grainy, as if taken from subpar security systems. "Here's a few of him following Nic. One of him following Nic and Bex."

"Good Lord, he was all over the five of them," Carwyn said. "How long?"

"We can find evidence of him from three months ago, which got more active in the past couple of weeks after Lee Whitehorn left. We think that whoever was targeting Lee must have pressured Peregrine after their primary target left."

Raj asked, "And this is all related to Paladin? What does this guy do?"

"The last job we have record of Mr. Peregrine actually working was as a bouncer at a club in Baton Rouge. That was over ten years ago. Since then, he seems to exist in a grey area. No residence on file. His driver's license is expired. He owns nothing under his own name. The only reason we have any name or picture is because he has an arrest on file from his time working as a bouncer."

"Interesting." Brigid leaned forward, her eyes narrowed on the screen. "Where's he from?"

"He's homegrown," Gaines said. "Born in Saint Tammany Parish, graduated from school in Covington. No further schooling, but he got good grades. He's no dummy."

"On-the-job training, I think." Gavin was tapping his thumb on the table. "He's exactly the kind I'd hire. Smart but underutilized."

"That's why you lured me from Singapore," Raj said. "Which I am very happy about, by the way."

Carwyn smiled. Gavin's security chief from Los Angeles had a casual manner and a keen eye. He would be easy to work with.

Gavin stared at the man on the screen. "He's working for an immortal."

"Any idea who?" Carwyn hadn't broached the likelihood that whoever was targeting Paladin employees was working for Marie-Hélène, and he didn't want to do it in front of Gaines and Raj.

"Saint Tammany Parish is Marie-Hélène's territory," Gavin

muttered. "I want to think about it before I put anyone in Brigid's crosshairs."

Brigid lifted an eyebrow. "What's the story on Nic?"

"Still no sign of him, but according to his mother, he has the key for a hunting cabin her family used to use in Vermilion Parish," Gaines said. "I should be getting a call from two people headed up there any time now; they left around four this afternoon."

"Raj, can you go pick up Savi and bring her to the office?" Gavin asked. They were sitting in his office in the Central Business District. He glanced at Carwyn and Brigid. "I want to ask her if there has been any unusual activity against Paladin's firewalls. And what she's doing to keep them secure with Nic missing. If they used amnis on Lee, they'll use it on Nic too."

"Right away." Raj nodded and left the room. "Gaines, can you come with? The kids know you better than me."

"Of course." Both men exited the room, leaving Gavin alone with Carwyn and Brigid.

Brigid tapped her phone. "You can't call Savi?"

Gavin's face didn't move. "Is that phone running Nocht?"

"Yes."

"Then what on earth makes you think it's secure?"

Carwyn leaned his elbow on the table. "Are you always this paranoid?"

"Yes, with good reason. I should be getting ready for a party to welcome my future wife's designer friend who's making our wedding clothes as a gift, and instead I'm here with you two." He rubbed his face. "No offense, but neither of you is better company than Chloe and Arthur when they've been drinking."

"None taken. I'd rather be there too," Carwyn said. In fact, he'd much rather be there. He'd met Arthur in New York. The tiny human was a riot.

"But I'm not wrong. If someone was using amnis on Lee,

they'd use it on Nic too, even though he's under Marie-Hélène's aegis," Gavin muttered. "Not only is it a threat to Paladin, it's an insult to both of us."

Brigid said, "You intentionally hired people who were under vampire aegis so our kind would be less likely to target them, and then it happens anyway."

Gavin glanced at Carwyn. "There were a number of reasons for the choice—prior knowledge of our specific electronic needs, no need to hide why meetings are always at night, confidentiality—but the fact that they'd be protected by us and their own aegis made sense."

"But someone isn't playing by the rules," Carwyn said. "And Nic is missing."

"They're right when they say Nic has done this before, but Bex is also correct; he usually tells someone he'll be out of touch. The longer he's gone, the more worried I'm becoming."

Carwyn decided it was time to broach the uncomfortable. "When we questioned Lee Whitehorn, he could pinpoint the first gap in his memory."

Gavin's voice was terse. "When?"

Brigid spoke softly. "It was the morning after a big party at Marie-Hélène's house. Their welcome party."

"The end of summer," Gavin said. "I remember that party, but I can't remember who Lee was spending time with."

"Is there any way you could get the guest list?"

"I'll talk to Marie-Hélène's security chief," he said. "He won't like it."

Carwyn frowned. "Won't like giving you the guest list?"

"No." Gavin stood. "He won't like knowing that whoever is targeting Paladin is someone Madame Charmont invited into her home."

SAVI BURST into the conference room with a panicked expression on her face. "I was just about to call you when Joseph picked me up. I found Nic!"

Brigid stood. "You found him?"

Carwyn frowned. "Who's Joseph?"

Gavin looked at him as if he were a slow child. "Gaines. He does have a first name."

"Literally no one here has ever used it as far as I can remember." Carwyn looked at Brigid. "Did you know?"

Brigid ignored him and focused on Savi. "What did you find? You found Nic? As in you know where he is?"

"Well..." The girl waved a hand and set her open laptop on the conference table. "Kind of. I tracked the IP address of the hacker who's making very clumsy attempts to get into Paladin's servers, but then I realized it was a proxy chain, so I tried to—"

"None of this is going to make sense to us," Carwyn said. "I am sorry, but the computer revolution left our kind in the dust."

Savi sat and let out a sharp sigh. "Okay, imagine someone was trying to attack you, and you have a blindfold on."

"What kind of attack is it?" Brigid asked. "Knifefight? Gunfight? Swords?"

"Just, like a..." She made a fist and pantomimed a boxer as she sat down. "Like a punching kind of fight, you know?"

"A fistfight." Carwyn smiled. The tiny woman was adorable. "I understand. And we have a blindfold on?"

"Yes, but everyone has a different way of fighting, right? Well, computer code is a language, and just like any language, everyone speaks it a little differently. So even though I can't see who is attacking the servers, I can recognize someone I've..." She waved her small fist again. "...fought with. Before, you know?"

Gavin's eyes were intent on Savi. "What are you trying to say? Who are you fighting... electronically?"

"I'm fighting Roland! Nic. I mean, I'm fighting Nic."

Brigid frowned. "Why?"

"It's like... It's a signal to me. A sign, I think. He's making very clumsy attempts to breach our firewalls from a proxy server, and he's not trying to hide it." She spread her hands. "So I found him!"

"Where is he?" Brigid was already standing. "Gavin, you have a car waiting?"

"Wait, I don't... I mean, I don't know where he is. Not in real life. I mean, I tracked the IP address to Rio de Janeiro, but I don't—"

"For fuck's sake, he's already in Brazil?" Brigid's eyes went wide. "Gavin, do you have a plane ready?"

"Wait!" Savi raised her hands. "He's *not* in Brazil. Or probably not. I mean, in theory he could be there, but there's no reason to think he's there any more than he's in New York, Baton Rouge, or right down the street somewhere."

Brigid sat again. "I am so confused."

"He's using a proxy chain." She paused and seemed to reevaluate her words. "Basically he is using a program that can mimic any geographical location, and he's using multiple layers of them. He could be anywhere in the world. I can try to track it back to him, but it will take a lot of time to do that because we're talking about a chain that he created, which could easily be fifty to a hundred proxies, which would all—"

"English, Savi." Carwyn patted her hand. "Keep it very simple."

"It would be far easier for me to try to send a message to Nic. It's possible he'll be able to then give us a clue about where he is if he knows we understand that he's trying to talk to us."

Carwyn must have still looked lost.

Savi took a breath and let it out sharply. "It would kind of be like writing a big message and hanging it on the wall he's trying to break down."

"Will that put him in danger?" Gavin said. "If you're right, it's obvious they have him trying to get into Paladin's servers. Would Nic actually be able to get into the system if he tried?"

Savi frowned. "Maybe, but I am very good." She snorted. "You know that; it's why you hired me. The algorithms I've set up..." She must have caught their expressions again. "My fighting style is much more... nimble than most. It's very flexible. So if Nic tries to punch through the firewalls, he's not going to break them even with a very powerful punch. It'll be more like his fist would go into the wall and turn to jelly."

Brigid nodded. "That's brilliant."

"I know." Savi smiled. "And to answer your earlier question, I don't think a message from me would put Nic in danger. I could write it in code even." Her eyes lit up. "I could write coded code! I love that."

Carwyn was lost and didn't like admitting it, but he had a feeling he knew what Savi was trying to say. "You can get a message to Nic that only he'll be able to understand because the two of you already have your nicknames and such, correct?"

"Exactly. Also, he's very familiar with my programming style. We've worked very closely together on the payment platform Nic is setting up because those have to be very, very secure."

Payment platform? A thought started forming in Carwyn's mind only to be thoroughly shouted down by the loud ring of the office phone in the corner.

"Good Lord, that sound is obnoxious." Brigid winced.

Gavin walked over. "You think so? I find it rather pleasant. It's a real bell, you know. Not an electronic toy." Gavin picked up the phone. "Hello?"

Savi spoke quietly to Carwyn as Gavin listened to the call. "My boss is a bit of a Luddite but a nice one. I think that's common for vampires, isn't it?"

"Quite." Carwyn smiled. "You're darling, by the way. Be very careful if a vampire tries to date you. They will be attracted."

Her eyes went wide. "Really?"

"Really."

Her dark brown cheeks reddened a little. "I think... I mean, well, we don't know each other that well, but—"

"That Miguel fellow seems like a nice sort. Have you ever asked him for a drink?"

She let out a tiny squeak. "We hang out."

Gavin slammed the phone down. "Damn."

Brigid crossed her arms, her face grim. "What happened?"

Gavin turned to Savi. "The good news is you and the rest of the team won't have to worry about the Ordinary Man following you anymore."

Carwyn looked at Brigid, who met his eyes. They both knew what was coming next.

"Gaines just got a call from the city coroner's office," Gavin said. "Auguste Peregrine is dead."

TWELVE

Brigid sat in a corner of Marie-Hélène's salon, a whiskey cocktail in hand and a burning desire to be anywhere but at a party in her heart. She also had a purse tucked next to her, a crystal-studded contraption that Carwyn had surprised her with just as she was getting ready to slide her phone under her tits again.

A tall, lanky vampire walked toward her, her face forcing a stir of recognition. Short, dark hair; flawless, immortal skin; and brilliant blue eyes.

"Hey." The woman held out her hand. "We met the other night, remember?"

"Chance with the cool name." Brigid rose and shook her hand, then motioned to the upholstered chair next to her. "Join me? I have a feeling you're as much a fan of these things as I am."

"Your feeling would be correct." Chance sat next to her, and the smile she offered Brigid was rueful. "But nevertheless, we attend."

There was something about the woman that Brigid couldn't place. She'd pointedly said that Marie-Hélène wasn't her sire, which had been Brigid's impression from talking to Marie-Hélène. Something about her amnis felt familiar in a way that Brigid couldn't articulate.

"I need to get Marie a dog," Chance said.

"A dog?"

Chance nodded. "That way when I'm at her parties, I have someone to talk to."

Brigid snorted. "I'm not much of an animal person, but I have been known to avoid a bad party by talking to indifferent cats." She nodded at Carwyn. "My husband adores dogs."

"You don't have any?" Chance asked. "I have about a dozen at the ranch. Two golden retrievers and a lab, which were intentional, then all the rest are a motley crew of strays that somehow wandered in and made themselves at home."

Brigid smiled. "You remind me of my sire. She lives on a farm in Wicklow, Ireland." She nodded to the velvet sofa where Marie-Hélène was meeting the guests of honor. "Have you met Chloe's friends before?"

"I haven't. From New York, right?"

Despite the revelations about the Ordinary Man, appearances had to be kept up. Brigid, Carwyn, and Gavin were attending a cocktail party to welcome Chloe's dear friend Arthur and his husband, Andrew, to New Orleans.

Chloe had only recently broken the news to Arthur that vampires existed, he was friends with several, and Chloe would be marrying one.

Arthur, a brilliant fashion designer with a taste for gothic design, the fantastical, and the dramatic, was thrilled. Andrew? Slightly less so.

"Arthur is a completely brilliant designer. He's created costumes for a number of Chloe's shows, and he has his own clothing line too. I think his husband is a banker or something."

Chance nodded. "Yeah, that looks about right."

Arthur was fawning over Marie-Hélène—they were already deep in conversation—and Drew was standing next to him, holding two drinks and looking uncomfortable.

Moments later, Carwyn sidled up to Drew and started a conversation. The human visibly relaxed and was smiling moments later.

"Your husband is one of the most charming men I've ever met," Chance said. "Wonderful sense of humor."

Brigid glanced at her bejeweled handbag. "His humor is second to none."

"Plus," Chance continued, "he seems to just... care. You can see when he speaks to people he's really listening to them."

Brigid smiled just looking at him. "He's my sunlight."

Chance was silent, but when Brigid looked back at her, her eyes were red-rimmed. "That's lovely."

Brigid immediately felt as if she'd taken off her clothes and run naked through the house. "If I don't murder him, I'll likely love him forever."

Chance laughed a little. "How long have you known Chloe?" She picked at a thread on her satin pantsuit. "I am so jealous of your pants, by the way."

"Why?" Brigid was feeling underdressed again, but she had no intention of buying more than the five dresses she'd already purchased for this vampire extravaganza. "I think you look brilliant."

"I hate dressing up." A thread of air gusted from a window, and Chance nudged it away before it reached the elaborate candelabra next to them.

"You're a wind vampire!" Brigid snapped her fingers. "That's what it is. There was something about your amnis that didn't seem to fit."

The corner of Chance's mouth turned up. "I'm a bit out of

place in this crew, which is why it's always nice when Gavin visits."

"Ben and Tenzin will be coming soon as well. Have you met them?"

Chance nearly spit out the sip of martini in her mouth. "No. I mean, I've heard of them. Especially Tenzin."

"They're not as scary as they're made out to be." Was that strictly true? Brigid would think about that later. "You know they're very close friends of Chloe's."

"I didn't know that. No." She swallowed hard. "Are they based in New York?"

"They are. They work in art retrieval these days."

"Not... assassination?"

"Not typically." Brigid sipped her Manhattan. She couldn't say that Tenzin had turned over a completely peaceful leaf, but art was her main target these days. Mostly.

"So how's the stuff with Paladin going?" Chance asked. "I don't know much about technology, but I know Marie-Hélène said there had been some problems with someone harassing the employees?" Chance frowned. "That's horrible."

"Things are progressing," Brigid answered with her standard response to ongoing investigations. "We're still following a number of promising leads. Have you met any of the young people working for the company?"

"Uh..." Chance pursed her lips. "Probably? I'm sure some of them have come to this kind of thing, but none of them stand out. I'm terrible with names though."

Brigid nodded. Chance didn't seem like the most social butterfly, so she wasn't surprised. "What about a man named Lee Whitehorn? He was a little older than the others." She motioned to her hair. "Has really long, beautiful hair he wears in braids. He's a Native guy from Oklahoma."

Chance might not have been the life of the party, but often wallflowers were excellent observers. If she'd noticed Whitehorn hanging out with any particular vampires, it might produce a lead.

"You know..." Chance stared into the distance. "He sounds familiar. It's been a while since any of the computer people were around." She lifted one shoulder in a slight shrug. "I'll keep thinking about it though." She brightened. "You know what? I'll ask Arabella. She remembers everyone, and I can hardly think with all this noise."

There *was* a lot of noise even though the band had been placed in the entryway again. Vampire ears were more sensitive than most.

Brigid reached for the card she carried with her business information. She kept a small stack of them in a pocket in her boot. "If you think of anything, call me."

"Of course." The woman looked at Marie-Hélène, and a soft smile crossed her lips. "I would never want anything to mess up one of Marie's businesses. She takes care of people. It's what she loves most."

"That's a lovely thing to be recognized for," Brigid said. "Far better than being known as the prickly fire vampire with a tendency to explode."

Chance pointed at the 9mm still attached to Brigid's hip. "If it helps, the staff was warned more about your tendency to carry firearms everywhere than the exploding thing."

"Oh, that's lovely to hear actually. Cheers."

———

BRIGID CAUGHT up with Gavin and Chloe later that night. Chloe was cuddled up to Gavin on a tufted chaise, her shoes kicked off and her feet curled beside her. The vampire had his arm around his fiancée and was rubbing her feet. Chloe looked half asleep but ecstatically happy.

"The craic was ninety, you two." Brigid dragged a chair next to Chloe. "I didn't want to explode even once."

"Awww, I know you're only saying that, but thank you anyway." Chloe reached over and patted Brigid's knee. "Sit with us for a while. I feel like I've barely seen you this week. I think Arthur had the best time, right? He loves anything over the top."

"That he does." Gavin played with one of Chloe's curls. "Only two more weeks to go."

Brigid wanted to laugh. They were only a third of the way done with a three-week wedding party. Good Lord, what was her life?

"It's good of you and Carwyn to attend the whole event." The corner of Gavin's mouth turned up.

"Don't worry, I'll send you a bill." Brigid smiled at Chloe. "For our investigative services, not the wedding parties."

Chloe whispered, "You can charge him for the parties too. He's rich."

Gavin pinched the back of her knee and Chloe squeaked.

Brigid smirked at Gavin. "Yer adorable, ye feckin' goon."

"Haud yer wheesht," he muttered.

Chloe blinked slowly. "I'm too tired to translate any of the Scottishness or the Irishness. But did I tell you I think Arthur and Marie-Hélène may be platonic soul mates?"

"Poor Drew," Gavin muttered.

Chloe's eyes opened wider. "Oh my gosh, I forgot about Drew."

"So did Arthur." Gavin smiled.

"Hush," Brigid said. "Drew's fine. Carwyn took him under a wing. They were talking about baseball."

"Does Carwyn know anything about baseball?" Chloe's eyes were closed.

"I think he knew just enough to keep Drew talking," Brigid said. "And that's all that matters."

"Drew is an outstanding human," Gavin said. "But he's far less accepting of the fantastical than Arthur is. Not a surprise from an investment banker, I suppose." Gavin kept rubbing Chloe's feet. "But I'm glad we told them. It will make planning dinner parties much less complicated."

"They kept inviting us to the Hamptons, and I felt awful making excuses for why Gavin isn't the biggest fan of beach life."

"Arthur kept making comments about vitamin D deficiency," Gavin said. "I'm sure he was only worried for my health."

"You just need to move to Dublin," Brigid said. "No one there will ever question your pallor."

"As a Scot" —Gavin let his accent run free— "I can confirm the same applies in Edinburgh."

Chloe turned to her. "Brigid, in Ireland when the sun comes out, do men immediately strip off everything but their boxers? It's something I've observed in Scotland, and honestly, it's... a little alarming."

Gavin shook his head. "It's not something we're proud of, but I can't deny it happens."

"You know, I think it's been too long since I was wandering around when the sun came out." Brigid smiled. "I'll have to ask. Gavin, I hate to turn the conversation to business—"

"Bullshit." He smiled. "You've been waiting all night. Love the purse by the way." He nodded at the rhinestones. "Definitely your style."

"I can use it as a weapon, you know. These crystals weigh a load." She tucked her purse behind her. "Any news from Savi?"

"I know she... painted the message on the wall, as she put it, earlier tonight, but I haven't heard anything since then. It's two in the morning, so she's probably sleeping. Savi seems to keep a more normal schedule than the rest of the team. Raj is with

Gaines at the lofts, coordinating the night crew while Gaines covers the day."

"I was talking with Chance earlier. She remembers Lee Whitehorn a little bit. She's going to try to figure out who was talking with him at Marie-Hélène's parties." She caught a look Chloe gave Gavin when she mentioned Chance's name. "Anything I need to know about Chance?"

"Nothing!" Chloe said. "It's not... She's good people. I'm sure if she remembers anything, she'll tell you."

Gavin opened his mouth, then closed it. He leaned closer to Brigid. "It's not anything to do with this case. I promise."

Gavin's amnis whispered over his skin, and a light dawned in Brigid's mind. "Are you and Chance related?" Their amnis was strikingly similar, but Brigid had heard Gavin only had one sister in France. Of course, hidden vampire children weren't that uncommon in the immortal world; wealthy, long-lived characters liked their secrets. "Sorry, none of my business. Just my inquisitive nature rearing its ugly head."

"We're in the same line." Gavin kept his voice very low. "But it is not public knowledge and I'd appreciate your discretion. We're both very private people, and she's completely under Marie-Hélène's aegis, so there are no questions about her loyalty."

"Of course. Don't think of it again."

Gavin glanced to his right. "Chloe has been giving me grief that I don't spend enough time with Chance. She thinks the woman is lonely."

Brigid sat back. "She strikes me as very content on her ranch."

"I'm telling you," Chloe said. "She's unhappy. I can see it in her eyes. You and Marie-Hélène are completely oblivious to it, but it's there."

"Chloe worries about everyone." Gavin's arm tightened

around her. "She's even worried about Tenzin being bored when she gets here. I told her that of all the people to be worried about, Tenzin should be the last. The vampire knows how to entertain herself."

"Yes, but unless Marie-Hélène wants a coup happening in New Orleans or a museum getting robbed or some priceless cultural artifact disappearing, we need to find something to keep her busy." Chloe rubbed her eyes. "Trust me."

Brigid knew Tenzin well enough to know that Chloe wasn't wrong. "Carwyn and I can ask her to assist on this case," she said. "Problem solved."

As long as she could keep Carwyn and Tenzin from killing each other. If there was any immortal who could drive her normally good-natured husband to murder, it was Tenzin.

She saw the same worry in Gavin's eyes, but she patted his shoulder. "It'll be fine. Trust me."

———

BRIGID AND CARWYN were cuddled in the library of their guesthouse, watching a laptop screen with six different security feeds going from the night Nic Cooper went missing. Brigid was watching the top three and Carwyn was watching the bottom.

It was excruciatingly boring work, but this was the last of the security footage they could find from businesses in the Marigny of the night in question.

"Anything standing out?" Brigid had the human inclination to yawn, which she didn't need to do, but she missed yawning. There was something intensely satisfying about a really good yawn.

"Nothing." Carwyn flipped a puzzle cube in his hand, solving it with one hand while he watched the three video feeds.

"Andrew Harrison's a nice fellow. Do you know that the Mets have one of the top lineups in Major League Baseball this year?"

"I don't even know what that means."

"I have a vague understanding. A better understanding after talking to Andrew."

"How's he doing with all the...?" Brigid waved a hand and focused on the corner of the screen. "I see him."

"Andrew?"

"Nic." She reached for the keyboard only to see the screen go wavy. "Fuck. Uh... Cara?"

Carwyn sat up. "He doesn't use Nocht, remember?" Carwyn reached for a pencil. "What do you want to do?"

"Expand that window. Top right corner."

He managed to expand the window. "Now what?"

"Go back. Rewind about two minutes."

"Okay..." He frowned and tapped the back button. "You saw something?"

"I saw Nic Cooper."

The footage was grainy, but she was sure it was him. "There. Do you see it? Pause."

The camera wasn't the best, but Brigid recognized him. "It looks like Nic to me."

"Agreed," Carwyn said. "And he's wearing that denim jacket we saw in pictures."

"I forgot about that." She waved. "Press Play again."

Nic had been sauntering down the street and stopped when a car pulled up next to him. He turned to the left, bent down, and smiled a little.

"He knows who it is," Brigid said.

"Not afraid at all."

After a few words spoken, Nic walked over, opened the car door, and got inside.

Brigid felt like jumping out of her skin. "Can we see the plate?"

"No, and it's a dark sedan. There's only about a million of them in the area, especially with all the vampires in town," Carwyn said. "The car is a dead end."

"But he knew them." Brigid sat back, her mind racing. "Whoever took Nic Cooper, he knew them and he felt safe."

NIC II

The cries were nearly more than Nic could bear, and he wasn't the one being attacked. The girl had screamed at first when the monsters fed from her, but now she sobbed in low and aching moans that ripped his guts out every time he heard them start.

"Hey!" He banged on the wall. "He-ey!"

They grew quiet, then spoke in hissing whispers. One stomped into the hallway, then into his room.

Nic resisted the urge to throw up.

"What?" It was the blond-haired vampire with the eerie black eyes. "What do you want now?" The monster still had her blood on his chin.

Nic forced himself to glare at the vampire. "If you want me to hack into one of the most sophisticated systems in the entire fucking world, you can't keep me awake all night and I need better" —he kicked at the tray near the foot of his bed— "fucking food!"

The "food" was ramen, and it was barely edible. The gumbo he'd asked for had never appeared, and he'd been living on ramen for days.

"You think my brain operates at full capacity on this shit?" He curled his lip and tried to pretend he was spoiled Preston Jefferson Davis, the most annoying little shit in his senior seminar class at GIT. "I know you probably think this shit food is sufficient for your rudimentary mental processes, but you're asking me to hack into a system designed by one of the most creative security programmers in the world. I. Need. Protein."

The monster sneered. "What are you fucking talking about?"

"Steak, you ignominious prick! Get me some fucking protein, or I'm not going to be able to work. You want your money? Get me a fucking steak."

It was easier to pretend to be Preston when he was very hungry. Ramen wasn't something Nic had ever liked to eat because the look of it reminded him of the permanent wave hairstyles he remembered from his grandmother's salon.

Plus it tasted like plastic.

The other vampire had come into the room by this point and was glaring at the blond one. They exchanged quick words in not-quite-French, and then the dark-haired vampire walked over, threw a searing punch just under Nic's rib cage, and watched as he crumpled to the ground.

Ow. Owwwwww. Damn it, he hadn't been punched like that since he was a smart-ass kid in fifth grade who didn't respect his elders.

"You want a steak? Shut the fuck up, you motherfucker." The dark-haired vampire was clearly annoyed with him. "I will get you your fucking steak. Then I'll piss on it and watch you eat it. Will that be enough protein? What do you think?"

Nic grunted from the ground. "Steak. No piss. Or you can hack into Paladin yourself."

His mother had always told him he had more sass than sense. This time it would probably get him killed.

More muttering from the two vampires, then they walked out the door and left him alone.

Next door, all he could hear was silence.

THIRTEEN

"Can you think of anyone he'd follow like that?" Brigid hammered at Bex. "An old pal, a former employer, a family member?"

Bex gripped her hair in her hands. "Nic didn't have many friends, and the ones he had didn't have fancy black cars. His only previous employer was Marie-Hélène; he started working for her in her communications security right out of college. And his only family is his mom and grandma. He doesn't have or aunts or uncles or anything."

Bex was sitting in the lofts with Brigid and Gavin on the couch opposite her. Carwyn and Raj leaned against the wall next to them.

Carwyn kept his voice soft. "Bex, we're just trying to help."

Raj had his arms crossed, and his brow was furrowed in concern. "Anything you can share that might help find Nic—"

"I've told you everything I know!" There were tears in her eyes. "I'm the one who told you someone took him, and it's been days now. You wouldn't even have believed me unless Savi told you about his hacks. And none of this makes sense, okay? Roland doesn't betray Paladin. Ever. They could probably torture him and he'd get through it." She was fully crying. "Once he gives his word, he won't break it. Not ever."

Gavin kept his voice even and kind; the girl was already shaking. "Bex, I don't think Nic would ever willingly betray you or anyone at Paladin, but whoever targeted Lee used amnis on him. It's possible they did the same to Nic."

The girl looked up helplessly. "But Nic was resistant to amnis. He said it was a perk of being neurodivergent."

Brigid looked at Carwyn, then back at Bex. "He told you that?"

The girl shrugged. "Yeah. There are a lot of people here whose brains work a little different. We always thought that was a plus with vampires, you know?"

Carwyn exchanged a look with Raj, then sighed. "Bex, I'm afraid that's not true."

Her eyes went side. "What?"

Raj explained more. "Some humans may have better natural defenses—I did when I was human—but *every* human brain is susceptible to vampire influence with enough pressure. Again, can you think of anyone—?"

"No!" She stood and stomped her foot. "You don't get it—Nic didn't trust people; you had to earn it. Whoever he got in that car with? They were from Paladin or from Marie-Hélène's staff. He wouldn't have trusted anyone else. He wouldn't have even given them the time of day."

"Okay." Brigid stood and nodded toward the door. "You can go. If you think of anything else—"

"You're supposed to be finding him." Bex was fully crying now. "Vampires are supposed to have better senses, sharper mental processing, all that stuff, right? So find him." She brushed angry tears from her cheeks. "Find him!"

Bex stalked out the door and slammed it shut before they could respond.

"I'm as frustrated as she is," Brigid muttered. "With Auguste Peregrine dead, we have no leads. Whitehorn wasn't a dead end, but he's not going to let any vampire search his mind to find more information after what happened to him."

Raj added, "I'd ignore that if it meant getting Nic back, but Whitehorn's vampire patron is not someone you mess with."

Brigid continued. "Nic's guard doesn't know jack shit because he was sparked out, so the only message we have is from Nic himself, and we have to take Savi's word for it."

Carwyn muttered, "And so far, he hasn't sent anything in response to the message that she sent."

"He may be trying to find more information," Raj pointed out. "There's no guarantee he knows where he's being kept, especially if it's outside the city. There's a lot of rural Louisiana that is very dense woods and bayous. Or he could be farther away than that. We have no idea."

Carwyn walked over and sat across from Brigid. "We don't even have a motive."

"The only one I can think of is sabotage," Gavin drummed his fingers on the arm of the sofa. "Nic's not irreplaceable, but his disappearance has thrown the entire company into panic, even in departments he doesn't run."

Carwyn crossed his arms. "He really is Roland, isn't he? Everyone looks up to him. And Bex is in love with him."

Raj said, "You got that too?"

"Absolutely gone over the boy," Brigid said. "She's frantic." She looked at Raj. "Have your people keep an extra eye on her. She could be unpredictable."

"I agree with Brigid." Carwyn shook his head. "The others are upset. Bex is beside herself."

"Did I sense guilt?" Brigid raised an eyebrow. "Could something she did have made him a target?"

Raj frowned. "From what I can tell, Nic and Bex were collaborators. If it was something they worked on together, I think she'd tell us. I didn't get guilt from her. Pure worry."

Brigid said, "Which puts us back at square dot. We're nowhere."

Gavin was silent. He stood and started pacing the room. He'd left his suit jacket at home that night and was wearing a pair of dark trousers and a charcoal shirt.

"He's my employee," the vampire said, "but he's a human under Marie-Hélène's aegis. She's known him since he was a child, and she feels personally responsible. Alonzo has people looking everywhere since you spotted him on video."

"We need more information," Carwyn said, "but we're running into walls. What can you tell us about the area where he was taken?"

"It's nowhere significant. He left the Black Cat—it seems like he did drug his own guard if he was walking on his own—and he was heading up Elysian Fields. It's not a busy street that time of night, but no one is going to notice a car pulling up to someone."

Carwyn painted a mental picture of a brilliant, intensely private young man who chafed at the idea of constant guardianship. He was in his hometown, probably wanted some peace and quiet.

"Any reason he'd be heading that direction? It's not the most direct way to his mother's house."

Brigid muttered, "That's why I was trying to figure out which friend he might visit. He was going somewhere."

"If he was trying to ditch his guard and go somewhere private, he was probably headed to the tram stop on Saint Claude," Raj said. "From there he could go pretty much anywhere."

Gavin frowned. "I suppose it doesn't matter at this point, but when I hired Nic, he had an apartment in Saint Roch. When he wasn't doing communications work for Marie-Hélène, he volunteered at an animal shelter there."

Brigid asked, "What exactly did he do for Marie-Hélène before you hired him?"

"He wasn't utilized to his full potential. He was running her websites, coordinating with the bookkeeping department to streamline the payment platforms for all her clubs. Things like that."

"Why did you pick him?" Carwyn asked. "It's clear he's fundamental to the company, but he has less experience than Bex or any of the rest of the team."

Gavin frowned. "I saw something in the young man. He doesn't speak much, so when he does, people listen. He has a patient way of explaining things. He's a leader. I fully intended to steal him from Marie-Hélène if Paladin didn't work out; he's the kind of employee every vampire wants."

"So you liked his leadership skills?" Carwyn asked. "Was that it?"

"That was his strength. He was direct and unusually perceptive. He also had a way of communicating with people that was both honest and kind. He's a very honest person. Very direct."

"That's a valuable and unusual trait in our world," Carwyn said.

Gavin nodded. "You weren't wrong that Savi is the least replaceable—technically she's the innovator—but if you wanted to grind the entire organization to a halt..." His eyes narrowed. "Taking Nic Cooper was probably the most effective way."

"So who would want to do that?" Carwyn looked at Brigid. "Who would Nic Cooper trust enough to get in the car with but would also want to slow Paladin Ventures to a crawl before it even got off the ground?"

Gavin turned to Brigid and raised an eyebrow.

"He doesn't know Nic from Adam," she protested.

"Maybe he had an accomplice?" Gavin was looking more convinced. "He has business connections everywhere now, Brigid. That's the benefit of owning Nocht."

Carwyn caught his wife's eye and held her attention. "It does make sense, darling girl. Deirdre didn't find anything, but you and I both know she's not the most—"

"Ugh!" Brigid rolled her eyes. "Fine. Crack on an' get me a secure video-chat connection and I'll call Murphy myself. I'll do it right now, and you know I'll be able to tell if he's chatting shit."

Gavin looked at Raj. "Find a room and a computer. Now. I'm tired of wondering."

———

BRIGID WAS SITTING in a tiny office in a corner of the lofts, and Patrick Murphy's handsome face filled the screen in front of her. Raj and Gavin had been banished so she and Carwyn could talk to Murphy privately.

"I'm deadly serious," she said. "I need a direct answer."

"Serious? Brig, you're talking about a Nocht competitor. That's an amusing prospect when we have one hundred percent of the immortal market." The corner of Murphy's mouth turned up. "Good luck pulling the tech-savvy ancient-immortal demographic away from subscribing to an already familiar platform when some of them barely understand email."

Carwyn sat next to Brigid and pinched her arse, but his wife kept her face serious as she talked to her former employer.

"So you're sayin' you don't consider Paladin a threat?" she asked.

Murphy laughed a little. "Brigid, you know me. My time and resources are valuable. Would I pull either away to chase a possible future threat that doesn't even exist yet?"

Carwyn piped up. "I remember what you did to the Deacon

crew, Murphy. Don't tell me you're not capable of sabotage on a rival."

The smile remained fixed. "That was just a little fun."

Brigid cocked her head. "Fun? You destroyed their business, and then you stole their dog too. And beat Old Man Deacon in a bare-knuckles match."

"I'd forgotten about the boxing." Murphy chuckled. "And for the record, the dog followed me. Who am I to argue with a stubborn pit bull?"

Brigid asked, "What happened to that dog? I can't see you hosting a hound in your house."

"Tom and Josie took him in. Damn retired fighting dog wears hand-knit sweaters and a sparkly collar now."

Carwyn leaned toward the screen. "Tom has a sparkly collar? I need a picture of that."

Murphy grinned. "I'm telling him you said that."

"I'd be disappointed if you didn't." Talking with Murphy was making Carwyn miss Dublin even if everything about Brigid's former employer annoyed him. "This case, Murph. A young man has been taken, his mother's only son. It's not a good situation."

Murphy's amusement fled. "If Gavin Wallace can't keep his people protected, that's not anyone's fault but his own, and honestly, it doesn't bode well for his future success."

"Gavin can't keep a human safe when the human doesn't want to be kept," Brigid said. "You and I both know young ones are more than capable of self-destruction even when others try to guard them."

Murphy shrugged. "I don't know what to tell you, Brigid. You know I wouldn't have a hand in this. It's not my style, and frankly, it's beneath my notice."

Carwyn had to smother the urge to reach through the screen and strangle the smug vampire.

Brigid put a hand on his knee and Carwyn calmed. She knew exactly how easily Murphy pressed his buttons. "Murphy, has anyone approached you with information about Paladin?"

He raised an eyebrow. "From the inside? No. I'd not turn them away if they did, but I wouldn't condone these tactics either. Whoever your kidnapper is, I don't think they're likely to come to me. Have you reached out to the Ankers? As far as I know, they're the only ones with a grudge against Wallace, and we all know morality is not their forte."

Carwyn said, "Mila Anker was briefly on the scene, but she isn't in the technology business anymore."

Or any business. She'd been executed in Los Angeles after running afoul of Ernesto Alvarez and kidnapping Chloe. It hadn't ended well for her or her team.

"I'm not talking about Mila," Murphy said. "I'm talking about her brother Otto. Mila was impulsive; Otto is not."

Brigid and Carwyn exchanged a look. "Tell us more."

"Sired from Rens, whom I'm sure you remember. Otto is an information merchant like his sire, but he's progressive and fanatically devoted to the family legacy. According to Tom, he's gathered a stable of young computer specialists who specialize in covert information retrieval."

"Hackers," Brigid said. "Otto has hired a bunch of hackers."

"*Hacker* is a very complicated word, Brigid." Murphy pursed his lips. "Doesn't information want to be free?"

"Very funny coming from you." Carwyn had never heard of the man giving away anything for free, especially not information. "So Otto has a hacker group of his very own. I imagine infiltrating an up-and-coming communications company like Paladin would be a goal then."

"They're constantly trying to breach Nocht's firewalls. It's not really a secret; we're on guard—it's to be expected. Our advantage is that our system was fully up and the operating system secure by the time Otto formed his little collective. Harder to storm a castle that already has walls."

"Whereas Paladin is still building theirs," Carwyn said. "If they could infiltrate the operating system before security was in place—"

"Is it unguarded though?" Murphy looked skeptical. "I've never known Wallace to be a fool about security despite this current mess."

"Maybe they're not trying to break it," Brigid said. "Maybe they're trying to make their own secret door into the castle. Can you do that with computer security?"

"Oh yes, you can," Murphy said. "And if you're good enough, your knights on the wall won't even know it's there."

"Can you get me names?" Brigid asked. "Of Otto's people, I mean. Do you have any idea who they might be in real life?"

"I can ask. They usually hide their identities, but I'll see what Tom has and tell him to email you."

"I appreciate it, Murphy."

Carwyn toyed with the seam of her pants. "You think we might find a tie to Nic Cooper?"

"I think information is useful." Brigid looked up at him. "And we have a group of programmers who might know the right questions to ask."

"Any names you can share?" Murphy asked. "I'm always looking for new talent."

"Good night, Murphy." Carwyn snapped the laptop shut. "You were done talking to him, right?"

FOURTEEN

The minute they mentioned Otto Anker's name, Gavin's expression turned so dark Brigid felt a shiver across her skin. Gavin was often hard to read, with his politic demeanor and unflappable calm. To see him so openly murderous was unusual.

"Otto Anker." His voice was a low hiss. "This time Alvarez won't be here to do my work for me."

Brigid said, "We don't know anything for sure."

"I'll try not to act rashly. The men who took Chloe also injured one of Ernesto Alvarez's humans. Chloe was unharmed, but Ernesto's man was not, so..."

"So Alvarez took his retribution instead of allowing you your own." Brigid nodded. It made sense, but any vampire wanted blood in their teeth if a loved one was attacked.

"If they had known who she was to me, I doubt they would have risked it." Gavin's face returned to a stoic mask. "I know it's better for me not to be involved. I don't like taking sides, but..."

Gavin's primary business was as a club owner, and for that he needed to be seen as neutral as possible. His clubs were meeting grounds where violence was strictly prohibited, but that neutrality was only as strong as Gavin was.

"If the Ankers are involved, they are fully capable of taking humans like this." Gavin's Scottish accent grew stronger. "They're shit stirrers who take pleasure in chaos. I'll reach out to my sister and see if she can find out more about Otto."

"Isn't she in France?"

"Yes, but she knows enough people in the Netherlands to be useful. Plus like recognizes like." His smile was rueful. "And my sister is the queen of shit stirrers." He nodded at Brigid and Carwyn. "Forgive me, but I'd like to get back to Chloe now. Let me know if and when Gaines has any updates about Nic."

"We will."

Savi and Nic were still parrying in the Paladin server with Roland making half-hearted attacks while Oliver repelled them. Savi thought there was some kind of pattern to his attacks that might be sending her a message, but she would need time and space to figure it out.

For now the team seemed reassured by Nic's clumsy attempts at their security. As long as he was "attacking" them, they knew he was safe. Carwyn and Brigid left Gaines with the staff while they attended yet another prewedding gathering.

The party that night was for Ben and Tenzin's arrival, which was supposed to have been at midnight, but the clock showed two in the morning and the notorious duo hadn't arrived, so the party at Marie-Hélène's estate was still hopping.

Brigid got up, walked to the bar, and retrieved two glasses of blood-wine for her and Carwyn. She strolled back and leaned in the doorway of the salon, staring at the beast of a man sprawled on a velvet sofa.

Mine.

His legs were long and his thighs the size of small tree trunks. His arms spread across the back of the dainty furniture, extending nearly the entire length of the sofa back. He was watching a pair of dancers who were demonstrating a soft-shoe routine, the corner of his mouth turned up in amusement.

He was wearing light-colored pants and a shirt with a bright green ikat print he'd found at a night market earlier in the week. If there was one thing her husband loved about New Orleans, it was the bright fashions everyone wore.

Brigid walked over and straddled one of his thighs, pleased to see his eyes light up.

"Wife."

She handed him the glass of blood-wine. "Husband."

His eyes drifted to the deep V of her shirt. "You look quite ravishing tonight. Can we do that later?"

"Ravishing?" She sipped her wine. "I'd be disappointed if we didn't."

Brigid wasn't gifted in the tits department, but that meant she could wear daring tops without fearing a wardrobe malfunction that would scandalize her internal Catholic.

That night she'd donned a shirt that was barely more than two rust-colored scarves flung over her shoulders. It covered the racy bits but not much else. Since daring was the rule at most of Marie-Hélène's parties, Brigid didn't stand out much.

"Oh my God."

Brigid turned and saw a short man with spiked hair watching them.

"Hello, Arthur." Carwyn smiled. "How are you and Andrew enjoying the city?"

Arthur, true to his profession, was wearing an immaculately cut blue suit with a bright yellow pocket square. "Forget us." He pulled up a chair. "Do you two realize how insanely hot you two are?" He made a square with his hands and framed them. "I want to do a photo shoot. You with that red hair, all those muscles, and that insanely hot beard. *Yes*, zaddy."

Brigid narrowed her eyes. "Did you just call my husband zaddy?"

Arthur turned his eyes to Brigid. "And you have the completely fierce badass warrior woman thing going even though you're, like, this tiny little pixie." His eyes went wide. "And oh my God, I just realized how many times I've teased you, but now Chloe tells me you're like a crazy dangerous fire vampire or something and you could burn me alive."

"I could." She almost wanted to snap her fingers and hold a fireball just to see him freak out. "But I wouldn't burn you alive, Arthur. Not when you're making Chloe's wedding dress."

"Right." His eyes were still the size of saucers. "You and Carwyn are just... you know, you're great. Love you both. Superhot."

"Arthur?" Carwyn kept his voice low and smooth.

"Uh-huh?"

"You're not in any danger from Brigid."

He relaxed. "Okay, good."

"Unless you try to put her in lace or a Peter Pan collar. Then I guarantee nothing."

"Okay." He stood and leaned against the chair. "I'm just going to go..." He pointed over his shoulder. "Back. To Chloe." He waved a hand in a circle. "Again, the two of you are smoking hot. Do you have an amazing sex life? I'm kind of reading that off you. I feel like that's accurate." Someone called his name. "Sorry! None of my business of course. But I mean, if you ever wanted to have photos taken, I know some great people."

———

IT WAS NEARLY three in the morning, and Ben and Tenzin still hadn't arrived. Most of the humans had left, and the party at Marie-Hélène's mansion had taken a distinctly vampiric turn.

Couples were feeding in dark corners, the blood-wine was flowing, and the music had dropped to an ominous background drone.

Brigid wanted to go home and shag her husband, but he was forcing them to stay. He was also running his hands along the sensitive skin at the small of her back, under her arm, and between her collarbones just to keep her distracted.

Evil. She had married an evil man.

"Hey!" Chloe bounced over to them. "I have no idea how I'm still awake; I guess I'm getting on vampire time now." She pointed at Brigid. "Bachelorette party next week—put it on your calendar."

"A what?" Brigid blinked.

"Hen party, darling." Carwyn stroked her back. "What day, Chloe? I'll make sure she doesn't duck out on you. She's liable to run screaming from anything like that, so make sure you keep a solid hand on her throughout."

"Beatrice and Tenzin are coming too, so I'll put them in charge of Brigid." She smiled and then bounced some more. "Excellent. This is going to be so fun."

"Is it?" Brigid was feeling slightly terrified. "Who else is coming?"

"It's just close friends, so you, Tenzin, Arthur, Beatrice, which is a little weird but it felt weirder to leave her out, so we're just going with it, Dema, Therese, Chance, and one of Chance's sisters, so that's nine of us, which seems like a good number."

Oh fuck no, this sounded like a nightmare.

"If Arthur is coming, why can't I come?" Carwyn asked.

Why doesn't Carwyn go and I stay home? It was what she wanted to ask, but she didn't want to hurt Chloe's feelings because hurting Chloe's feelings was like kicking a wee pup.

"You'll be at Gavin's bachelor party, which if I was going to guess is likely to be a bunch of old vampires sitting around and drinking scotch while they talk about the days when real vampires rode horses or something like that." She scrunched up her face. "Sorry."

Carwyn huffed. "This is completely unacceptable."

Chloe raised her hands. "Take it up with Gavin because I'm not in charge of him."

Brigid felt the disturbance in the room before she heard it.

Chloe turned her head. "Oh, they're finally here."

They turned and saw Ben and Tenzin enter the room. Arabella, Marie-Hélène's flamboyant greeter, opened her mouth with a smile only to fall silent when she saw what Tenzin was dragging in behind her.

Angels of death.

It was the phrase that jumped immediately to mind. Ben was six foot, lean, and his cheeks looked hollow in the candlelight, his beautiful ash-grey eyes pierced the crowd. Tenzin moved beside him, her night-black hair cut at a severe angle along her jaw and her feet not quite touching the ground. Her luminous skin was marred by a faint splatter of blood along her cheek.

Probably from the body she was carrying.

Everything and everyone in the room went quiet as they entered.

Tenzin raised the hand that wasn't dragging the body. "I promise he's not dead."

"Yet," Ben muttered.

They were both dressed in black, so it was impossible to tell how much blood covered their clothes.

Carwyn poked his head out. "Dear God, are they bringing humans as party favors now? There's something wrong with that woman."

"Kind of like a cat," Brigid mused.

Chloe looked at her with wide eyes.

"You know, if a cat finds a mouse and..." Brigid shrugged. "Probably a bad comparison."

Ben lifted the head by the hair to show the face of the unconscious human. "Does this man belong to anyone here?"

More silence.

Marie-Hélène finally spoke. "Gavin, your friends certainly do know how to make an entrance."

"That they do." Gavin stepped forward. "What was he doing?"

"He was perched in a tree at the edge of the property," Ben said. "Taking pictures with a very large lens." He dropped the man's hair. "We startled him and he fell."

"He had a knife; it's my knife now." Tenzin withdrew a hunting knife the length of her forearm. "Decent quality, nice bone handle."

Most vampires near her visibly shrank back, and one of them hissed. Still others shifted closer, drawn by the scent of fresh blood.

"Come now, my darlings." Marie-Hélène clapped her hands. "Are we all so squeamish? Don't worry your heads about this little human. We'll have that camera destroyed sooner than you can snap your fingers. Am I right, Miss Arabella?"

"My lady, we know you are," Arabella called back. She snapped her fingers, and the band started up again. "Did y'all think this party was over?"

Scattered laughter and brighter music distracted the crowd, diverting their attention away from the bloody human.

Brigid walked forward and lifted the man's head, took a picture of it with her phone, and nodded at Ben and Tenzin. "I'll ask around." She turned to Gavin. "Does Marie-Hélène...?"

"There's a secure room on the property," Gavin said. "Ben, if you'd follow me, I'll catch you up."

Carwyn rose. "I'll go with Gavin." He turned to Chloe and

gave her a sideways hug around the shoulders. "No worries, my girl. I'm sure this is nothing to worry about. Probably just the damn paparazzi. You're famous, after all." He winked and followed Gavin.

Tenzin lifted the man by the collar and handed him to Ben. "He's still alive."

"We'll talk about it later," Ben muttered. "You have blood on your face."

"Oh." She wiped it with her sleeve, which only smeared it more. "Chloe!"

Brigid turned to Chloe, whose head was cocked at a slight angle. "You okay?"

"I'm fine." Chloe walked forward to greet Tenzin. "To be honest, I didn't really expect anything different."

FIFTEEN

"He was found on Marie-Hélène's grounds." Her security chief was standing firm. "We will conduct the interrogation."

Gavin wasn't backing down either. "Paladin has an ongoing investigation to find Nicolas Cooper's whereabouts, and it's likely this man was hired by the same people who took him."

"I think that's a stretch," the vampire said. "We don't know who hired him right now."

"It's just a coincidence that someone was spying on that party?"

"With as many prominent guests as we have on the estate right now, it definitely could be a coincidence."

Marie-Hélène's security chief went by the name of Alonzo, and he was nearly as massive as Carwyn. He was a water vampire with a scarred face, buzz-cut hair, and features that marked him as some blend of European, African, and Native blood. His accent told Carwyn he was a New Orleans native, and his demeanor said he was not new at his job.

"Mr. Wallace." Alonzo crossed massive arms over his barrel chest. "We're hosting over four hundred immortal guests in town over the next three weeks. Do you realize the kind of security coordination we're dealing with here? This intruder could have been hired or could have been targeting any one of those guests."

"Yes, but Nic has already been targeted and is missing," Gavin said. "Check with Marie-Hélène. I know she'd want Brigid and Carwyn to question him."

Alonzo glanced at Carwyn and Brigid, and the look on his face made it seem like he'd just smelled something he didn't like.

"Check with her." Gavin's voice was low and menacing. "Or I will. Who do you think will come across as the reasonable one then?"

Carwyn straightened to his full height, stretched his shoulders back, and stared silently at the security chief. Brigid had once told him that his silence was more intimidating than any threat he could make because as soon as he opened his mouth, his natural friendliness was impossible to hide.

"I'll check with Madame Charmont," Alonzo said. "But understand this: Paladin Ventures does not have a monopoly in New Orleans. You're *one* of Marie-Hélène's businesses, not all of them, and every single one of her people are my priority."

"Nic Cooper isn't one of your people?" Brigid asked quietly.

The look on Alonzo's face told Carwyn there was some history there. "Nic Cooper is an ungrateful brat who thinks he's smarter than everyone. You ask me? He pissed off the wrong people in this city and now it's caught up with him."

Well, this was interesting. Carwyn remained silent, but he saw Brigid's brain go into overdrive, analyzing the situation as Alonzo stormed out the door.

As soon as the vampire was gone, Brigid turned to Gavin. "Why the animosity?"

Gavin grimaced. "I worked hard to keep the security for

Paladin out of Alonzo's hands." He held up a finger before Brigid could speak. "Not because I don't trust him but because he is maniacally devoted to Marie-Hélène. Not the businesses, not the organization—Marie-Hélène personally."

Carwyn finally spoke. "Problematic when his loyalties are so narrow."

"It works for her and her other businesses," Gavin said. "But Paladin is her first joint venture with someone outside her own power structure. My people needed equal access, and Alonzo wasn't going to allow that, so we decided to create a completely different infrastructure for the new company. He wasn't happy."

Carwyn asked, "How do he and Gaines get along?"

"Barely civil, but they're professionals." Gavin waved a hand. "I'm not worried about this. Marie-Hélène will let you interrogate the human."

Carwyn was still mulling over what Alonzo had said. "Over four hundred vampires and their parties. It's a massive undertaking. The man could be right; this could have nothing to do with Nic and Paladin."

"And if it doesn't, I have faith that you and Brigid will be able to determine that quickly. If this human's presence is unrelated, then we hand him back to Alonzo."

"And then what?" Carwyn asked.

"This isn't the church, Father." Gavin's face was impassive. "I don't dictate to other vampires how they deal with threats."

"He's human," Brigid said. "He's vulnerable."

"And he took a job spying. Don't ask me to feel sorry for him." Gavin loosened his tie and pulled it down to hang loosely around his neck. "If this man is working for one of the Ankers or one of your many enemies, we need to know, and I don't much care how we get the information."

"Information revealed under duress isn't reliable," Brigid said. "I can question him better."

"I have no doubt," Gavin said. "But information gathered with amnis is even more direct, and it's fast."

Brigid's chin went up. "I don't need to manipulate his mind to get what I need."

Gavin cocked his head. "You'll use your fangs to feed, your speed to chase, but you won't use amnis to safely gather information that could save Nic's life?"

Carwyn saw her resolve falter.

"I don't need it," Brigid said. "I'll be able to see if he's lying."

Gavin grimaced. "Maybe Alonzo had the right idea. I don't need morality plays, Brigid. I need information. I need that young man to be safe." He glanced at Carwyn. "If he dies—if he's even hurt—you know what kind of ripples this will cause in our world."

If a human under vampire aegis was harmed, it was open season on any human under immortal protection. Mortals would refuse to work for vampires, and vampire organizations would be utterly useless without human staff. Rivals would use humans as hostages and combatants.

They were a tenuously balanced society of apex predators; even one slip could prove disastrous.

"Nic Cooper trusted me to keep him safe when he signed a contract with Paladin," Gavin said. "And right now we have no other leads than that human and whatever Savi might find. I will use whatever means necessary to get the information he holds."

"Wallace, don't worry about me and Brigid. We'll get what you need." Carwyn's voice was clipped. "We'll get Nic back."

———

"WHAT THE HELL kind of amateurs does he think we are?" Brigid fumed in their room. "I've more than half a mind to leave tonight. We don't need this headache, Carwyn."

"Shhh." He rubbed her back. "Darling girl, we came for Chloe and we're staying for Chloe. And for all those young people at Paladin. You know we're still their best chance at finding Nic."

Not that they'd been able to question the human that night. According to Marie-Hélène's physician, the man would be stable and talking by the following night, but until then, he needed to rest and get his bones set. He'd suffered two broken arms when Tenzin had tossed him out of the tree, along with scrapes, bruises, and a concussion.

Brigid sat on the chaise at the end of their bed. "Remind me never to send Tenzin on a fugitive retrieval assignment."

"Unless you want the human damaged, she's somewhat useless." Carwyn unbuttoned his shirt and draped it over a chair. "Delicacy is not her forte."

"She's getting better." Brigid reached over and ran a hand along his back. "She's mellowing."

"You and Ben think that, but I've known the woman far longer." He turned and cupped Brigid's chin in his large palm. "She'll never been entirely civilized. She doesn't want to be."

"What has civilization ever done for her?" Brigid asked. "I don't blame her for not trusting institutions and political structures. At least her worldview is honest."

"Treat everyone like an enemy or a pawn until they prove otherwise?"

"She's survived this long because of that." Brigid stroked a hand down his bare abdomen. "It's not your way, but I do understand it."

Carwyn's fangs dropped when Brigid's hand touched his skin. "Enough talk about Tenzin, Ben, Gavin, or anyone else distracting you." He kept her chin in his hand and nudged her mouth open with his thumb. "Have you fed tonight?"

She gave his thumb a friendly nick with her fang. "I did." Then she captured his finger in her mouth and sucked hard, milking the drop of blood from him while her fingers ran along the waistband of his trousers.

The corner of his mouth turned up. "I think you may still be hungry."

"For you." She flicked the button on his trousers open and drew the zipper down with agonizing languor. "I was watching you all night."

He kept one hand cupping her face while the other teased amnis along her neck, behind her ears, and up her delicate throat. "That's quite the coincidence. I was watching you too."

Her shirt was a mere scrap of bronze-colored silk he slid to the side as he reached down and cupped her delicate breast. Brigid closed her eyes and hummed in pleasure, then opened the placket of his pants and stroked her hand along the firm length of his erection.

She turned her face as she drew it out and ran her lips and the tip of her tongue along the length.

The low growl built at the back of Carwyn's throat, and he pinched her nipple. "Take it."

She opened her mouth and enveloped the head of his cock, opening her eyes to look at him as she worked her lips, tongue, and hand over his erection.

Carwyn stroked his hands down her throat, over her nape, and down her shoulders, teasing her breasts as she teased him.

Brigid slid her hands into his trousers and worked them down over his legs; her fingers played along the sensitive skin of his groin and his inner thighs.

He could barely think straight with her mouth busy on his cock, but he knew she wanted more. She wanted to feed.

Carwyn kept one hand on the back of her head as he kicked off his pants, and his knees nearly buckled as he lifted one foot and placed it next to her on the chaise where she was sitting.

He was moments from climaxing when he pulled her off his cock. She looked up at him, her mouth red, swollen, and glistening. Her eyes were wide and hungry, and her fangs were long in her mouth.

He wanted to fall at her feet and worship her.

Carwyn nudged her toward his inner thigh. "Go on."

She didn't wait even a second but plunged her fangs into his vein and pulled hard.

He shouted and closed his eyes, images of her mouth red with his blood too much for him to see without spilling his seed like a randy boy. Carwyn kept his hand on her head, pressing her teeth to his skin and focusing on the thread of pain instead of the intense pressure to climax.

Brigid pulled away and delicately pierced the tip of her tongue, laving it over the fang marks in his thigh; then she stood and pushed her leggings down at the same time, baring her body to him.

He picked her up, tossed her on the bed, and leaped on her, knowing as he seated himself to the hilt that her body would already be primed for him. Her wet heat, already swollen with blood and desire, enveloped his erection, and she wrapped her legs around his waist as he drove into her over and over again.

Carwyn pulled back when he felt the fire licking beneath her skin, but she grabbed him by his shoulders, pulled him down, and sank her fangs into his shoulder.

"Don't stop," she rasped. "Don't stop."

He felt her fingers burning the skin of his lower back, but the rise of their amnis pulsing together drove him forward, and he felt her body climax around him a second before he let himself come.

Her whole body shuddered and she went still beneath him.

Carwyn let out a long breath. "Brigid."

Her voice came back nearly pained. "More."

He rolled them over, their bodies still joined, and put his hands on her hips. "So take more."

She rode him again slowly—his erection had only partially subsided—and he quickly hardened again watching her head thrown back, her face a mask of ecstasy, her nipples hard points he wanted to bite.

She saw his eyes and pulled him up, pressed his mouth to her breasts. He kissed and sucked them until her nipples were bright red and swollen, then sank his teeth into the left side, sipped from her blood, then pierced the right side too.

Carwyn leaned back and watched thin rivulets of blood trickle down her body, and he lifted her to ride him harder.

Brigid's second climax came more violently than the first; she arched her back and opened her mouth in a silent shout, tears pooling at the corners of her eyes. Seeing her release, Carwyn came with a hard groan and collapsed back on the bed.

He lifted her off his body, placing her gently on the sheets as he lazily licked up her body, catching every drop of blood with his tongue like a satisfied cat.

She was blinking rapidly. "I needed that."

"We both did." Carwyn kissed every inch of her skin, reveling in the pulse of amnis that spread from her body to his, then back again. "Let me know when you're ready to go again."

She smiled a little. "So it's going to be one of those mornings, is it?"

"Morning. Evening." He kissed her hard. "If we weren't working, you'd be in this bed for a week."

SIXTEEN

Brigid stood against the back wall of the interrogation room, watching her husband ask the human questions. The man's face was bandaged and swollen, making it harder for Brigid to read him. His right arm was set in a full cast, and a brace wrapped around his left wrist.

He looked like he'd been tossed from a perch in a tree and hit every branch on the way down, which was exactly what had happened.

Ben Vecchio stood at her side. "I don't think she actually meant to hurt him that badly—the tree was higher than she realized."

"Your mate having issues with depth perception in her old age?" Brigid muttered.

Ben shrugged. "Maybe." He nodded toward Carwyn. "Is he going to actually ask any questions?"

"Wait for it."

The human was alone in a room with four vampires, two dressed entirely in black. Alonzo stood in the corner in a grey suit, and then there was Carwyn.

Her mate sprawled in a folding chair that looked poised to

collapse under his weight. His hair was unbrushed and sticking out at odd angles, and he wore a blue shirt with sailboats on it and a pair of cargo pants.

He paged through a file on the table in front of him. The terrified human was on the other side, trembling, his eyes darting from Brigid to Ben to Alonzo, then back to the strange man across from him.

Carwyn slapped the file shut. "See, this is... Most of this isn't pertinent. I think they just want me to embarrass you, but your arrest history is really none of my business, is it?"

The man opened his mouth, clearly disarmed by Carwyn's apologetic tone. "I don't think so?"

Carwyn kicked his feet out. "I'm not a judgmental man, Bert. May I call you Bert?"

The human's voice was barely over a whisper. "My name is Albert, and I usually go by Al."

Brigid watched the man's face as he focused on Carwyn. He'd been frightened before; now he was confused but less fearful.

Carwyn persisted. "You really seem more like a Bert to me."

"Ooookay." The man frowned. "You can call me Bert if you want."

"Excellent." Carwyn sat up a little straighter. "Now, your history of hiring sex workers isn't pertinent in this situation, Bert. I mean, I'm sure your mother is disappointed, but that's between you and your mother."

Embarrassment, confusion, more embarrassment. The man was entirely baffled at this point.

"Are you from New Orleans, Bert?"

"Yes."

"You're what? Thirty-five?"

"Thirty-one."

"Hmmm. Smoker?" Carwyn nodded. "You know it's bad for you, but you're an adult. That's all I'll say."

"Okay?"

"Catholic or protestant?"

"Catho— Do you want to know who hired me?"

"We'll get to that." Carwyn opened his file again. "Bert, you've got a grandmother living in Vacherie, is that correct?"

"Outside of there, yeah." His eyes went wide. "Now wait, my grandma doesn't have anything to do with this!"

Dead silence.

"What are you implying?" Carwyn slapped the file down. "Are you implying that I'd attack an old woman because of the sins of her grandson?"

The man was even more confused. "Aren't you the one... I mean, aren't *you* implying—?"

"What kind of vampire do you think I am?" Carwyn slowly shook his head. "I thought we'd built a rapport, Bert."

"I'm... sorry?"

"If you mean that, I appreciate it." He picked up the file again. "When did you get the job to spy on Madame Charmont's party?"

"On Thursday, and I didn't know—"

"So three days ago?"

"No, last week."

"A week ago? So they approached you at Pete's on Thursday?"

"How did you know I was at Pete's?"

"That's where you pick up your girls, Bert."

"Right." The man's face showed signs of embarrassment again. "All they said was I needed to take some pictures of that fancy house and get pictures of all the people going in, okay? I wasn't doing anything else. I didn't even break in or anything, and the money was really good. Five hundred for a few hours of work."

Brigid read the man's face and saw the honesty on it. Carwyn's disarming demeanor had worked. The man was giving them everything he knew to try to save himself.

"But you knew it was a vampire house, didn't you?"

Bert was silent.

"Bert?"

"Everyone knows the rumors about Madame Charmont, okay?"

"Rumors are rumors..." Carwyn paged through the pictures in the file. The pictures that Bert had taken the night before. Close-ups of every guest who had walked through Marie-Hélène's door. Gavin and Chloe. Chance. Arthur and Therese and Drew. "Rumors are rumors until you can prove them. Am I right?"

"I guess so?"

"Who do you work for?"

"I don't know."

"Don't you?" Carwyn looked at him. "Human or vampire?"

"I don't know. Not all of you look—"

"You have instincts, Bert! Good instincts. Human or vampire?"

"Vampire."

"Good. Local?"

"No. Definitely not."

"American? European? Asian?"

"He was a White fellow." Bert blinked. "Uh... he looked... I don't think I remember how he looked exactly. I usually remember faces, but..."

The vampire had used amnis to erase Bert's memory. An interesting twist they likely wouldn't have known if they'd used amnis to question him. The human's memory would have been even more muddled.

But knowing the vampire had used amnis, Carwyn reached out and touched his hand. "Think about being at Pete's."

Brigid saw the man's eyes go distant as Carwyn's influence crept into his mind. "Fucking hate this."

Ben frowned at her. "Using amnis?"

"He didn't consent to this."

"He took a job from a vampire," Ben said. "And he knew it was a vampire. Amnis is the safest and quickest way to get answers about your missing kid."

But would the information be accurate? Human memory was a tricky thing. Brigid pursed her lips and watched Carwyn lead the man back to Thursday.

"You were sitting at the bar?"

"I like the bar at Pete's."

"Steve's a great bartender, isn't he?"

"Yeah!" Bert was all smiles. "I was having a whiskey sour."

"Not a bad drink for a cool night. It was cooling down, wasn't it, Bert?"

"Cooling down." The human nodded. "Felt the cold air when the door opened."

"But it wasn't a regular."

"Nope. Pete's ain't a bad place for new people though. Friendly place."

"Did they walk around or sit at the bar right away?"

"Sat right next to me!"

"Is that right?"

"Said they'd talked to Jerry."

Alonzo and Brigid both stood a little straighter.

"Is that so?" Carwyn asked. "Who's Jerry?"

"Jerry Conklin. He's a... He's not my boss, but I take pictures for him sometimes."

"Is that so? Is Jerry a police officer? A detective?"

"Naw, he's a lawyer. Like... one of the cheap ones." Bert snorted. "Whaddya call 'em? Ambulance chasers?"

"Oh, I see. And you take pictures of clients for Jerry?"

"Yeah, that's why they must have asked me."

"Who is they, Bert? Who sat next to you? A vampire?"

"And the other guy."

"What other guy?"

Bert frowned. "White guy. Dark hair. Real... just normal-looking, I guess. He reminded me of my landlord, but he wasn't my landlord, you know?"

Brigid would bet that Bert was talking about Auguste Peregrine, the ordinary man. He and whoever had been pulling his strings must have hired Bert before Auguste had outlived his usefulness.

Which didn't bode well for Bert's long-term health.

"Think about the vampire again," Carwyn said. "It was a man?"

"Yeah, I think maybe... He was White. Or she? Maybe it was a she. They had... glow in the dark. Glow-in-the-dark red..."

"The vampire was glow-in-the-dark?"

"I ain't never seen anyone so pale." Bert licked his swollen lip. "And he had an accent, but I'm real bad at accents. I could understand him good though."

Ben raised one eyebrow. "So the vampire we're looking for is a pale White guy with an accent? That narrows it down so much."

"Who was here over a week ago but isn't local," Brigid said. "And not just pale but glow-in-the-dark pale." Or glow-in-the-dark red? What did that even mean? Something was scratching at the back of Brigid's memory, but she couldn't identify it. "It narrows it down some. At least we have another lead with this Jerry Conklin fellow." She glanced at Alonzo. "And we can look at guests of Marie-Hélène's who arrived last week. You okay with that?"

"Just because they're guests at a wedding doesn't mean I trust any of them," Alonzo said. "I'll send you a list."

Bert and Carwyn were still talking. "Are you gonna let me go?"

"I'll be straight with you, Bert. That might not be the best thing for your health. Why don't you recover here at Madame Charmont's estate for a while?"

"Okay, but..." Bert looked from Carwyn to Alonzo. "Do I have a choice?"

Alonzo shook his head. "No."

———

BRIGID WASTED NO time hunting down Jerry Conklin in the phone book. A quick internet search with Kit turned up Conklin's office and home address. She'd been about to grab Ben to go question the man while Carwyn went back to the lofts, but then she realized that would leave Tenzin at loose ends or at Carwyn's side, neither of which were good options.

So she took them both.

"You gotta stop floating," Brigid said as they parked the car on a quiet residential street in the Lakeshore neighborhood where Jerry Conklin made his home. "People do notice."

"But they assume they're imagining things," Tenzin said. "Why do you care?"

"I care because I don't wanna attract any more attention than I already do."

"You're mated to a red-haired giant who wears flowered shirts," Tenzin said. "Anonymity was never going to be an option."

"Still." Ben reached over and gently pushed Tenzin back to

the ground. "The better we blend in, the easier this will be. We don't want Brigid to attract any unnecessary attention."

"Fine." Tenzin walked beside them. "Why are we questioning this human?"

"He's the one who gave Peregrine the lead for a sneaky photographer," Brigid said. "Conklin uses Bert to take pictures of clients, cheating spouses, disability fraud, things like that. I think whoever he gave Bert's name to might also be a client."

"You think it's the dead guy?" Ben asked. "The Peregrine guy?"

"Possibly. Peregrine seems like the type to need a sleazy solicitor," Brigid said.

"Isn't that privileged information?" Ben asked. "Would the solicitor—lawyer—tell us?"

Brigid stopped, staring at Ben. Then she looked at Tenzin. "Is he serious?"

"I'm just saying," Ben added. "You don't seem to want to use amnis these days, so how are you going to make him tell you?"

"I'll question him, read his body language and facial expressions, and if that fails, I'll threaten him of course."

"And that's better than using amnis?"

"Obviously," Tenzin said. "He will *decide* to tell Brigid because he'll be frightened of her, not because he has no choice in the matter."

Brigid nodded. "Thank you, Tenzin. I'm glad you understand."

"I don't," Tenzin said. "I would threaten him and then use amnis if he withstood torture."

"But we're not torturing humans anymore," Ben said. "Because that's inhumane."

Tenzin looked back at Brigid. "Yes. We're not torturing humans anymore."

And she just seemed so sincere about it too. Brigid

continued walking. "Just let me do the talking when we get there."

They walked up the steps of a midcentury ranch house with a neat green square of a lawn and a Lexus in the driveway. Brigid knocked on the door and waited for it to open.

The man who answered the door was in his early sixties and had a grey comb-over and a light green seersucker shirt that stretched over his beer belly. "Can I help you?"

"Jerry Conklin?"

He immediately turned suspicious. "If you're looking for Jerry, you should try his office during the week."

He started to close the door, but Ben stuck his hand out and halted it.

"I think you'd prefer answering my friend's questions here."

Ben's cool stare and long arm did the trick.

Conklin turned back to Brigid. "What do you want?"

"I've heard about Southern hospitality, but to see it in action like that..." Brigid shook her head. "So gratifying."

The man was unamused. "What do you want?"

Brigid handed him a card with her number. "I'm an investigator working for Paladin Ventures, and we're looking into the kidnapping of an employee, a young man. Do you know this man?" She held up a picture of Bert.

"Yeah, I hire him sometimes. Freelance work only, he doesn't work for me." The man's swallow revealed his nerves, and his eyes stared straight at Brigid. "He's an independent contractor."

"We know that, but we also know that Auguste Peregrine is a client of yours."

It was a shot in the dark, but Brigid was hoping her instinct was right.

Bingo. Jerry Conklin's eyes flashed between shock, worry, and denial in a fraction of a second. "I don't know who that is."

"You're lyin'. We know you gave Bert's name to Peregrine. He hired Bert to trespass on private property and stalk Paladin employees."

Conklin's eyes flared. "Now wait a minute—"

"Mr. Conklin, did you know Auguste Peregrine was found dead earlier this week?" Brigid held up a picture of Peregrine from the morgue. "Did ya know that, Mr. Conklin?"

Jerry Conklin looked like he was on the verge of puking. "They killed Gus?"

"Yes, they did, and it wasn't pleasant." It was a single shot to the head, but Brigid didn't think that qualified at a pleasant way to die. "What did Gus Peregrine hire you to do, Mr. Conklin?"

The man was pale, and fear crept into his expression. His mouth tightened and he swallowed hard. "Listen, Gus may be dead, but he was still my client and I'm not allowed to tell you—"

"We're not from the police or the licensing board or the state bar, Mr. Conklin. We're looking for an innocent young man whom Gus Peregrine was following before he disappeared. We have pictures; we know he was involved. We just want to know what you did for Mr. Peregrine. Were you involved in the stalking as well?"

Tenzin spoke quietly. "Did you follow those children?"

"Children?" The pulse in Conklin's neck was visible. "Hell no, I'm not involved in— Gus hired me to broker some property deals he was working on! He wanted to be private and didn't want his name all over the place. That was all! He had... uh, quite a few rental places, a strip mall, that kind of thing. That is all I did for the man. I don't know anything about stalking or kids or any of that vampire shit he was involved in."

Tenzin smiled, revealing two arching fangs. "So you know about vampires."

Conklin took a step back. "I don't want anything to do with this."

"We'd like a copy of any files you have on Auguste Pere-grine," Brigid said. "You can email those copies to the address on my card." She looked at the man's hand. "Do you have my card, Mr. Conklin?"

He held it up. "Yes. I have it."

"If you email those files, we won't have any reason to come back to your home," Brigid said. "Do you understand?"

"I get it."

"It might be a good idea to email them as soon as possible," she continued softly. "After all, a young man is missing and I'm sure you want to help."

He nodded quickly. "I can do that. I'll do that right now."

"Excellent." She stepped back. "Paladin Ventures appreciates your cooperation, Mr. Conklin."

He slammed the door as soon as they turned and started walking away.

"I like the way you question humans," Tenzin said.

"It's all a matter of studying reactions." Brigid's mind was racing. Property deals? What did any of this have to do with finding Nic? Could Peregrine have been keeping him at one of his rental properties?

And was there any chance he was still there now?

SEVENTEEN

Carwyn sat next to Savi as the young woman attempted to do something on her computer for the third time. None of it made sense to Carwyn, so he had no idea how to be helpful, but he wanted to gauge the mood of Nic's compatriots at the lofts. He also wanted to touch base with the security team.

"I don't know why he's not responding." The girl was near tears. "He keeps sending the same code over and over, the same attacks with random variations. It doesn't make sense."

"It this something he could have automated?" Carwyn said. "Do you know that he's still the one typing?"

"I don't." The poor girl's expression crumpled. "It's possible this is a program he initiated days ago and it's still going. He might not even be on the other side."

"He could be gone." Bex's face was a grief-stricken blank. "You guys are going to parties and running around, and Nic could be dead."

He saw Gaines from the corner of his eye. The man's brow was furrowed and his lips were pursed. He did not like the implication that he wasn't taking his duties seriously.

Carwyn knew Bex didn't understand all the dynamics of

what was going on, but she needed some perspective. "I know it may seem like we're not doing everything we can, but you have to remember that Nic's disappearance has come at a precarious time for Marie-Hélène and Gavin."

"How is it precarious for them? Are any of *their* family members missing?"

Savi whispered, "Bex!"

Kit and Miguel exchanged grim looks.

Carwyn looked past Bex's anger and saw the heartbreak behind it. "I know how it feels when someone you love is missing."

The wave of grief rose, crested, and washed over his heart before it settled him. It was always there—would always be there—but it didn't pull him under anymore. He could remember his son without feeling only grief. "My son was taken by an enemy," he told Bex. "I know how you're feeling."

Bex's eyes went wide. "I'm sorry."

"So am I. I wish this had never happened to Nic, but I promise you this: while we are putting on public appearances and presenting an unworried face to the many very dangerous vampires visiting the city right now, I guarantee there is not a moment when Brigid and I are not thinking about how to get Nic back. We have to be very careful what facade we present to greater immortal society because any weakness on Marie-Hélène's or Gavin's part would invite attack, and that would create even more danger for all of you."

"That's why you're still having parties and stuff," Kit said. "Even though Nic is gone. To like, keep up appearances."

"Marie-Hélène and Gavin need to appear completely in control as they host Gavin's wedding. There are hundreds of eyes on them, watching Marie-Hélène's control of the city, watching Gavin's businesses. Not everyone invited to this wedding is a friend."

Miguel raised a hand. "So... why were they invited?"

Carwyn smiled. "Vampire weddings are rare and usually political, so they become more theater than friendly get-together. Gavin and Chloe know that, but it will be politically advantageous for them, and it will also present Chloe to the broader immortal world, which should offer her more protection."

Bex said, "I didn't think of that."

"So if you didn't go to the parties and things like that," Savi said, "someone might notice and it might put Nic in more danger, not less."

"It's possible, yes. Added to all that, Gavin must not be seen moving publicly against anyone until they have proven to be an enemy. His position and business depend on his neutrality." He looked from one young person to the next. "Which is why he called Brigid and me in to help. He trusts us, and you can too."

His phone buzzed in his pocket. He reached for the bulky case and pushed the button that answered Brigid's call. "Hello, my love."

"I'm bringing some files to the loft. We'll need some help doing some online research, but this could be a concrete lead to Nic's location."

He turned and gave Bex a thumbs-up. "Excellent. I think I know just the people to help. We'll be ready."

———

"WHAT IS THIS?" Bex looked at the file Brigid dropped in front of her. "This is... so much paper."

"These are legal files." Brigid dropped another manila folder in front of Savi. "And this is a list of names. Has anyone here ever heard of Otto Anker?"

Brigid and Carwyn were alone with the remaining team.

She scanned the four human faces. "Otto Anker?"

Savi was confused; Miguel was curious; Bex looked angry.

Kit's face was very carefully blank.

Brigid spun their chair around and pulled up a chair of her own. "Otto Anker, Kit. What do you know?"

A slight smile was fixed on their face. "I don't know anything."

"Bullshit."

A twitch around their mouth. Anger. "I really don't know anything about Anker or his group."

"But you know he has a group."

Kit saw their mistake immediately. "I just mean—"

"Did he try to recruit you? Did he try to recruit a friend? What do you know about his collective?"

"Nothing." Kit stood abruptly and started pacing. "I promise, I really don't know anything important."

Carwyn saw Brigid's impatience growing. "Kit" —he jumped in— "why don't you tell us what you do know, and we can decide if it's important or not."

Kit was already shaking their head. "I can't help you with this."

"Why not?" Brigid tapped her foot.

"Because I don't want to go back to jail," Kit said quietly. "And if my probation officer finds out I'm searching for or looking up anyone involved with Otto's crew, I will break the terms of my probation and I might go back to jail."

"So it's serious," Brigid says. "Otto's group?"

"Who's Otto?" Bex said. "Is that who took Nic?"

"I don't know," Kit said. "I had no idea that the Anker Group was involved in any of this. I don't know him or anything. My dad kind of knew his dad." They twisted their hands on their lap. "He knew I was studying computer programing, so he offered me a job right out of school. I did an online interview with him, and when he found out that I was arrested when I was younger—"

"You were arrested, Kit?" Savi looked horrified. "What did you do?"

"I hacked into the Pentagon when I was fifteen. And... a few other places I wasn't supposed to go." They looked at Carwyn. "I didn't have to spend long in juvenile detention, but it was hideous and I nearly killed myself. I will not go back."

Carwyn leaned forward and rested his elbows on his knees. "What happened when Otto found out during your online interview that you'd been arrested?"

Kit's cheeks flushed. Shame.

"At first he got excited," Kit said. "He has this... weird, almost-dead face, right? He hardly makes any expression. That creeped me out, but then when he found out I'd been arrested, he smiled. Then I told him I didn't want to ever do illegal shit again, and he kind of lost interest. Especially when I told him I was still in contact with my parole officer." Kit turned to Brigid. "Which is why I cannot help you with any of this. I still have to report to someone in the government about my activities, and I'm a terrible liar."

"You are." Brigid covered her eyes. "But let me remind you I'm not a police officer or anyone official. I'm not going to report you, Kit. I need your expertise, and I need to know if Otto Anker is involved in any of this. I don't have time to fuck about."

"There are ways they can track my movements." Kit looked as if they were about to cry. "And why would Otto have anything to do with Nic being missing?"

"Because he might hold Gavin responsible for the death of his sister last spring," Brigid said. "His sister kidnapped Chloe, thinking she was someone else. In the process of doing that, he severely harmed a human under Ernesto Alvarez's aegis."

Carwyn could have heard a pin drop.

"Mila Anker was killed because of it," Brigid said. "It's possible that Otto took Nic in an attempt to recruit him, to break into Gavin's new company and sabotage it. Or just to sabotage Paladin for revenge."

"Is Otto Anker in New Orleans right now?" Savi asked.

"Not as an invited guest," Carwyn said. "But there are so many people in the city right now, it wouldn't be difficult for him to remain hidden."

Carwyn added, "The Ankers are known for hiring independent contractors too. Otto could be orchestrating all this from Europe."

Brigid flipped open the folder in front of Kit. "Do any of these names look familiar?"

Kit frowned and read the list. "Yeah, three. One is based in Morocco, and the other two are Russian guys."

"These must be fake names." Carwyn read over Kit's shoulder. "Who names their child Lord Boris?"

"Lord Boris is on that list?" Miguel asked. "I know them. Well, know *of* them. It's actually these two cousins out of Eastern Europe. Like Moldova or somewhere around there."

Carwyn caught Brigid's eye and smiled. Miguel had hidden depths. Savi, Miguel, and Bex all gathered around Kit, looking at the list of names.

"I know Baby Lucy." Bex pointed at a name near the bottom of the list. "She's from Southern California, but I never talked to her. She was pretty infamous though. I thought she was more of a hacktivist."

"If she's working for Otto, she's after the money," Carwyn said. "The Ankers have no political ideologies, good or bad. They're a very old family of vampire spies, and they used to be very feared."

"Used to be?" Savi looked up. "What happened?"

"Their patriarch was killed in London about ten years ago,"

Carwyn said. "Since then, they've been scattered. As Brigid mentioned, Mila Anker was killed after she kidnapped Chloe."

"Who would take Chloe?" Kit asked. "She's like, the nicest person ever."

"She brought me macaroni and cheese when I first moved here," Savi said. "I'd never had it before, but I'd heard about it in movies."

"Could Otto do some damage with these people on his team?" Brigid asked. "Could Otto have snatched Nic?"

"Honestly?" Bex shook her head. "If this Otto guy *really* has all these people working for him, he's not after companies like Paladin. At least not yet. Once our servers are holding really sensitive information? Maybe. But right now Paladin's not worth their time."

"I'd agree," Kit said. "The three names I know are notorious for sophisticated ransomware attacks. We don't have anything to ransom right now. Not really."

"Ransomware?" Carwyn asked.

"It's like locking up computer systems and holding the key for ransom," Kit said. "Send us fifty million in cryptocurrency or you don't get access to your computers back."

"Jaysus," Brigid said. "Do companies pay that?"

Carwyn was still wondering what cryptocurrency was. Ben had tried to explain it, but it made absolutely no sense.

"Do they pay?" Miguel nodded. "Oh yeah. There might be some negotiation, but most of the time, they don't have a choice."

"Fuckin' hell," Brigid said. "So Otto's probably made a fortune already."

Kit shrugged. "I have no way of knowing, but these are very competent people, at least the five names we've identified. And there're twenty on the list."

Another thought occurred to Carwyn. "Would Nic ever work for people like this? Could they have recruited him?"

Bex snorted. "Roland?"

Miguel smiled. "Nicknames aside, Nic Cooper really is a white knight. I can't see him ever doing anything with a collective like this unless they could convince him it was for the greater good."

"And that would take a lot of convincing," Savi said. "Nic is not trusting by nature."

Carwyn turned to Brigid, who was staring at a wall, stewing about something. "Darling girl?"

"He's not trusting," she said. "We keep hearing that from people over and over again. You four, Gavin, Alonzo, Gaines."

"Nic wasn't trusting," Miguel muttered. "He was a pain in the ass and questioned the guards constantly."

"So why the hell did he jump in that car?" Brigid asked. "What on earth made Nic Cooper get in his kidnappers' car?"

———

MARIE-HÉLÈNE CHARMONT SAT ON A CHAISE, her elaborate hairstyle gone and her hair twisted into two braids that fell over her shoulders. She was wearing a dressing gown and little to no makeup.

She looked younger and far more distressed than her public persona. "I just can't believe there hasn't been a single sign of him." She gripped Chance's hand. "I'm sick, Chantelle. What must Caroline think of me right now? Nic is her entire world."

"She knows you're looking for him," Chance pressed Marie-Hélène's hand to her cheek. "Marie, you must calm yourself. Alonzo and Gavin will find the boy."

Carwyn sat across from Marie-Hélène, Brigid at his side. "Whoever has taken him has been very quiet and very discreet, but we have reason to believe they want Nic for a purpose—likely something to do with Paladin—and they're not going to harm him if they want something from him."

Marie-Hélène let out a rueful laugh. "But will Nic cooperate? He's the most stubborn boy I've ever met, including you, Carwyn. More stubborn than the oldest vampire I know and twice as ornery. He gave Alonzo fits when he was under our protection."

"He gave me fits, but he was never kidnapped," Alonzo muttered, glancing at Gavin.

"We're looking at two leads right now." Gavin ignored Alonzo and spoke directly to Marie-Hélène. "We're looking into Auguste Peregrine and any properties he might have owned to see if any of them are isolated enough to hide Nic with no trace. And we're also looking into Otto Anker's movements in the United States. Officially he's not here, but we have reason to believe he might be the one behind the attempted sabotage of Paladin."

"Anker?" Marie-Hélène's eyes went wide. "Mila's brother?"

Gavin nodded. "The same."

"That animal." She curled her lip. "I shouldn't say anything."

"It's just us, Marie." Gavin took her hand. "The Ankers have burned all their bridges with me, so they'd be a fool to alienate you too, but they may not realize how exposed they are."

"What has the world come to, cher?" She gripped his hand. "The children used to be safe, even from the worst of us."

"Nic isn't seen as a child anymore," Gavin said gently. "He's a man to them, and a valuable one with the knowledge he holds of Paladin and your organization."

Alonzo interrupted. "You think this could be an attempt to target Marie-Hélène?"

"Surely not!" Chance looked at Alonzo, then at Gavin. "Gavin, is Marie in danger?"

"I don't think so," Gavin said. "We don't have any evidence that Marie-Hélène is being targeted personally, though Nic is under her aegis. His going missing doesn't make her look good."

Brigid spoke softly. "We've been utilizing the development team at Paladin to help us try to find him. He is active online, so we're trying to communicate with him that way."

"He's active online?" Chance frowned. "What does that mean? Like he's posting on social media or something?"

"Nothing so open. He's been trying to hack into Paladin's servers," Carwyn said, "but he's doing a poor job, probably on purpose. Bex Romero is probably the closest to Nic on the team, and Bex is working day and night on this. She won't stop until she finds a way to communicate with him."

There were tears in the corners of Marie-Hélène's eyes. "Good. Give this girl whatever money she wants to find Nic. Give her anything."

Carwyn smiled and patted Marie-Hélène's knee. "She's not doing it for the money, Marie. She cares about him as much as you do. Maybe more."

NIC III

Nic III

"I'm Nic," he said quietly. There was a thin spot in the wall, and he and the girl next to him were trying to communicate loudly enough to hear each other but not loudly enough to be heard by the human guards who watched them during the day. "I'm six foot, one hundred eighty pounds, and I have short red hair. I don't wear glasses or contacts. And I'm White. I'm a computer programmer at Paladin Ventures."

"Reena," she said. "I'm Black and I have shoulder-length hair in braids. I'm twenty, and I'm going to school at Southern, studying social work. If either of us gets out, we can tell the police."

"Yeah, that's a good idea." He didn't tell her that the chances of them escaping weren't good. That wouldn't do anything but make the woman more miserable. "Are you okay? I know they're biting you."

She was silent. "I don't want to talk about it."

"Okay." He wanted to punch something. "Are they feeding you?"

"Ramen."

"Same." He had a thought. "Did you see where we were when they took you?"

"Yeah, I was up in Vacherie visiting my grandma. She lives outside town. They grabbed me and... Actually, I guess I don't know where we are now because I don't remember how long I was out."

Vacherie? Saint James Parish would fit within the radius he'd mentally drawn from his time in the trunk. "I was in the city when they grabbed me. Well, I got in the car, but it's a long story. I was in the trunk for about an hour I think."

"I don't remember how I got here. Or how long I was in a car. I don't even remember a car."

There was shouting down the hall, and then someone was banging on Nic's door.

"Hey, Mr. Genius!" a human guard shouted at him. "We're coming in, and we're moving you. There are three of us and we all have guns, so don't even think about any funny business."

Fuck. This wasn't part of the plan. "Reena, did you hear that?"

"Yeah." She sounded panicked. "Nic, if you leave—"

"I'll try to escape, okay?" He kept his voice low. "Wherever they take me, I'm going to try to escape. Stay alive. And whatever you do, don't leave the house at night."

He sat back on the floor with his legs straight out and his hands folded on his lap, staring straight ahead at the opposite wall when the human guards burst in. One had handcuffs, and another kept a 9mm trained on Nic.

"You're not going to shoot me." He glanced at the man with the gun, then looked away dismissively. "You need me."

"Maybe." The guard was American. "Maybe not, smart-ass."

They flipped him over, cuffed his hands, and dragged him out of the room by his ankles before they tossed him in the back of what looked like a delivery van. He quickly took in as much of his surroundings as possible.

Old Creole-style plantation house between the cane fields and the river.

Two large outbuildings.

Dirt road.

Alley of pecan trees falling in on itself.

He didn't recognize the road as they were going over it; then someone tugged his hair back and looped a blindfold around his eyes.

Everything went black.

EIGHTEEN

Bex was the one who brought the computer to Brigid. "Okay, these are the properties we found on our first search. There are seven houses, one strip mall, and then it looks like some kind of farm or something out in Terrebonne Parish."

Brigid glanced at the tablet but didn't touch. "Tell me about the houses."

"Okay, so we hacked into the power-company records—not Kit, the rest of us—and we looked at the records for all the different houses. We figured he's not going to keep Nic anywhere that people are living, right? Six of the seven houses don't have any interruptions in the power usage for the past six months to a year, right? So we figure those places have regular renters."

Brigid nodded. "Good thinking. And the seventh?"

"It has no power use at all, which makes me wonder if it's even inhabitable. It's in Saint Roch, which isn't that bad, so if it was a nice place, he'd probably be able to get renters for it."

Brigid tapped a pencil on the table. "Peregrine's girlfriend's house was in Saint Roch. And Nic used to live there."

"He had a shitty apartment with two other guys, yeah. He hated it."

Brigid cocked her head. "What's between you two? You and Nic."

Bex opened her mouth, closed it. She was nervous and embarrassed. There was a flush in her cheeks, and Brigid was jolted by the realization that she hadn't fed that night.

Damn. She'd need to go back to Revel tonight.

"We're friends," Bex said. "But pretty close. Yeah. I mean, we're close friends."

Too many words not to be hiding something.

"You're romantically interested in him."

Now the flush was unmistakable. "He's not interested in me that way."

"How do you know?"

"He's just not. He doesn't really date or anything. He... uh." She smiled. "I think he's convinced himself that he wouldn't be a good boyfriend, so he just doesn't try."

"Is he right?"

"I don't think so." Her voice was soft. "I think he just needs someone who understands him, you know?"

Brigid nodded. "I suspect you're right."

Bex tapped the tablet. "Can we keep going over the—?"

"We should check the vacant house, though I'm thinking if Nic is being kept there, there would be at least a mild draw on city power."

Bex nodded. "Miguel and I were thinking the same thing, so we looked at the strip mall—only one vacancy there and it's an old video store with giant windows. Not a good place to hide someone, I don't think."

Brigid frowned. "Did you go out and search all these places today?"

"No, we just used a mapping program with street views."

She blinked. "With street views?"

"Yeah, you can click on a street address and they usually have a view like you're walking down the sidewalk."

Well, that was terrifying and useful. "I agree on the strip mall. Were you able to find out anything about this old farm?"

"Nothing. We have a general area, but there's no actual address, and I couldn't find it on the map. The file the lawyer gave you had some old photographs, but they look like they're from fifty years ago or something. And since there's not a proper address, there isn't any information online about the power use."

"Right." She craned her neck to look at pictures of a run-down house with a wide front porch and long, tall windows in the front. There were broken stairs leading to the porch from the gravel driveway and an alley of tall trees marking the entrance. "Can you print that out for me?"

"On paper?"

"Yes, Bex. Paper. Something I'm not going to short out if I touch it."

"Oh, this is a device designed for vampires." Bex pointed to the case. "From the company that shall not be named around here."

"It's designed for *most* vampires," Brigid said. "Not fire vampires."

"I don't think I knew you were a fire vampire." Bex's eyes widened. "That's wicked."

Brigid nodded. "It's somethin'." She tapped the tablet and the screen blinked. "Printouts please?"

"Yeah, sure." She hurried away, and Brigid waved Gaines over. "We may have a lead on a house. Can you set up a team to check it out in person? Daylight is probably best, just to be safe."

Gaines nodded. "Agreed. I'll get a pair of eyes on the place in the morning to check it out. Whereabouts?"

"Terrebonne Parish. Bex is printing out the file. Have her make you a copy." Brigid finally felt like she was making progress, plus she was missing a reception Chloe and Gavin were hosting for Gavin's staff from Singapore. Carwyn was attending and would join her later.

Brigid wondered if she had enough time to slip out to Revel and feed. She scanned the workroom they'd set up in the lofts.

Savi was hunched over her computer with Kit beside her, leaning on her shoulder and speaking quietly as they watched the screen together.

Miguel was cooking something in the kitchen that smelled spicy and delightful. He'd shared a Bahamian fish and grits dish with Brigid the night before that nearly seared her tongue off, but it was tasty.

Not as tasty as blood.

She walked over to Gaines. "I'm out for an hour. I'll be at Revel if anyone needs me." She glanced at the four young people. "Don't let them leave."

"I don't think any of them has left this place for over a week now," Gaines said. "I don't know how they're not stir-crazy."

"They have the balcony and their computer screens," Brigid said. "The world is at their fingertips."

Gaines smiled. "Go on. I'll keep them safe."

———

BRIGID'S SECOND visit to Revel was distinctly more crowded than her first. She even saw a few familiar faces in the crowd and decided to be friendly for as long as her hunger allowed.

"Brigid!" Beatrice waved from a booth near the back of the club near the private rooms. "We haven't seen you in days." She patted the seat next to her and slid closer to Giovanni. "How's it going?"

"Finally making progress." She looked around and didn't spot anyone suspicious, but she still kept her voice low and her words cryptic. "This project has been more complicated than we initially imagined."

"I understand the... goal has been somewhat enigmatic." Giovanni was also scanning the room, fully understanding her caution. "No clear signposts?" *No messages from Nic's kidnappers?*

"None, and the initial actor hasn't communicated what their goals are. It's amazing how well an objective can stay out of reach when no communication happens." *We can't find shit if all they want is to stay hidden.*

Beatrice nodded. "I have firsthand experience with that."

Brigid had almost forgotten Beatrice had once been taken by a water vampire and kept on an island for months. No ransom demand. No taunting messages to follow. It had taken Giovanni months to find her, which made Brigid feel slightly better about not being able to find Nic.

"Are you fairly sure the goal is still within reach?" Giovanni asked.

"I honestly have no idea." She took a deep breath. "We're making some recent progress though. I have an excellent team."

"That's important," Giovanni said. "Especially when you're in unfamiliar territory."

Brigid was itching to start a fight with the man but knew it was only her amnis being a bitch about another fire vampire so close when she hadn't eaten in days. Luckily, Giovanni was as aware of the issue as she was.

She leaned toward him. "I'm going to go feed before I want to rip your head off. Are you and B hanging out for a while?"

He looked amused. "We are, and I'd love to catch up."

"I just fed," Beatrice said. "Jordan was excellent."

"Tried him a week ago. I agree."

Giovanni said, "I believe Minerva mentioned they have

several vegans on staff. Might be refreshing with all this humidity."

Brigid pointed at him. "Excellent idea; I'll ask."

She bid her farewell, walked back to the hostess stand, and asked Minerva for her vegan recommendation.

A delightfully plump girl named Macie met Brigid in the back room and chatted about her studies in psychology at Tulane while Brigid fed from her wrist. Her blood was clear and bright with a zing of citrus that Brigid particularly enjoyed. It was the exact type of blood draw that made Brigid feel like she really didn't have to be a monster for eternity.

Just as Macie was leaving, Brigid's phone buzzed. She took it out and answered it when she saw Carwyn's name. "I was just thinking of you."

"Have you fed tonight? It's been three days."

"Yes, that's why I was just thinking of you. I just had a delightful meal with a lovely girl named Macie. She's going to be a child psychologist."

Brigid was fed and her amnis untangled and even. Macie had gotten to rattle on about her schooling to a captive audience, and she'd earned a nice fat paycheck and tip for her efforts.

"Good for her," Carwyn said. "A noble profession. This party has been unexpectedly entertaining. How is it going at the lofts?"

"Makin' progress. I'll brief you before morning, but there's an old house in Terrebonne Parish Gaines will be investigating during the day tomorrow. We may be visiting tomorrow night, depending on what they find. Why is the party entertaining?"

"Three words. Tenzin knife throwing."

"Dear God, does everyone still have all their eyes?"

"Ben nearly lost a finger, but everyone is intact."

"You know she can manipulate the trajectory with the air, right? She doesn't have perfect aim. No one does."

"Darling girl, in no way does that make the spectacle any less entertaining."

She could imagine the delight and amusement on his face. "I adore you, Carwyn ap Bryn."

"The feeling is quite mutual, Miss Connor." His voice was gruff. "Where are you right now?"

"Still at Revel. Giovanni and Beatrice are here, so I'll probably catch up with them. Are they helping with this at all?"

"I'm sure they'd be willing, but they have their daughter with them, so I thought it was a better idea to hold off on their help unless we really need it."

"Good point."

Sadia Vecchio was a precocious child, and Chloe was one of her favorite people. Brigid suspected that Sadia might even have a small part in the wedding, which would make Beatrice and Giovanni far less likely to expose her to any unnecessary attention by participating in an investigation. They'd help if she asked, but Brigid was determined to avoid it.

She checked her teeth in the bathroom mirror and walked back out to Beatrice and Giovanni's booth where she saw Zain, their driver and one of Sadia's bodyguards.

"Brigid Connor." Zain smiled and stood to shake her hand. "How are you and that earth vampire getting along?"

"Did Carwyn show you pictures of our van?" she asked. "We're regular campers now."

"Did he cut a skylight over the driver's seat so he could fit?"

"It's surprisingly roomy." She smiled at Zain, the fresh blood putting her in a placid mood. "Chloe's going to be officially off the market in a couple of weeks. Have you given up hope?"

He sucked his teeth and smiled. "You know that girl's like my sister."

"I know that, but Carwyn has never lost hope that a torrid love triangle will develop between you Chloe, and Gavin, leading to amusement and melodrama he could vicariously live through."

"He's gotta cut back on the telenovelas, Brigid."

"I don't know if that's realistic when he's well over a thousand years old." She smiled at Zain as Giovanni and Beatrice laughed. It felt good to be among friends; it fed something in her soul that had been missing for months.

She glanced at Giovanni and saw him slide a finger around the collar of his shirt. The curls at his nape were shorter than the last time she'd seen him, a subtle indicator he'd used a large outpouring of fire.

He caught her eye and raised an eyebrow in question.

Brigid touched the edge of her hair and grimaced slightly.

Giovanni gave her a knowing look and leaned over to Beatrice. His mate nodded and smiled at Brigid before she turned her attention to Zain. Giovanni slid out of the booth, and Brigid followed him out of the club.

He glanced over his shoulder. "I told her we were going out for a smoke."

Brigid smiled. "Clever."

"She understands." They walked a good distance from the entrance, stopping in a dark and relatively deserted part of the parking lot. "Are you having issues?"

"When does it get easier?" She stared at the ground in front of him, the pavement wet from a sudden shower. Rainbows rippled in the puddles as light touched oil. "I've made peace with the immortality, but..." She clutched her hand in a fist and pressed it to her chest. "The fire. I just want to know when—"

"It doesn't." His voice was quiet. A little wistful.

Brigid looked up. "I knew you were going to say that."

"It's constant," Giovanni said. "Unrelenting. Inside, it's a constant burn. I suppose when I'm in water—as in completely enveloped in water—I can relax. A pool at your new house wouldn't be a bad idea. But I can't live my *life* underwater." He shrugged. "It's a battle, and I know it always will be. I don't know what kind of ancient control Arosh has mastered to live as long as he has, but—"

"Do you think that some of us, some of our kind... Do they just give up? Do they let it take them?"

Giovanni's eyes were haunted. "I would never judge them if they did."

"I'm supposed to be happy. Of all the lives I could lead, I found a path that fulfills me, a husband who loves me, and a life where I feel like I can make a difference."

"We're both fortunate that way."

"But sometimes I want to rage. I want to destroy everything, and I don't know where that comes from."

"It comes from you and it comes from the fire. It's part of you now—don't try to section it off or treat it as a foreign thing within you. Don't try to run from it when it's what gives you your strength. I know your life wasn't easy. Carwyn hasn't shared everything, and he doesn't need to. I can see the ghosts."

"That's why, don't you see?" Brigid shook her head. "I can't become the destroyer."

"But you can't avoid it either." He kept a strict distance between them, but his words reached her like an embrace. "Both live in you. This is the thing that I have learned, Brigid Connor. Fire is no simple thing. It consumes and creates, destroys and revives."

She nodded. "The volcano erupts and burns everything in its path, but it also creates new land. I know."

"Part of you knows, but not all of you." Giovanni frowned.

"Maybe our gift is the most human of all the elements for that reason. Human creation is usually destructive." His eyes turned inward. "The mother who gives birth to life also gives birth to death. There is no new life without death laying the path for it to be born."

NINETEEN

The old house that backed up to cane fields was run down, suffering from decades of neglect. Whatever owner had built it to be a showpiece had long since joined the dust he came from, and the ancient trees surrounding the property wept long tendrils of Spanish moss over the swiftly encroaching wilderness.

There were two faint lights from the first-floor windows, and the sickly-sweet smell of decay suffused the humid air that rustled the canes.

Carwyn and Ben sat at a distance, watching the lights and waiting for the rest of their party to arrive. Tenzin had carried Brigid to the site, and Ben had carried Carwyn. Raj, Gaines, and his men were coming in a van but would probably be another half hour.

Carwyn watched the man at his side, the vampire he'd watched grow to adulthood, his dearest friend's son, who was now a vampire of considerable ancient power. "How is your sire?"

Ben glanced at him from his side. "Zhang is well. He's back

in Penglai for now. Tenzin and I are planning a visit at the end of the year."

"She's willingly going to see her father?"

The corner of Ben's mouth turned up. "It's one of her New Year's resolutions."

Interesting.

"And how are the two of you doing? I understand you came into an object of considerable power."

"Right now that particular object is living in an undisclosed location and is very well guarded." Ben smiled. "Giovanni is still certain he'll be able to decipher the language with enough time and enough experts in ancient languages."

"Hard to think of a language that Saba doesn't know."

"Oh, I'm pretty sure she knows it, but she's not sharing." He stared at the grass. "Apparently my ancestor didn't leave too many records. Just... really dangerous artifacts."

It was a long story, but Ben was distantly related through his human bloodline to an ancient and legendary vampire who had long since disappeared from history, leaving a scroll with unspeakable immortal power that no one seemed to be able to wield.

"Do you want it?" Carwyn asked. "The scroll?"

"Not particularly." He narrowed his eyes and looked off into the distance. "Tenzin says that's the reason she gave it to me."

"I may not agree with her often, but in this, she's right. Don't tell her I said that."

Carwyn glanced at the ring Ben wore on his right ring finger, a thick gold band that echoed the design that Tenzin wore on the same hand. Though the two hadn't taken any formal vows to each other, he could feel their ridiculously powerful amnis flowing together. They were true mates.

"And how is married life?" Carwyn asked. "I can't imagine she makes it easy for you."

Ben's smile was wide. "Where would be the fun in that?"

"Are you happy?"

"Yes." His grey-and-brown eyes turned to Carwyn. They had been rich brown in mortal life, but now they looked like a thunderstorm hovering over a desert. "I'm happy, and I think she is too."

"Uncles are supposed to say that's all they ever want for the children they care about."

Ben raised an eyebrow. "But not you?"

"I want far more than happiness for you," Carwyn said. "Happiness is a feeling that comes and goes. Joy is a way of life. Joy and goodness. And immortal life will challenge both those things in ways you cannot imagine yet."

"I know." Ben bit his lip and frowned a little. "I don't think that Tenzin will ever be *good*. Not by your definition, I mean. But... she's becoming more. More than what she used to be. And I'm with her for the journey."

"She's all you've ever really wanted."

"No. Not all. But I can't imagine this life without her beside me. Does that make sense?"

Carwyn craned his neck and saw Brigid sitting with Tenzin at a distance. She was watching the house with intense focus, her hand on a hunting knife.

"It makes perfect sense, Benjamin."

"I've been working on something fun." A mischievous smile came to Ben's face. "Want to see?"

"Absolutely."

Carwyn angled his shoulders and watched as Ben picked a pebble from the ground, then searched for something in the grass. He found a small feather and cupped both those things in his palm.

He kept his focus on his hands, and Carwyn could feel his

power building. It almost screamed out from his body, and the air around him started to rustle the grass.

"Ben—"

"Almost." He drew his cupped hands away from each other, the pebble and the feather floating in the space between, then turned his right arm, wrenching his hand up. At that moment, the pebble and the feather fell soundlessly into his left palm, both landing in sync.

Carwyn narrowed his eyes. "What was that?"

"A vacuum." Ben grinned. "I've been working on creating vacuums. Manipulating the air is easy." He swirled a hand, and the pebble and feather both turned and lifted in front of him. "That's nothing."

He released the air, and the pebble dropped with a small thud while the feather floated to the ground, pulled and twisted by the air.

"They fell at the same time." Carwyn realized what he'd seen with wonder. "You pulled the air back so completely that you created a vacuum between your hands."

Ben nodded. "When we were in Ethiopia, I had recurring dreams about being torched by Arosh. Then I realized that fire needs air to live. I can't put out big fires yet, but small ones?" He nodded. "I'm working on it."

It was a massive show of strength and a use of amnis so subtle that only those with extreme discipline would ever be able to master it. Moving your element was child's play, but creating a vacuum in midair was... something else entirely.

"That's very impressive." Carwyn didn't know whether to be impressed or a little afraid. "Incredible, Benjamin."

He smiled. "Well, it's no fire tornado, but it might come in useful."

THERE WERE nine vampires surrounding the house, creeping in silently while the five guards made their circuit. One was on the door, three more patrolled the grounds, and another must have been in the house, guarding whatever treasure they held.

As they approached, Carwyn walked over loose ground that cried out to him. A stab of anguish made him freeze.

"There are two bodies buried here," he whispered.

Raj, Gaines, and Brigid turned to look at him.

"Later." Carwyn shook his head. "First we go inside."

There was at least one human inside, and they were bleeding. The smell of it was everywhere.

The first guard went down without a sound, ambushed by Brigid, who sliced a knife across his throat to silence him, dragged him back into the tall grass, and finished him with a slash to sever his spine. The water vampire's body twitched, but his amnis was already dissipating into the damp air around them.

Tenzin and Ben had disappeared into the trees. They were waiting and watching the house while Gaines, Raj, Brigid, and Carwyn took out the guards on the south side.

Marie-Hélène had already confirmed that none of her people or her guests were staying at the old farmhouse. Whatever vampire had set up shop there, they had done so without permission of the local authority. Couple that with the scent of decaying bodies, and Carwyn had little moral conflict with taking these rogue vampires out.

He saw the second guard craning his neck to look for his partner. "Thirty-one?"

The vampire had a hint of an accent, but Carwyn couldn't place it. French or possibly Spanish. The guard started toward the first vampire's position. "Thirty-one?"

They had numbers instead of names? Interesting.

Before the man could take another step, Carwyn sank his

hands into the earth and pulled with all his energy. From the way he moved, Carwyn had thought he was a water vampire; he would have no defense against the earth. The ground beneath him opened up and swallowed the man to his waist.

"Fuck!" He began to curse in French; then his training took over. "Perimeter breach!"

Carwyn rushed forward and twisted the man's neck, breaking it with a quick snap as Brigid went hunting for the third guard. Gaines was behind him, his gun drawn, looking for the four men—two mortal and two immortal—he'd brought with him.

"Rickert, respond." He spoke quietly into a small radio. "Two guards down on the south side approach."

A voice crackled back. "Vine and Jones took out a third on the north side."

"Copy." Gaines nodded at Carwyn. "That leaves the one inside and the other on the porch."

Raj nodded. "I'll go."

"No." Carwyn spotted a broken window near the trees and Ben standing over the body of the vampire guard at the door. He looked back at Gaines. "They're already taken care of. Unless there are surprises your men didn't catch at sunset, it's done."

THE GIRL WAS HARDLY MORE than a child, possibly eighteen or nineteen. Her rich brown skin showed signs of bruising on her arms and legs. Her lip was split, and she had one black eye.

"There were five... maybe six of 'em." Her voice was barely over a whisper as Gaines interviewed her and Tenzin stood at her shoulder like an avenging angel. "I, uh... I was visiting my grandma about a week ago. I go to school in the city. Can you call my parents please? I don't... I don't know what to tell them."

The girl was covered in a blanket Ben had found in the house, and two of Gaines's men had already called for a medical team from New Orleans.

The fatherly human reassured her. "We will tell them whatever you're comfortable telling them, Reena. You understand that we can't go to the regular police with this?"

The girl nodded and blinked back tears. "They weren't... normal. What they did to me... They're some kind of monsters, right? Like from a book or a movie or something."

Carwyn could see evidence of fang marks on the girl's neck, arms, and legs. They were unhealed, and a few of them looked infected.

"Yes, they are." Brigid knelt down next to the girl. "They've all been taken care of, Reena. Do you understand what I'm telling you?"

The girl looked up at Tenzin, then back to Brigid.

"Yeah." She nodded. "I understand."

A spatter of blood on Tenzin's neck was the only evidence of violence, which was surprising considering the vampire's head had been ripped completely from his body.

The four bodies had been dragged outside where Raj and Gaines's men were taking pictures of their faces in an attempt to identify them, so the only evidence left of Reena's tormenters was arterial spray marking the far wall. Carwyn was trying to block it from the girl's view.

Ben stood by the door, watching the activity and waiting for the van. Brigid and Tenzin had shoved the rest of the men back except for Gaines, who clearly had experience with trauma victims.

"The most important thing right now is to get you safe and

healthy. Make sure your family knows you're okay. We have a doctor coming to treat you privately. Is that okay?"

She nodded. "I live with my cousins off campus, so they know I've been gone." She sniffed. "What do I tell them?"

"Whatever you feel comfortable telling them," Brigid said. "If you want them to know the whole truth about who did this—"

"No!" She put her hand out and gripped Brigid's arm. "I don't want them knowing anything about... whatever those things were. I don't want that. My daddy, he won't know how to handle that."

Brigid nodded. "Then we'll figure out an explanation he can understand. I promise."

"There was another guy here. Another guy they were keeping. He... uh, he had red hair and his name was Nic and he worked at a place called... Palestine?"

"Paladin?" Brigid offered.

"Yeah, that's it. He didn't hurt me; they took him too. They kept him in another room. If either of us got out, we were gonna call the cops."

Brigid sat on the floor. "We've been looking for Nic. He was here?"

"Yeah, but they took him away. He was there when they first caught me, and then..." She blinked and looked down, clearly searching her memories. "He was doing something for them, because they didn't treat him the way they treated me."

"That's so helpful, Reena." Gaines handed her a water bottle. "Is there anything else you remember?"

"He got... I feel bad, but I think he was trying to protect me." She sniffed. "When he heard them coming to my room, if I made a sound or something, he'd start yelling about not being able to work. Needing food or Coke or something like that. He'd bang on the walls and everything. I think they maybe hurt him a little bit." She blinked harder, and a few tears rolled down her cheeks. "It didn't really stop them from biting me, but I'm pretty sure he was trying to help."

Brigid nodded. "Nic's friends say he cares a lot about people. I'm sure he was trying to help. He's not much older than you."

Reena furrowed her brow. "When you find him, I'd like to say thank you, you know? I hope he's okay."

Lord in heaven, the backbone of this young woman. It enraged Carwyn all over again to see her thinking of others in the middle of her own trauma. Forget vampire strength or elemental ability. Humans amazed him on so many levels.

"I don't think they were gonna hurt *him* though. They seemed real interested in whatever he was doing. I think I heard him typing on a computer sometimes. And there was another one who came sometimes, but I didn't see who it was. They would talk about someone coming, and then they'd blindfold me and put tape over my mouth." She touched the edge of her lip. "They put me in the closet, so I don't know if that other one even knew I was here. I heard 'em though. They had a different accent than the other ones."

"What kind of accent?"

"Maybe... I think it was Russian, or Eastern European maybe. There's a Russian deli I go to, and the owner sounds a little like that."

Gaines and Brigid exchanged a look.

Lights shone through the window, and Ben stood straight. "Van coming. I think it's the doctor."

Brigid and Tenzin helped Reena to her feet, keeping the blanket wrapped around her to give her as much privacy as possible. They walked with her to the door, and Carwyn followed, relieved to see Chance exiting the van with a young woman in a medical coat.

"Hey there." Chance walked up to the girl and clasped her hands in front of her body. "Are you Reena?"

"Yeah, that's me."

"I'm Chance, and this is Dr. Kaur."

A cheerful young woman in a white coat lifted a hand in greeting. "Hey, Reena. I'm going to take care of you if that's okay."

Reena looked doubtful. "You're a real doctor?"

Dr. Kaur smiled, and it took over her whole face. "I promise. I just look like I'm still in school. I'm actually thirty-three."

"Okay." Reena nodded and started walking toward the van.

"I know it probably seems strange not taking you to a hospital," Chance said, "but Mr. Gaines is coming with us. You've already met him. And we'll give you your own cell phone." She was helping Reena into the vehicle with gentle hands. "You can call anyone you want. We don't want you to feel uncomfortable or trapped or anything like that. We just want you to be able to rest and heal. Does that sound okay?"

Reena turned and looked at Tenzin and Brigid. "Do you know where I'm going?"

"No secrets here," Chance said. "We're going to my ranch, which is about an hour north of the city."

"We know where you're going," Tenzin said. "And we know who's going with you."

Chance touched Reena's shoulder gently. "Do you like horses? My ranch is a horse sanctuary, and it's really quiet and peaceful."

Reena smiled a little. "Yeah, I love horses." She looked at Brigid and Tenzin. "Do you have, like, a phone number?"

Brigid immediately held out a card. "We're going to keep looking for Nic, but you call anytime. I might not answer during the day, but I'll get your message at night. I promise."

The girl nodded, the door closed, and the van drove off, kicking up dust from the old gravel road.

Tenzin stared at the disappearing vehicle. "We've killed everyone who needed to be killed, but now I want to kill someone else."

Ben put his arm around her and kissed the top of her head. "I know, Tiny."

Tenzin turned to Carwyn. "We're helping whether you want it or not."

Carwyn wanted to snarl at her tone, but he knew it came from a place of hurt and recognition. "Don't worry, you mad little heathen. There's still plenty of hunting to do."

TWENTY

Marie-Hélène slowly flipped through the pictures of the wounded girl, cold fury on her face. "Alonzo."

Brigid watched the security chief scurry to his mistress. "Yes, madame."

"When we find who ordered this, bring them to me. I will kill them myself."

"Yes, madame."

"Chance is with the young woman now?"

"Yes, they're staying at the ranch. I have increased security, but I've had to pull some resources away from your guests."

Marie-Hélène's expression flipped from fury to political calculation in a split second. "Gavin?"

Gavin stepped forward. "I've already spoken to Raj. We can pull people from Atlanta, Houston, and Chicago. I don't have any significant resources closer, and we're probably only talking about twenty, maybe twenty-five people. Most of my New York staff is already here."

Marie-Hélène nodded. "It should be enough. Alonzo, we need to rank the guests by threat level and vulnerability. Focus our resources on guests who didn't bring their own security."

"Understood, my lady."

She looked at Brigid. "I cannot be seen as unable or unwilling to control my territory. Whoever has infiltrated will be dealt with. What news of Nicolas?"

"The girl who was taken said that he was at the house but was taken away two days ago, right about the time we located Peregrine's attorney. It's possible the man tipped someone off. Gaines has already gone to question him."

That wasn't what Brigid was thinking though. Nic got into the car without a fight. Whoever was keeping him knew the farmhouse had been located almost as soon as they found it. They'd been a step ahead of Carwyn and Brigid the entire investigation.

Marie-Hélène had a mole.

Was it Gaines? Alonzo? Brigid didn't trust anyone at this point, and if she could take their only witness out of the area, she would, even though Tenzin had flown up to Chance's ranch that night to check on Reena and she'd continue to do that every night the girl was there.

"What do we know about the vampires who were holding the girl and Nic?" Marie-Hélène asked Alonzo.

"Gavin's man and I identified three of them by their pictures," Alonzo replied. "All three independent contractors working out of Western Europe. Two don't have any record in our databases."

"Another sign pointing to Anker involvement," Gavin said. "They tend to use independent contractors, and they're based in Amsterdam."

One of the benefits of owning vampire clubs and bars all over the world was that Gavin and Marie-Hélène had two of the most extensive vampire directories in existence. It made it much easier to identify faces in the camera-shy immortal world.

"Whether it's the Ankers or not," Marie-Hélène said, "we

cannot point fingers. We can't be seen in open conflict. This needs to be taken care of privately and quickly."

"Agreed," Gavin said. "Plus I still need to get married in ten days. I'd prefer not to have the ceremony marred by violence from disgruntled spies."

The Anker clan had once been powerful shipping magnates, but as the world changed and modernity crept in, they'd shifted their network to traffic in information instead of freight. While their organization had been significantly damaged when Otto and Mila's sire Rens was killed in a bombing, Otto seemed to be determined to regain prominence, and he didn't have any of the grey moral boundaries that Rens had followed.

"They've lost their hideout now," Brigid said. "And five of their people. There were internet lines routed to that house that looked recently installed."

Marie-Hélène cocked her head. "Meaning?"

"They can't take Nic just anywhere and have him able to work. They're gonna have to take him someplace isolated that also has good internet access. We can probably work with that. Plus we have faces now. We can track movements, see where else they might have traveled."

"There was a sixth vampire," Carwyn said. "Reena said someone came and they hid her—possibly they weren't authorized to take another human captive, I don't know. But there was another vampire, and that's the one who took Nic. He's on his own now, and Nic isn't a man without resources."

"Focus on your guests and the incursion into your territory," Brigid said. "We'll find Nic."

———

"I CAN'T BELIEVE we still haven't found him," Brigid said. "Over a week now and nothing." They were walking through the

French Quarter, and Brigid felt like she was tripping over vampires. "This is ridiculous."

"Not finding one human or the glut of immortals in this city?"

"Both."

Pale vampires in their best attempts at modern fashion lingered at bars and meandered through streets. Most of them seemed charmed by the old-world feel of the oldest part of New Orleans, though many stared at the garish neon lights, "foot-long cocktails," and clubs with music pounding out of their doors.

"I just saw an old acquaintance from France," Carwyn said. "He was wearing roughly the same outfit I saw him in when we met in the twenties."

"The nineteen twenties?"

"Yes."

Brigid snorted. "I'm trying to imagine what this wedding is gonna look like, and I just can't."

Carwyn looked at her with narrowed eyes. "Good Lord, you have been sheltered, haven't you? I just realized you've never been to a large immortal event like this."

"Our wedding doesn't count since it was literally only the two of us in bed. And I managed to escape Gemma and Terry's with a last-minute emergency, remember?"

"Huh." His smile was smug. "You'll love it."

"Why?"

"It's the best people-watching in the world," he said. "And quite interesting from a historical perspective. Generally, older vampires will wear formal attire from whatever era they were born. It's one of the ways we can guess how old vampires are, though" —he wagged a finger— "some of us do play with that to confuse others."

"And some eras didn't really have formal wear." Brigid

frowned. "Good heavens, your formal wear would be a drab church frock coat thingy from the Norman era, wouldn't it?"

"Not quite, but you're not far off." He bumped her hip a little. "Don't worry. I've already ordered our clothes from a tailor in Dublin."

Brigid froze. "You didn't."

"Oh, I absolutely did."

Visions of garish silks and overwrought lace filled Brigid's mind with horror until Carwyn bent down and planted a kiss on her mouth.

"Do I love you, wife?"

"Yes?"

He grinned. "Would I order clothes for a formal event that I know you'd hate or be embarrassed to wear?"

Probably not?

"No?" She was more hopeful than convinced.

"Trust me." He grabbed her hand and pulled her back to walking down Bourbon Street. "You're going to love it."

"Are we walking to the lofts?"

"Yes."

Brigid felt her phone buzzing in her pants pocket. She reached down and got out the bulky case. "It's Savi." She touched the button to answer. "Savi? What's going on? Has there been a change?"

"Two things." The girl sounded like she was crying. "Nic's hacks have changed, and Bex is missing."

"Fuck!"

———

"WE DIDN'T LOSE HER." Gaines fumed. "She ran away."

"It didn't occur to you that she might?"

He threw his hand out. "Of course it didn't. We told them they were all targets! What kid in their right mind—?"

"She's *not* in her right mind." Brigid tried not to yell. "She's a suspicious genius who's in love with another suspicious genius and neither of them trust authority and one of them is missing. She thinks she knows more than we do, and now she's missin' too."

Brigid wanted to set something on fire. She desperately needed to set something—anything—on fire. "Ben!"

He'd been leaning on a wall near the kitchen, but he came to attention. "What's up?"

"Fly me to that island I told you about." She stomped toward him. "I need to think."

He shrugged. "Sure."

Brigid spun before she left the upper loft. "Carwyn?"

Her mate was sitting with Savi, Kit, and Miguel. "My love."

"I know it's an invasion of privacy, but search Bex's room. See if there's a note, an email, any kind of communication that looks like it was from Nic. She's not an idiot. She wouldn't just run away, but if she got a message she thought was from Nic—"

"She might have followed directions, trying to help." Carwyn nodded. "I'll look."

Savi patted his giant forearm. "I can get you into her work email and her personal."

Miguel and Kit nodded eagerly.

"We'll do anything we can to help," Kit said. "I'm sure if Bex ran away, she thought she was helping Nic."

Brigid spun and walked toward the stairs, following Ben, who was already downstairs. "That's what I'm afraid of."

They walked out to a dark corner of the parking lot outside. Ben turned and crouched down. "You're not Lois Lane, shorty. Hop on my back."

"I feel like a child."

"An angry, armed child." He patted his shoulder. "You want to go burn things? Hop on."

Brigid reluctantly climbed on his back. Carwyn forced her to hang on his shoulders this way when he tunneled longer distances; at least riding piggyback on Ben was better than feeling like a badger's backpack.

She directed him out to the mouth of the river and toward the barrier islands that protected the Louisiana coastline. She spotted the one that Gavin had pointed out the night she cleared the brush on the first island. "There."

Ben followed her pointed finger and landed them on a small island barely larger than a speck in the vast Gulf of Mexico. Like the first, it was covered in brush and grasses that were overgrown, waving the night breeze from the ocean.

She stepped forward, grabbed a lighter from her pocket, and built a fireball in her left hand, feeding it until it was the size of a soccer ball. Then she hurled it at a hedge of grasses and watched the dry brush burst into flames. She swept her arm out, letting her amnis delight in the rush of the growing fire. She walked toward it, reveling in the heat and the energy.

Ben hung back in the sky behind her, letting her sweep the flames over the dry grass. The crackle fed her and cleared her mind.

Who was it? Who was lying?

All of them. Everyone was lying about something. That was the problem with vampires. They were all cagey, suspicious creatures who were hiding something. Most of their secrets would have nothing to do with her current missing person.

Who was hiding Nic?

Who was hiding devious intent from Marie-Hélène and Gavin?

Brigid allowed the flames to grow, licking her fingers and teasing the air around her. The fire loved her, dancing in the dark night as she played it like a conductor over an orchestra of destruction.

Tell me your secrets, it whispered. *Show me your sins.*

She poured her frustration and failure into the inferno, releasing the scream that had been building for a week, and watched as the flames jumped higher and spread wider, enveloping the grass but leaving the roots safe under the sand.

The land sighed and stretched. The fire would leave room for new shoots to grow. She could feel the twin urges in her amnis, burn and renew.

When the land was black and smoking, she pulled the fire back, wary of letting it burn too hot.

Ben circled the island, using wind to toss misty waves up on the shoreline of the island to staunch the flames. After an hour of burning, the dead grass was gone and steam rose in the humid night air.

Brigid knelt in the sand, and Ben landed beside her.

"Feel better?"

She nodded. "Someone's lying."

"Someone's always lying."

"I know." She stood. "But right now there are only three people I want to question. The problem is, suspecting any of them is going to rightly piss off the people who hired me."

Ben kicked the sand. "Well, that's fun. Any ideas?"

"No." Her mind was clear and churning. "But give me a few minutes and that should change."

TWENTY-ONE

Carwyn sat in bed, watching his wife pace. "You're sure it's one of those three?"

She shook her head. "Of course not. I'm sure of nothin' in this crazy situation, but you agree with me, don'tcha?"

"I don't want to, but I do." There was no way someone outside the organization could have been keeping ahead of them so neatly. There had to be a mole. "We're sure about Gavin."

Brigid nodded. "He wouldn't have hired us if he was involved, and it makes no sense for him to sabotage his own company."

"And Marie-Hélène."

"Again, it makes no sense for her to sabotage her own company." Brigid stopped pacing and stretched her arms out, swinging them back and forth to stretch her sides. "Plus she's genuine in her concern for Nic. She's up the walls about him bein' missing."

"So if we're looking at people who had full access to the information about the farmhouse, whom Nic would have trusted enough to get in the car with them, and who might have been able to get to Bex, we're left with three people."

"Two vampires and a human." Brigid bent over and touched her ankles, stretching the back of her legs. "Alonzo, Gaines, and Raj."

All three trusted security operatives for Gavin, Marie-Hélène, and Paladin.

She straightened and looked at Carwyn in anguish. "It can't be anyone else."

"I agree they are the most probable suspects."

"And I hate that they are." She closed her eyes. "But I can't ignore it. I can't. They're all hidin' things; I've seen the secrets for days."

"We can probably find a way to question Gaines and Raj discreetly," Carwyn said. "Alonzo is another matter. He won't cooperate."

"But he's hiding somethin'," Brigid said.

"We all hide things. Even me." Secrets were a way of life for their kind. There was no other way to protect the ones you cared about. Often those secrets were kept for good reasons.

"I realize that, but we need to find out who's keeping a secret about their involvement with the Ankers."

"If the Ankers are even involved."

Brigid sat on the edge of the bed. "You're right. We're just speculating at this point."

"It's a theory." Carwyn rubbed her back. "And a good one. Come here."

She crawled in bed next to him and allowed Carwyn to comfort her. He could feel she was more relaxed and was grateful Ben had flown her out to a safe place where she could release the fire.

"Have you fed tonight?"

"No. I just had blood-wine."

"You should have fed after an elemental purge like that."

"I know, but I wanted to see you. I'll be fine until dusk."

It was too close to sunrise to visit Revel, and the place was jam-packed with vampires unless you arrived early.

"I think Minerva has her hands full with the increased vampire population in the city right now," he said. "I'll send a message for her to have someone ready for you at dusk."

"Thank you." She already sounded drowsy. "I love you."

"I love you too."

"I love that I can trust you."

He brought her closer and enveloped her in a tight embrace. "It's a valuable thing, isn't it? We can't trust many in this world."

"I feel like this city is crawling with threats right now. So many vampires in one place, all for what's supposed to be a joyous celebration, but..."

"But it feels more like a den of vipers."

"Exactly."

"I know. Aren't you glad we had a small, intimate ceremony instead?"

"If you're talking about exchanging vows while we were having sex and breaking my old house, I don't know how you get more intimate for a wedding."

Carwyn chuckled. "Do you wish we'd had a formal ceremony? In front of your aunt and Deirdre and the lot?"

"God no." She shook her head and pressed her face into his chest. "That sounds like a feckin' nightmare."

Carwyn ran a hand down her back, over her bottom, and trailed delicately over the back of her thighs, intimately familiar places where he knew she loved to be touched.

She lifted her face and pressed a slow kiss to his lips. "You're the only thing in the world I trust."

"Don't say that. We're surrounded by excellent people. Beatrice. Giovanni. Ben. That lovely old fellow who customized our van for us."

She laughed. "He was lovely, wasn't he?"

"We're fortunate to have the friends that we do." He stroked a hand over her soft cap of hair. "We have far more than most."

"Still, it's a good thing you're immortal, old man."

Since he'd never have met the singular woman in his arms if he'd remained mortal, Carwyn had to agree. "I do love that I have lived long enough to see the glory of..." He sighed. "The foot-long margarita."

She dissolved in laughter, and it made his heart sing. "You're ridiculous."

"That's why you love me."

She pressed up and threw her leg over his hips. "There are so many reasons I love you."

He was already inching the black tank top up and over her breasts. "Is that so? I'd like a detailed report on those reasons, Miss Connor."

"Well, according to Arthur, we are *smoking hot*." The corner of her mouth turned up. "Zaddy."

"Oh fuck, now you've done it." Carwyn yanked her shirt over her head and tackled her to her back. "I'm going to have to punish you for that."

Her laughter filled the bedroom, and it was the sweetest sound in the world.

———

THEY STARTED the following night at Revel, where Minerva had found another lovely young vegan for Brigid to feed from. It was a young man this time who talked about his ambitions to enter medicine.

Carwyn carefully watched Brigid drink from his wrist,

tipped the nervous student a generous amount, then tossed him out the door so he could enjoy a quick fuck with his wife. He never thought he'd be the type of man to have sex in the private room of a club, but one had to be flexible while traveling.

They cleaned up in the private bath attached to the room, Brigid carefully concealing her firearm and knives in the tailored pants and vest she'd donned for the night.

"You know, I really do think Arthur could make a fortune if he designed a line of clothes for vampires. He made this one for me last year after we visited Chloe in New York and I love it. I think he makes all Tenzin's clothes now."

"Arthur makes a small fortune designing clothes for humans at this point." Carwyn had to admire the way the vest hugged her body while still concealing her 9mm. The man was gifted. "I don't know that he needs vampire clients."

"But he could make a *massive* fortune designing tactical couture," Brigid said. "I'll talk to him about it."

"I think I saw him outside in the club." Carwyn rose and followed her toward the door. "He was sitting at a table with Chloe, Zain, and Raj."

Her eyebrow went up. "Raj?"

"Indeed."

She turned and looked up at him. "I'll piss off Gavin if I'm too obvious."

"You'll piss off Gavin anyway." Carwyn touched her cheek. "Raj is no amateur; he's going to know what you're doing."

"I know." Her mouth settled into a grim line. "I'm not looking forward to this."

"You'll get further if you approach the table without your interrogation face, Brigid."

"If I approach with a smile, they'll for sure know something is up." She turned and walked out the door. "Everyone knows who the cheerful one is in this relationship."

"That is very true." He ushered her out of the back hallway, giving Minerva a deferential nod as he passed, and scanned the room to find Chloe's table. "There they are."

"I see 'em."

Chloe, Arthur, Raj, and Zain were at a booth in the corner, sharing a bottle of wine and watching the dance floor where a DJ was keeping the party going strong. Carwyn saw Audra, Chloe's personal bodyguard, stationed at the bar where she caught Carwyn's eye as they approached.

Audra nodded and kept her eyes moving for threats.

"May we join you?" Carwyn asked with a smile.

"Brigid!" Chloe yelled and held out her arms. "You better! You two are working too much, and I know the reasons, but I'm trying not to think about them because I'm marrying the love of my life in nine days!"

"That was a mouthful," Brigid said.

Arthur whispered, "I bet it is." He glanced at Carwyn, then looked away quickly. "Pull up a chair!"

Such a strange little human. Carwyn pulled over a chair from a nearby table while Brigid slid into the booth next to Arthur.

She stared at him. "It is."

Arthur's cheeks were red. "Just saying. *Super*hot."

Chloe leaned forward. "What are you talking about?"

"Nothing." Carwyn hadn't felt like blushing in roughly a thousand years, but that had changed. "I wish we could attend more of the festivities, Chloe, but I trust Marie-Hélène is sparing no expense to show you the best of the city."

Chloe nodded and raised her voice over the music. "I was just telling Raj that she hired out an entire spa the day before the wedding. Brigid is invited."

"Not me?"

"You are too if you want to come." Chloe winked. "We'll get you all buffed and polished."

"Polished Carwyn?" Brigid looked at him in wonder. "That's a sight I'd like to see."

He scoffed. "No mere human aesthetician could polish a Welsh mountain like myself."

Arthur muttered, "Oh my God."

"But I could do with a pedicure," he said. "I'll let you know."

Zain raised a glass. "If you want something a little less buff and polish and more trim and shave, let me know. I know a good barber in town."

"That does sound excellent."

Brigid turned to Raj. "I feel like we've only spoken in passing, Raj. How did you come to work for Gavin?"

The vampire smiled, and Carwyn sensed youth and cheer with an undercurrent of cunning.

"It's kind of a story," Raj said. "He poached me from a rival."

Carwyn smiled. "Sounds dangerous."

"Well, a friendly rival," Raj clarified. "I was working background security for a club in Singapore when I first met Gavin. Kind of stuck where I was because the organization I was in—"

"Who were you with?" Zain asked.

"The Banyu Group?" Raj said. "They're based in Jakarta."

Zain nodded. "I've heard of them. Midsize, right?"

"Yeah, and that was the problem. There were too many new people they brought in around the same time, so there were limited opportunities to move up in the organization." He looked back at Carwyn. "I say it was a rival, but my boss and Gavin are pretty friendly. There were no hard feelings when I left."

The waitress brought two more glasses to the table, and Brigid poured an inch of wine in hers. "I don't know much about Jakarta," she said. "Indonesia, correct?"

"Yes, but like I said, I was based in Singapore."

"Interesting. Did you ever travel to Indonesia though? I've heard it's beautiful."

"I've traveled some for work." Raj nodded. "But it's a huge country."

Brigid turned to Zain. "How about you? Have you been? Carwyn teases me about taking me to Bali and keeping me naked for a week."

Chloe laughed and Arthur nearly choked on his wine.

Brigid turned to Raj. "That's Indonesia, right? Bali?"

Raj smiled. "It is. I can't give you any naked travel tips though. Sorry."

"Such an interesting country." Brigid was on a roll. "Very diverse, isn't it? I've always wanted to travel there." She sipped her wine and turned to Raj again. "The *Dutch* colonized that part of the world, didn't they? Curious if they have any influence anymore."

Carwyn watched Raj, who kept a placid face, but he could see faint tension around the man's eyes. "That was a long time ago."

Zain piped up. "Ah, imperialism." He lifted a glass. "Europe's most obnoxious export."

"What?" Chloe asked. "I thought Europe's most obnoxious export was Eurovision."

Arthur yelped. "You shut your mouth, Chloe Reardon! Eurovision is a treasure of talent and inspiration."

The whole table burst into laughter, but Carwyn kept his eyes on Raj.

There. He finally saw what Brigid had seen days before. He'd known it, but he hadn't recognized it at first.

Raj was afraid.

NIC IV

"Wake up, Mr. Cooper."

It took Nic a minute to understand what he was seeing. The vampire sitting on the bed across from him nudged something with their boot. The immortal's skin was the palest Nic had ever seen—nearly translucent—and they had gold-red hair that reminded Nic of a flame. They looked neither male nor female, but Nic had a feeling they were old. Very old.

The vampire smiled, just a little. "I brought you a present."

He blinked and knew that one of his eyes was nearly swollen shut. "Will it give me a faster internet connection?"

"Sorry. Your previous location had been thoughtfully outfitted with the best rural Louisiana could offer, but this one had to be thrown together when the other one was compromised."

"Tragic."

"It was." The vampire seemed doubly amused that night. "Don't you want to know what your present is?"

"Body armor?"

"Where would be the fun in that?"

Nic had lost count of the days he'd been at the new place. He only knew it was even more isolated, they fed him oatmeal instead of ramen, and every night—whether he cooperated or not—they beat him until he could barely move the next day.

Him not moving the next day was probably the plan.

Nic tried to act defeated, but he was already secreting away the supplies he'd need to escape. Dying trying to escape was better than the endless loop of hell he was living in now.

"I don't need any presents unless it's water," he said. "I could use more water."

"I'll see what I can do." The vampire nudged the pile on the ground again.

It moved, then it groaned, and the sound was familiar.

"Fuck."

No. The bottom of Nic's world fell out. Not that. Anything but that.

"Say hello to your pretty comrade," the vampire said. "And she thought she was so clever."

Bex raised her head, and her eyes were still swimming from amnis. "Nic?"

He tried to make his face appear impassive, but he knew it wasn't working. "Taking her was stupid. They're going to be searching even more now. She's under Ernesto Alvarez's aegis."

Bex looked around, the reality of where she was beginning to dawn on her. "You sent me... There was a note."

"Don't be foolish," the vampire said. "Marie-Hélène Charmont won't inform Alvarez until it's far too late. She won't want to appear weak. Her obsession with appearances will eventually be her end, but not before you make all of us a lot of money."

Bex was just staring at Nic, her eyes filling with tears as she realized what had happened. "Nic—"

"Shut up." He kept his eyes on a spot over the vampire's shoulder. "I told you this was stupid. If you don't understand why, I'm not going to tell you."

The vampire rose. "I'll leave you for now." They bent down to pinch Bex's cheek. "And let the lovebirds have a few minutes together before I take you away."

The vampire left the room, and Nic immediately scrambled to Bex. "Are you okay? I'm sorry I said shut up." He tugged the dirty blanket from around her. "Did they hurt you? Did they bite you?"

Bex threw her arms around Nic's neck, and he was too tired to flinch at the unexpected contact and the pain from his ribs. "I thought you were dead. When the server hacks started to feel scripted—"

"They were supposed to be scripted. I was being watched all the time." He ran his hands over her shoulders, examined her neck. "Did they bite you?"

"I got the note in my mail and I should have known, but I was just so... so hopeful. I thought you'd escaped." She was crying. "You're all bruised." She put her hands on his cheeks and examined his face. "What did they do to you? Are you okay?"

"I'll be fine." He ran a hand over her hips and gripped her thigh. "Did they bite here? There's a vein in the thigh that—"

"I'm fine." She was in his lap, and she caught his hand before it wandered any more. Her cheeks were red, and Nic realized that he'd been putting his hands in intimate places.

"Sorry." He blinked, and suddenly her eyes caught his; Nic couldn't look away and he didn't move his hand. "I didn't mean to make you uncomfortable. I apologize."

"I understand. You were worried about the vampires biting me."

"Yes." *And now I can't stop looking at your eyes.* "I didn't write you a note. I would never want you within a hundred miles of any of these things."

She nodded. "I'm getting that. They fooled me to get me out of the lofts."

"They fooled me too."

"They must have taken me for another reason."

"I don't need you to do what they want me to," he said. "I don't know why they took you."

Except he did. He'd been angry about the girl next to him at the other house, but he was on the cusp of flying into a manic state knowing that Bex was under these monsters' power. Any thought of running away or taking a chance with his safety was gone.

Until he could ensure Bex was safe, Nic would do anything they asked.

TWENTY-TWO

She found Raj in the parking lot outside Revel, talking quietly on his phone. It must have been with another vampire because even with enhanced hearing, she could barely make out the words.

"...asking..." He paced. "No, I didn't—" He turned and spotted Brigid at a distance. "I gotta go."

He stuffed the phone in his suit pocket and the look of cunning returned. "I know when I'm being questioned. You think I'm hiding something."

"I know it." She stopped a good distance from him. Carwyn was hanging back, watching from behind the corner of the building. "Then again, as my husband pointed out, we all hide things."

He shrugged, the polite smile never leaving. "The work we do doesn't lend itself to being an open book."

"What work *do* you do, Raj?" Brigid stuffed her hands in her pockets, her fingertips brushing against the knives hidden in her vest.

"I think I've already told you that."

"Have you?" Brigid moved to the side, ducking into a shadow

created by a sprawling oak. "I know what I'm doing in New Orleans. What are you doing here?"

"I'm working for Gavin." Raj moved with her, keeping their distance even. "I'm looking for Nic."

At this point there was no point in being discreet. "What do you know about the Ankers?"

A split-second twitch under his right eye. "I know as much as you do."

"No, I don't think that's correct." Brigid froze and looked directly at him. "I think you're lying about the Ankers, Raj."

He walked toward her. "When I tell you this is none of your business and you need to let it go, I mean it. I'm loyal to Gavin. That's all you need to know."

"No, I'm sorry." She shook her head. "That's not gonna be enough. I need to know about the Ankers."

"And I don't need to tell you anything." He puffed out his chest slightly. "You want to tell Gavin you suspect something about me, go ahead. Gavin knows I'm loyal."

"So he knows about your relationship with the Ankers?" It was a guess, but it got a reaction.

The corner of Raj's mouth pulled down a tiny bit. He did not like that implication.

"You've made up this... this *fiction* in your mind." His voice rose. "And now you want to ruin my life? You want to force me out of Gavin's trust? For what? You think I know anything about who took Nic?"

Raj was in her face before she could blink. The man was faster than she'd anticipated; her fingers curled around a knife. Brigid felt the ground beneath her shudder as Carwyn began to run.

"I don't know who took Nic." His gaze was open and forthright. There wasn't even a hint of deception when he spoke of the young man.

Carwyn had the man in a headlock before Brigid could pull a blade.

Raj didn't even seem to notice the giant holding him. "Nic is one of Gavin's people. If I knew anything, I'd tell you."

"Goin' to need you to calm down, boyo." Her mate's voice was tightly controlled fury.

"I don't know where he is." Raj didn't break his gaze with Brigid. "But if I did, I would sacrifice my own life to get him back because he's important to Gavin and that man got me out of hell."

There was not even a hint of dishonesty. "You believe that."

"I know that."

Brigid glanced at Carwyn. "He's all right, old man."

Carwyn released Raj, who never let his eyes leave Brigid's. "Do you believe me?"

"I believe you about Nic, but you're still hiding something about the Ankers."

Raj shook his head. "We don't even know they're involved in this."

"Oh, cop on to yerself!" She spat out the words. "Don't feckin' patronize me. Gavin was responsible for Mila Anker's death, and we both know it. Ernesto took the kill, but only because he got to her first."

"The only person responsible for Mila's death was Mila."

There was something about the way Raj said the name.

Brigid stepped forward and cocked her head. "You knew her."

The corner of his mouth turned up. It was nearly imperceptible, but Brigid caught it.

"No one knew Mila."

Carwyn's massive hand was at Raj's throat. "Start talking."

"I can't."

The hand tightened, but Brigid put a hand on Carwyn's forearm.

"Can't, not won't." She could see it was true. "You *can't* tell us about the Ankers?"

A dark car pulled up behind them, and Brigid turned. A driver exited the vehicle and opened the door for Gavin Wallace, who was dressed casually in a black kilt and a dark grey shirt. "Carwyn, I'd politely ask you to release my man."

Carwyn exchanged a look with Brigid, who nodded slightly. Carwyn let the vampire go, and Raj walked directly to Gavin's side.

Brigid turned to Gavin. "He *can't* tell us about the Ankers. Can't, not won't."

Raj's eyes pleaded with Gavin. "Boss—"

"You're fine." Gavin put his hand on the young vampire's shoulder. "Go join Chloe inside. I'll deal with this."

Brigid watched the interplay with intense interest. Nothing about this situation had been a surprise to Gavin, though she could see he was angry.

Gavin watched Raj walk back to the club and enter the employee door before he walked to Brigid and Carwyn. "I'm only going to say this once." He kept this voice low. "Nothing about Raj's employment history is unknown to me."

Brigid watched his eyes. Gavin believed that, and he was as good at reading people as Brigid was, probably better. "He doesn't know who took Nic."

"If Otto Anker is behind Nic's kidnapping, there's no reason Raj would know anything you don't."

So Raj had been involved with Mila Anker, not Otto. It was interesting but not pertinent to their investigation, and if Gavin was satisfied, Brigid would have to be too. Either way, Raj had told her flat out that he didn't know where Nic was, and Brigid believed him.

Gavin continued. "I'm not angry you suspected him, I'm annoyed you didn't come to me first."

"He was here," Brigid said. "It was an opportunity."

"I understand that, but he's young and immortal life before he came to me had not been kind to him." Gavin was talking to Brigid, but his eyes were on Carwyn. "He has a reason for his secrets, Brigid. I would think you of all people would understand that."

"Don't be mad at Carwyn," Brigid said. "I provoked Raj to get a reaction out of him. Raj reacted and so did my mate."

Gavin's stony expression didn't change. "I'm going into Revel to spend time with my fiancée and her friends. I'll let them know the two of you needed to leave."

We're the ones doing you *a favor, you arse.*

She thought it; she didn't say it.

"We'll go to the lofts," Carwyn said. "We need to check on the rest of the lads."

"Good." Gavin started walking away. "See if you can keep any more of them from going missing, will you?"

Brigid bared her fangs and nearly lunged at the man, but Carwyn caught her by the collar.

"Not worth it." He picked her up around the waist and walked them toward their car. "He's got his knickers in a twist because we questioned his judgment about an employee, Brigid. Just let him walk away."

"He can shag right off, the fuckin' tool. If he had any fuckin' brains, he'd be dangerous. Fucking eejit—he can kiss my arse and thank me for it."

Carwyn laughed. "I do love it when you get angry."

———

BRIGID STEWED in the back of the car, all the way back to the lofts where Savi, Miguel, and Kit were working. While they were trying to help the investigation, Miguel in particular was juggling like an acrobat, trying to balance the loss of two of Paladin's project directors.

An overwhelmed man with a thin blond mustache and a Canadian accent was talking to Miguel when Carwyn and Brigid reached the top of the stairs.

"I just don't know what I'm supposed to be telling people." The man was sweating and red in the face. "First Lee, then Nic of all people, and now Bex? I just don't understand—"

"Nic and Bex will be back soon." Miguel tried to soothe him. "I know this puts everything off target—"

"Our quarterly report is due in two weeks, and it's a disaster!"

"Martin, I can't tell you what's going to happen next week, so take a deep breath and focus on what we do know. If you can help me coordinate the payment integration..."

The conversation switched into the kind of techno-jargon that left Brigid feeling like a trained seal who had no idea it was in the circus.

"Do you understand any of that?"

Brigid turned and nearly jumped out of her skin when Tenzin appeared at her shoulder.

"No. It's complete bollocks to me."

"Ben understands it," Tenzin mused. "As long as one of us does, we won't have a significant tactical disadvantage."

"Carwyn and I are fucked then." She shook her head. "Utter gibberish to both of us."

Tenzin frowned. "You need a Chloe."

Carwyn said, "There's only one Chloe, and you don't even have her full-time anymore. Have you thought about that? Eventually she's going to be too busy to work with you and Ben. Her life is about to get significantly more complicated."

It was clear from Tenzin's expression that she absolutely had not considered it and didn't appreciate Carwyn pointing it out.

She glared at him, then retreated to Kit's side, sitting uncomfortably close to them as they tried to work. Kit froze, unsure of what Tenzin's proximity meant.

"Hey." Kit glanced to the side. "Hi... Brigid's friend."

Tenzin leaned in and examined Kit's face like she was examining a bug under a microscope. "Do you like New York? What about birds? Do you like birds?"

Kit looked up and around in desperation before their eyes landed on Brigid. "Help?"

Brigid wandered over and took Tenzin's hand, guiding her away from Kit. "You can't poach Gavin's employees."

"Why not? He's poaching my employee to *marry* her. I should be able to pick Chloe's replacement from his computer people."

"You don't need a computer person." Brigid led Tenzin over to the conference table where Savi was working. "You need an assistant who is reasonably proficient in computers, which is probably ninety-nine percent of people under thirty in New York. You don't need one of Gavin's programmers."

"But what if I want one?"

They would be bored and cause trouble, just like you. Wait. Better not say that. Tenzin would probably think it was a brilliant idea. "I think you should ask Chloe who she would recommend. She has the best idea of what she does for you and would be the best person to choose her replacement when it's time. *Only* when it's time." Brigid had the sudden fear she was kicking Chloe out of a job, and that was the last thing the woman needed.

"Good point." Tenzin watched Savi. "What about this one? She looks friendly."

"She's a security specialist."

"Perfect."

Brigid sighed. "Tenzin, you don't need one of those either."

"Who doesn't need a security specialist?"

"It's a very specific kind of security." How was she supposed to explain this to a vampire who'd only entered the modern world fifteen years ago? "Okay, imagine you took the world's greatest lock-picker—"

"Ingrid Svarsdotter, born in Kalmar in 1822," Tenzin said. "An artist unappreciated in her own time."

Brigid blinked. "Right. Well, imagine Savi was Ingrid, only with computers. She needs a challenge you don't have."

Tenzin sat across from Savi, who stared at her with wide, dark eyes.

"You're very beautiful," Tenzin said. "People probably underestimate how intelligent you are because you're very beautiful."

Savi blinked. "Sometimes yes."

"I can tell." Tenzin didn't take her eyes off Savi. "So why can't you find your friends?"

Sometimes Brigid really felt like punching the elfin tyrant, but that probably wouldn't end well.

Savi opened her mouth. "I am trying—"

"You don't have to answer her," Brigid said. "You don't work for Tenzin, Savi."

"No, it's a fair question because this *shouldn't* be so difficult. In fact, I think what Carwyn mentioned the other day is probably what is happening."

This was new information.

Brigid sat across from her. "What do you mean?"

"I think the program that Nic initiated is automated. The..." She sighed. "How do I explain to people like you? Okay." Savi sat up and spread her hands out, wiggling her fingers. "Imagine you're trying to open a locker with a combination lock."

"Okay." Brigid nodded. "I'm imagining it."

"You're not going to try numbers randomly. You're going to think of obvious choices the person who set the combination might make, correct? You'll try dates or alphanumeric codes. Because anything not set as random by a computer isn't *truly* random. The human mind always interferes with randomness."

Brigid was beginning to understand. "You're saying the keys that Nic is trying to break the lock aren't random?"

"No, I'm saying they *are*."

Tenzin nodded. "If he was the one entering the codes, they wouldn't be random, they would be intuitively reacting to the defenses of a known enemy. You."

"Exactly." Savi smiled. "But they *are* random, so I believe they are automated."

"Could that be intentional?" Brigid asked. "Could that be a way to legitimately try to break the firewalls?"

"Not in this case."

"So why would he do it?"

The corner of Savi's mouth turned up. "Imagine you were working for someone who wasn't very computer savvy..."

Brigid smiled. "Like a very old vampire?"

"You said it, not me," Savi quipped. "What he's doing might make it look like he's working very hard to break in when he is actually doing nothing."

"So he's doing nothing?"

"Nothing that I can detect," Savi said. "But I could be missing something because I've been focused on these clumsy hacks."

"Where does Bex come in?" Brigid asked. "Why would Nic's kidnappers want to take Bex?"

Savi bit her lip. "I'm afraid they know he's not doing

anything. He may not be fooling them anymore. They may want progress."

"And Bex can help?"

Savi's expression turned fearful. "What do you call help?"

Tenzin kept her eyes on Savi. "He loves her; that's why they took her."

Savi nodded.

Brigid's stomach sank. "So maybe Nic would risk his own safety to protect Paladin, but he won't risk Bex."

"They fight," Savi said. "It's their own way of flirting because they're socially awkward."

Tenzin sighed. "Love screws everything up."

Brigid patted Tenzin's shoulder. "Such a lovely sentiment for a wedding. I'll make sure to share that with Chloe at her hen party tomorrow night."

TWENTY-THREE

Carwyn stared at the massive television in the corner where a rugby game was on the screen. Gavin, Raj, and Ben were fixed on the game while roughly two dozen other guests, human and vampire, milled about.

They had taken over one of Marie-Hélène's clubs in the Central Business District at her direction, and Giovanni was the ostensible host for the evening even though Gavin's people had coordinated the staff.

A discreet waiter passed through the room, serving cocktails and taking orders for whiskey, blood-wine, or whatever the guests requested.

There was a long buffet table laden with charcuterie, more blood-wine, and a few Scottish sweets. There was a gaming table with four men and one woman playing poker, a billiards table with still more vampires, and clutches of vampires in suits gossiping in small groups all over the club.

Giovanni set a glass of neat whiskey on the table before he pulled out a chair and sat next to Carwyn. "I don't think I've ever seen you brood before."

"Humph." Carwyn took a swallow of the excellent port he

was drinking. "Chloe warned me this was going to be a party with a bunch of old vampires sitting around, reminiscing about carriage days, but I was hoping she was wrong."

"They're not reminiscing." Giovanni nodded at the television screen. "They're watching large humans bash each other in ritual combat."

Carwyn looked at his best friend. "Chloe said the girls and Arthur were going out for spa treatments and karaoke."

Giovanni sat up straight. "Damn it, did we lose the human? Where is he?"

"Which human?"

"Arthur's human. Beatrice will murder me if we've lost him."

"Don't fret. He's watching the rugby match."

Giovanni relaxed. "He's very hard to keep track of when there are so many suits around."

Carwyn and Giovanni were definitely two of the more casually dressed figures in the room; even Gavin had donned a suit for his own bachelor party.

To be fair, Gavin had been a diplomat and invited most of the more prominent vampires attending the wedding to the gathering, which meant it was distinctly more formal than spa nights and karaoke parties.

"I could throw this scotch in your face and wrap your head in a towel," Giovanni said. "That's the only spa treatment I know."

"I'd much rather drink the whiskey than wear it, thank you." He sipped his port. "Fuck, even Alonzo is here—there's a plank if I ever met one."

"I'm surprised he left Marie-Hélène's side for the night."

"He's probably calling in every ten minutes to check on her." Carwyn glanced at Giovanni. "Brigid has a theory."

Giovanni lowered his voice. "Inside job?"

"Guessed it in one."

Giovanni nodded slightly. "She's right. It has to be."

Carwyn nodded at Alonzo, who was watching the billiards match.

Giovanni arched an eyebrow. "That one?"

"He's a suspect."

"He's a vampire."

"It presents difficulties."

Giovanni barely spoke over a whisper. "He's a security chief in charge of Marie-Hélène's entire organization; he presents more than just difficulties."

Carwyn wished he had the ability to read people the way Brigid did. He was far better at seeing the best in people than interrogating them. He was well aware that his compassion overruled his survival instincts at times, and knew that his size, age, and elemental power afforded him the privilege of being charitable.

Still, at times like this, he wished he was more suspicious.

"You're good at reading faces," Carwyn said. "Maybe you and I could question Alonzo now?"

"At Gavin's bachelor party?"

"It's his employees we're trying to find."

Giovanni shrugged. "That's a decent point, but I don't think Gavin would see it the same way."

"He's still angry with us for questioning Raj."

"He's protective of the young man. I have a feeling I know why, but it's none of my business. I will say that any dealings we've had with Raj Bhata in Southern California have been straightforward. I have never sensed any deception in him other than what is natural for our kind."

Meaning: all vampires were liars, but some lied more than others.

Carwyn's gaze drifted back to Marie-Hélène's security chief. "And Alonzo?"

"I only know the man as relates to our time here, but my impression has been that he is ferociously loyal to his mistress and he very much considers her his regent. He's old-fashioned. Very old-fashioned."

Carwyn had the same instinct. "I can see him going after Gavin, but taking Nic and Bex affects Paladin, which reflects on Marie-Hélène as much as it reflects on Gavin."

"So would he risk it?"

"It would help if we had a peek inside his head," Carwyn said. "But since cracking his skull isn't an option, I'm stumped."

"You could simply ask him if he's a traitor," Giovanni said. "That might get a reaction."

Carwyn looked over at Giovanni and nodded. "You're a brilliant fella."

Giovanni's eyes went wide. "I wasn't serious."

"No, I think that's exactly what I need to do." Carwyn stood and walked toward the billiard table.

"Carwyn!" Giovanni hissed. "You mad Welshman, stop!"

"Alonzo!" Carwyn barged between two men speaking quietly as they watched the game. "Oi, Frenchie!"

Marie-Hélène's lieutenant raised an eyebrow as Carwyn pushed himself into the crowd. A low murmur skittered around the room as attention shifted from polite conversation to something far more interesting.

Carwyn narrowed his eyes and leaned down to get into Alonzo's space. "Is there something you're not telling us? Brigid and me, I mean."

Alonzo kept his gaze steady, a mannered vampire trying to defuse a volatile bear. "I'm sure I don't know what you're talking about." He glanced around the room with a slight smile curving the corner of his mouth. "Who have you been drinking from, my friend?"

It was said with amusement, and Carwyn knew he was

treading a very fine edge. The vampires in the room were unaware that there had been a threat to Marie-Hélène's authority or her and Gavin's business. It was imperative that the Paladin facade remain intact.

"I just wonder." Carwyn didn't back off but got into Alonzo's face. "Because you know how I am, don't ya? I'm far from the diplomat! Don't exactly know the time or place of things, do I?"

Scattered laughter. The priest was making a fool of himself.

Giovanni put a hand on Carwyn's shoulder. "My friend—"

"But *you* know the time and place, don't you?" Carwyn cocked his head, examining Alonzo. "You know all the times and places. In fact" —he pressed in and put a finger on Alonzo's chest— "if anyone knew what you knew, your queen—and all her interests—might be quite exposed."

The feigned amusement fled from Alonzo's expression. "Vecchio, it would be good if your friend stepped back and contained himself."

"You know what I'm implying, don't you?" Carwyn didn't move away; he inched closer. "You have all the information. You know all the moves."

"I know who I am and what I do," Alonzo's voice was a tightly controlled blade. "Are you angling for my job, Priest? I know I make security in this city look easy, but I assure you, it's not." He glanced around the room; he was performing now. "Marie-Hélène knows that her interests are safe with me, Father. No need to fuss over your old friend."

Giovanni didn't move to interfere—that would only escalate tension—but he kept his hand on Carwyn's shoulder.

"Nothing out of place?" Carwyn cocked his head. "No cracks in the armor? No slips? Not a hair, not a word, not a hum—"

Alonzo cut off Carwyn's musings with a punch to the mouth. It was wicked fast and landed with a solid pop. Carwyn's head flew back and he laughed, his lips splitting.

Blood spiked the air, and his amnis flared.

Alonzo followed up the punch to Carwyn's lip with a body blow he felt in his gut. The man might be small, but he was sturdy and he knew how to land one. Carwyn let himself fall back, and the ground shook when he hit the floor.

All attention in the room shifted to the two vampires fighting in the center of the room. A ring formed around them as Carwyn stood and lifted his fists.

Alonzo knew how to fight. He circled Carwyn, eyes scanning his much larger opponent. He took in the set of Carwyn's feet, his hip stance, and shifted accordingly.

"Gentlemen!" Gavin's voice carried over the chattering vampires and humans who were already placing bets. "Whatever disagreement you may have—"

"Oh come on, Wallace." A voice from the crowd piped up. "We're not in one of your clubs tonight, and this is far more entertaining than rugby."

"No amnis!" someone called to the general agreement of the crowd.

Gavin glared at Carwyn. "Fists only. No amnis. No fangs." He muttered a particularly inventive Scottish curse under his breath and crossed his arms over his chest, his eyes narrowed on the giant redhead who'd started a fight at his bachelor party.

Carwyn saw Giovanni shove two humans behind him before he crossed his arms and glared. He could read his old friend's expression as easily as he could hear the crowd's growing excitement.

This was not a good idea.

Carwyn shrugged and grinned.

Alonzo was quick on his feet, and Carwyn's fist glanced over his jaw without landing properly. He danced away as the crowd laughed and money started exchanging hands.

He ducked to the left when Alonzo tried to land a third

punch. He wasn't an obvious fighter, but he telegraphed his moves with his hips.

Carwyn's second punch landed squarely in the man's solar plexus. He pulled it back, but Alonzo still stumbled only to be shoved toward Carwyn by their audience.

He was keenly aware that he needed to let Alonzo win in the end, but that didn't mean he couldn't have fun in the meantime.

"You know all her secrets, don't you?"

Alonzo's lip curled. "If you're trying to say—"

"Not *trying* to say anything. I'm saying it." He shuffled to the left just in time to avoid a stout blow to the jaw.

"Just because you have no loyalty—"

Carwyn threw his head back and laughed. "And who would I give fealty to, lad?" He slapped a hand to his chest. "They bow to me, not the other way round."

He had to keep a laugh from erupting when Alonzo landed another punch. The man was angry, but Carwyn caught his expression in a flash when he doubled down on the gut punch he'd landed.

He could have taken the man by the shoulder and flicked him away, but Alonzo's face flipped between anger, frustration, and confusion. He wanted to best Carwyn, was angry at the implication he couldn't be trusted.

And he genuinely didn't know why Carwyn had started the fight.

His fist shot out and snapped Alonzo's jaw back. The vampire's eyes rolled back in his head for a second, and Carwyn started to panic.

Shit! That was harder than he'd intended. This was going to end very badly if he actually knocked Alonzo out.

Just when Carwyn was really starting to panic, the man shook his head, sneered, and came at Carwyn with renewed vigor, landing a flurry of blows that could reasonably be expected to bring down the small mountain that was Carwyn ap Bryn.

He flew back and landed on the ground with a grin on his face and a bloody nose. He laughed, gripped his stomach, and pointed up at Alonzo, who was watching him with narrowed eyes. "You're a lad, and you broke my rib." Carwyn's voice was jovial. "I'm out, friends."

Laughter chased groans around the room, and more money exchanged hands along with a few promises for debts repaid in other currency. Carwyn sat up, shook his head, and looked up at Alonzo, who was standing over him with a hand held out and a suspicious expression.

"Good man!" Carwyn popped to his feet, and Alonzo's eyes widened slightly at how quickly his opponent seemed to recover.

Oh right. Carwyn pressed a hand to his side. "You've a punch to make the stars shine, Frenchie, and we did manage to liven up the room, didn't we?"

Alonzo was catching on to Carwyn's ploy. "If you wanted a fight, all you had to do was ask."

"It's been too long, and these tossers are too feckin' proper, aren't they?" Carwyn looked around the room. "Come on, boys! Back to drinking." He saw a shipping magnate from Cyprus grimace. He pointed at him. "George, I am sorry you lost your boat betting on me, but we all know you have a fleet to spare."

Good-natured laughter made George smile again, his fangs peeking from beneath his neatly trimmed mustache. "I should have known you were only looking for amusement, old friend."

"Aren't we all?" Carwyn lifted a glass of beer someone shoved in his face and looked for Gavin in the crowd. "To Wallace! May he outlive me and keep that pretty nose out of fights."

The guests cheered, and Carwyn gulped the beer down,

then slammed the pint glass on the table, reached up, and cracked his nose back into place.

Alonzo winced and Giovanni slowly shook his head.

"Carwyn," Alonzo said, "would you like a smoke?"

Alonzo was taking the opportunity to get him alone.

Carwyn nodded, then turned to Giovanni and slapped him on the shoulder. "I know, you don't have to tell me."

"I'll tell you anyway. You're an idiot."

He pointed at Giovanni before he followed Alonzo out of the room. "Just be glad there wasn't a folding chair."

———

UNLIKE CARWYN, Alonzo actually did want a smoke. The stocky vampire lit a cigarette and held one out for Carwyn, who shook his head. They were standing in the alley behind the club, and the scent of burning tobacco was a welcome mask to the scent of garbage in the dumpster halfway down the block.

"One of the best fucking things about immortality." Alonzo's voice was a low growl. "I don't have to worry about lung cancer."

"I suppose that is a benefit."

"I fucking love smoking." He shook his head. "Can't do it much these days; the humans in the building don't like it, and Marie says it makes her clothes stink."

"She has a fair point."

Alonzo shrugged. "I didn't much care for the idea of you and your wife poking around, but I've decided that I like your wife. She's suspicious and she's honest. I get why Gavin wanted you to look into the shit at Paladin."

"What about me?"

Alonzo raised an eyebrow. "You're an asshole masked in a clown."

Carwyn's laugh was long and low. "Damn, but I do hate when people see through it."

Alonzo gave him a quick nod. "I know there's someone on the inside, but it's not me."

"I figured that out during our fight. Could it be Gaines?"

"Joe wouldn't be my first guess." Alonzo took a drag from the cigarette. "He's a Boy Scout, but I'm running out of ideas."

"Brigid and I questioned Raj last night; that's why Gavin's annoyed with me."

Alonzo's eyes cut to him. "What did Brigid think of Raj?"

"He's hiding something, but Gavin knows what it is and it's not about Nic." He shrugged. "We both figured that out."

"Sure." Alonzo dropped his cigarette butt in a standing ashtray near the back door. "We've kept Nic's disappearance locked down. The last thing I need is a wedding guest with delusions of grandeur deciding to push boundaries because someone took one of Marie's kids."

"Is she your sire?"

Alonzo shook his head. "Gerard, her mate, was my sire. I promised him I'd look after her, and I do. I would never do anything that might threaten her safety, and I keep this city in order. New Orleans is a trouble magnet. Every new vampire in the past fifty years has come here, thinking it's some kind of free-for-all vampire heaven." He cursed under his breath. "Just the thing I need. Fucking vampire movies."

"Does Gavin's presence help or hurt?"

Alonzo narrowed his eyes. "Generally? Gavin's a positive influence; he keeps his clubs clean and running smooth. Minerva makes sure I don't get any calls."

"Minerva? The hostess at Revel?"

The corner of his mouth turned up. "You think she's just a hostess?"

"Well, clearly I don't think that anymore." Carwyn's mind was whirling. "So you don't have a problem with Paladin?"

"On principle, no. It's just another one of Marie's businesses to me, and she has dozens of them all over the world. I deal with this city and her personally, and I gotta tell you, the longer all this drags on, the longer Nic is missing, the more she's rethinking all this shit."

"Paladin? The partnership with Gavin?"

Alonzo nodded. "She was doing fine without it. The money was a draw, but it's not worth risking her people, and Nic going missing hit hard. I don't like that little asshole, but that's mostly because he never follows orders and is completely useless in any kind of hierarchy. She loves him though."

"So if Raj isn't the leak, and if Gaines is a Boy Scout, who does that leave?"

Alonzo's expression promised that he had an answer.

And that Carwyn wasn't going to like it.

TWENTY-FOUR

Brigid woke the next nightfall and immediately knew there was something wrong with her head. It took her a few seconds to remember.

She closed her eyes, and images of the night before flashed in her mind. "Oh fuck me."

Carwyn popped into the room with a giant grin on his face. "Good evening, wife!"

She put a hand over her eyes. "Don't. Just don't."

"I knew you'd have fun at the hen party, but I had no idea how much."

"Carwyn—"

"Also, I want to point out..." He walked over from the bedroom door with a thermos of what Brigid was desperately hoping was warmed blood even if it was preserved. "I married a woman of principle, and if I didn't know that before tonight, I know now." He handed her the thermos and planted a kiss on her lips. "I love you, and I'll get the scissors."

"The scissors?" She sat up and heard rustling. "Oh fuck, I forgot about that part."

The short crop of hair she'd been sporting had been

"enhanced" by extensions threaded with tinsel so her entire head appeared to be covered with long, sparkly, rainbow hair.

How many people did she have to kill to keep the entire incident quiet?

She opened the thermos and began to plot as she gulped down the much-needed blood, only to narrow her eyes when she felt familiar amnis just outside her door.

Tenzin slipped in with a grim expression and her own glitter extensions in bright red and silver. "How do you get them out? Ben won't stop laughing. I've been trying to unthread them all day."

"You have to cut them out."

Tenzin looked like she wanted to kill something. "Bachelorette parties are an appalling rite of passage and should be banned from civilized society."

"I didn't even want to go, but you were the one who suggested—"

"You're blaming me?" Tenzin pointed at her. "You're the reason we ended up in the jail."

"We couldn't use amnis on that many cops, Tenzin!"

"We could have tried." Tenzin narrowed her eyes. "Was there video evidence? Am I going to be on YouTube now?"

"I told Chloe to delete the pictures she had. I don't think Beatrice, Chance, Dema, or the rest of them had phones."

"Security footage at the police station?"

"I told Gavin's people to make sure any security footage at the police precinct was destroyed." She finished drinking the blood and set the thermos to the side. "I'll check with him later. I'm pretty sure he'll be busy with Chloe for a while."

Carwyn bounded into the room with a set of shining silver scissors. "So how did you like karaoke, Tenzin?"

The small, lethal wind vampire glared at him. "I can kill him?"

Carwyn snorted. "So you think."

"No." Brigid threw back the sheets and motioned for Tenzin to come closer. "Let's work on your hair first. You don't have as many extensions as I do." She crawled to the foot of the bed, and Tenzin sat on the corner. "Did I tell you that I really like your singing voice? I think you took everyone by surprise."

Tenzin shrugged. "I don't know why they'd be surprised I can sing when I have known associations with the Corsican vampire mafia."

Brigid blinked and looked over at Carwyn, who just shook his head.

"I understood the individual words coming out of her mouth," he said. "But I'm as lost as you are."

"That's not important," Tenzin said. "What is important is that we get the shiny hair out of my nice hair without chopping all of it off. I have a birthday party to attend in a few months, and I don't want to be bald."

Brigid was able to remove the first few strands without losing any of Tenzin's hair. She glanced at Carwyn, who was having way too much fun with all this, much to Tenzin's obvious irritation.

"Make him stop smiling."

"Trust me, if I could, I would." She snipped out another extension that had become tangled in Tenzin's hair. "This next one, I might have to pull a little."

"I will brace myself." Tenzin kept her head still. "Brigid, after last night, I now consider you a friend."

You didn't before? "That's good, Tenzin. I consider you a friend as well."

"Therefore, I feel like I should tell you that I have plotted to kill your husband on three occasions in the past five hundred years."

"What?" Carwyn squawked. "What did I ever do to you, you mad little heathen?"

Carwyn looked genuinely shocked. Brigid, on the other hand, wasn't shocked at all. "Only three?"

"Did I say three?" Tenzin sighed. "I meant twenty-three."

Her husband glared. *"Twenty-three?"*

"Did I kill you? No. Stop complaining. But you smile so much," Tenzin hissed. "Constant smiling. And you made Giovanni stop being an assassin. For around a hundred years, I was very angry about that."

"He made that decision himself."

"He made it after he talked with you."

"Because he was depressed, Tenzin! Not everyone can justify killing people the way you can."

"If a vampire's fate has led them to the edge of my knife, who am I to argue with fate? We didn't kill indiscriminately."

"But you did kill for money."

Tenzin turned to Brigid. "No, we killed for gold. A *lot* of gold."

Brigid did like Tenzin, but she had to side with Carwyn on this one. "I think Giovanni is happier being a librarian instead of an assassin, so it all worked out in the end, don't you think?"

"Yes, we got to keep all the gold." Tenzin turned around. "And I didn't kill you, Carwyn. See? Growth."

"You may want to kill me when I tell you about my conversation with Alonzo last night," Carwyn said.

Brigid stopped snipping. "What? Why?" Alonzo had been the first person Brigid wanted to question that night.

"He has a theory about who the mole might be, and you're not going to like it."

———

BEN AND TENZIN looked as unhappy as Brigid was feeling.

"If he's right," Brigid said. "We might as well put a knife in Marie-Hélène's heart."

"I don't want him to be right," Carwyn said. "No one wants him to be right, but if we considered Raj and Gaines, we have to consider her too."

Ben's voice was low. "It makes sense."

Tenzin and Brigid turned to him. "How?"

"I mean, it makes sense as a possibility. We've eliminated pretty much everyone else who had inside information."

"Chance isn't everyone else," Brigid said. "She's related to both Marie-Hélène and Gavin."

Carwyn turned to her. "I didn't know she was related to Gavin. How?"

"I don't know; I just know that he said they were in the same line. I didn't ask questions, and he was secretive about it."

"Chance is friends with Chloe," Tenzin said. "She went to her rite of passage. And she came to get the girl who was injured at the farmhouse. Wouldn't the girl have recognized her if she was involved?"

"Not if Chance kept herself hidden," Carwyn said. "Remember what the girl said. There was another one, but they locked her away and she never saw them. The girl thought the accent was Russian, but what if she misheard?"

"Why would she take her afterward? Why would she take care of her?" Brigid turned to Tenzin. "You've been checking on the girl every night."

"She's safe and being cared for. Chance hasn't harmed her. She's been very kind." Tenzin's jaw was clenched. "She could be covering."

"Covering her involvement by taking care of the victim?" Carwyn asked. "If she's involved, it's the smart move."

Tenzin nodded. "And it gives her access to the girl just in

case there was something she missed, some memory that crops up."

Ben asked, "Why would she betray Marie-Hélène? It doesn't make sense. What kind of motive could she have?"

"Money? Anger?" Brigid shrugged. "Who knows?"

"It's a fair question," Carwyn said. "Marie-Hélène treats Chance like her own daughter. She bought her the ranch, gives her whatever she wants. Why would Chance threaten that arrangement?"

Brigid looked at Carwyn. "Did Alonzo say why he thought it was Chance?"

"Just that he came to the same place Ben did. When you question and eliminate everyone who had knowledge of our investigation, you're left with very few names. Marie-Hélène confides in Chance like no one else in the world. There's nothing she would keep from her."

"And nothing she wouldn't give her," Tenzin said. "The horse ranch is far more than a quaint little farm. It is a country estate fit for nobility with a large mansion, guesthouses, various outbuildings, a huge barn, and a bunkhouse."

Ben raised a hand. "I hate to bring it up, but that could be the perfect place to hide a couple of computer programmers when you run out of other options."

"We need to search that ranch." Brigid looked at Ben. "Can you fly us north?"

Ben and Tenzin exchanged a look, then both nodded.

"We don't tell Gavin," Ben said. "Not until we're sure."

"Agreed," Brigid said. "I don't know how attached he is to the woman, but it's clear there is a tie there. If she's involved..."

If Chance was involved, they wouldn't ever be welcome in New Orleans again. Even if Marie-Hélène believed them, she would never forgive them.

"We'll fly you to the ranch," Ben said. "We shouldn't wait. We'll go tonight."

"One problem." Carwyn raised a hand. "We're supposed to be at a giant reception with Gavin and Chloe, Marie-Hélène, and the majority of the wedding guests tonight to celebrate the bridal party."

Tenzin frowned. "And?"

Brigid cocked her head. "Tenzin, you're Chloe's maid of honor."

"Right," Tenzin muttered. "Though I am very far from a maid."

"Semantics." Brigid fiddled with her wedding ring. "You have to be there; too many questions otherwise."

"And Marie will notice if I'm gone," Carwyn said.

"Fine." Brigid pointed at Ben. "You fly me to the ranch." She pointed at Carwyn. "You and Tenzin attend the reception."

"Together?" Tenzin's face was stony. "Do we have to?"

"Whoever has taken Nic and Bex is likely to be at that party tonight," Brigid said. "We don't want to tip Chance or anyone else off that they're under suspicion until we know for sure. Plus you are Chloe's maid of honor. You *have* to be at this event."

Carwyn nudged Tenzin and grinned. "Time to put your dancing shoes on, Sparkles."

Tenzin stared at him for an uncomfortable length of time. Then she turned to Brigid and said, "Twenty-four."

TWENTY-FIVE

C arwyn stared at the dance floor where a series of beautiful women, vampire and human, paraded in elaborate couture. One by one, each bridal attendant was presented to Madame Charmont in the ballroom at Bonnevue estate, announced by name and family; then they were introduced to their counterpart among the groomsmen.

"Therese Carla Mansfield, daughter of Hank and Joy Mansfield of Brooklyn, New York. Currently pursuing her master's degree in business administration at Columbia University."

Polite applause from the assembly as a curvaceous woman in a coral-colored gown walked toward the dais, holding a bouquet of abundant fall flowers.

The room was lit with electric light mixed with candles to give the air a vibrant, living quality. The string quartet playing in the foyer lent the entire event an aristocratic, old-world energy, Marie-Hélène playing the regent on a dais at the end of the ballroom with Chloe and Gavin sitting beside her, Alonzo, her faithful knight at her left shoulder, and Chance, her beloved daughter, on her right.

Carwyn felt sick to his stomach when he saw Chance. Gavin

had accepted his excuses for Ben and Brigid with no questions, but he still felt conspicuous without his mate.

"Zhang Rinpoche Tenzin, daughter of Zhang Guolao, protector of Penglai Island and commander of the Altan Wind."

Since there were humans in attendance, immortal titles had been foregone for the evening, leaving Tenzin sounding more like a dungeon master in a role-playing game than the fearsome warrior and daughter of vampire nobility that she was.

Tenzin walked into the room, the last of the attendants to be announced, and took the arm of a tall vampire who looked South Asian. A very old friend of Gavin's, if Carwyn remembered correctly.

Carwyn tried to remember if he'd ever heard Tenzin's full name before and didn't think he had. Yet she'd revealed it for Chloe's wedding. More evidence that despite his beliefs about the ancient vampire, she might possibly be capable of change.

Tenzin was dressed in a plum-colored formal gown that showed off her elegant neck and slim figure. Arthur had told Carwyn he'd used the same color palette for all the bridal attendants but customized the dresses for each woman.

The designer had achieved a stunning display, himself included, as all the attendants stood on the dais with Chloe and Gavin, who were both smiling warmly at the assembled guests as Marie-Hélène addressed them.

"...our great thanks to all who made the effort to attend tonight, some from the other side of the world. Your friendship and effort will never be forgotten."

Polite applause from the audience.

Marie-Hélène continued in a Southern accent so lyrical it fairly danced across magnolia-scented air. "When my dear friend Gavin told me he was marrying this delightful, intelligent, and talented woman, I first checked with Chloe to make sure he was not playing some elaborate prank on me."

Scattered laughter and a good-natured smirk from Gavin.

"Then I sent her to my good friend Dr. Fontaine to make sure that she hadn't suffered a tragic head injury."

More laughter from the crowd.

"And then I simply insisted that they allow me to host this *glorious* event."

Enthusiastic applause from all corners of the room.

Marie-Hélène turned to Gavin and Chloe. "I am so grateful they agreed, because family are the people who mean the most to us, and Gavin's friendship, loyalty, and constancy over my many years of life have meant more to me than most of you will ever know."

More applause, this time directed at Gavin, who bowed slightly, pressed his fingers to his lips, and blew Marie-Hélène a kiss.

It was political theater of the highest order, but Carwyn could see the sincerity behind it. There were few people that Gavin Wallace had been able to trust and confide in over the years without betraying the many confidences with which he was burdened. Marie-Hélène played an important role in his life.

It made seeing Chance standing next to her like a dutiful daughter a bitter pill to swallow.

"Now dance!" Marie-Hélène spread her arms. "Drink. *Behave.*" She wagged a finger at the crowd and winked. "But not too well, because where's the fun in that?"

More laughter from the crowd, and the music grew louder as the guests followed their hostess's direction and took to the dance floor.

Tenzin, for her part, gave nothing away. She immediately made her way to dance with her partner for the wedding, along with all the other attendants, smiling demurely, partly to be polite and no doubt partly to hide her ever-visible fangs.

The tiny vampire could be unruly, unpredictable, and hostile to polite society, but when she knew she needed to play a part, she played it to perfection. Far better than Carwyn did if he was honest. Unlike Tenzin and Giovanni, he'd had no kind of court training. Facades were difficult for him.

"Carwyn!"

He turned to see the last person he wanted to talk with walking toward him. "Chance." He forced a smile. "How are you tonight?" He bent slightly and pressed two kisses to her cheeks.

"I'm holding up." Her smile seemed genuine. "Wishing all this was over and they could just get married already, but I know how much Marie is enjoying this. She *adores* Gavin." Her eyes smiled. "We both do. And we were so thrilled to meet Chloe. Marie treats her like one of the girls she sponsors, and that means she considers her family."

"I've known Chloe a long time, so I love hearing that. She hasn't had the easiest time with her human family, so it's wonderful that she's been so welcomed by Gavin's friends."

Chance's eyes turned to Marie-Hélène, and there was a wistful sadness in her expression. "Families are complicated." She shook her head a little. "And this one does love their extravagant social events."

Carwyn smiled. "I can tell, though I think I'm more in your way of thinking. I love a good party, but it seems like there have been weeks of receptions and events. Brigid and I live a quieter life most of the time."

"Where is Brigid?" Chance scanned the room. "Did I miss her?"

"Oh, she's..." Damn, what was the story they'd agreed on? "She's at the lofts with the rest of the Paladin team tonight, trying to soothe their nerves, you know? She hated to miss the party, but she and Ben wanted to stay there and help the kids."

Chance's expression immediately turned sympathetic. "It's

so strange, right? We have to put on these happy faces to celebrate Gavin and Chloe, and the whole time, Marie and I are both *wrecked* about these two young people going missing."

"Hmm." Carwyn nodded sagely and bit his tongue.

Chance leaned closer and dropped her voice to just over a whisper. "I'm sure they're safe though. I just have this feeling. Maybe it's foolish optimism, but I have to think whoever took them wants something from them, you know? They have no reason to hurt them."

"Keeping them alive? I agree with you. Keeping them safe?" Carwyn shook his head. "I think the girl we rescued from that old farmhouse is evidence that these aren't the kind of people who can be trusted with anyone's safety."

Carwyn watched her carefully and saw the glance down and away when he mentioned the girl from the farmhouse. Guilt? Anger?

"You're right. That was... awful." Chance looked up, and righteous anger was in her eyes. "I'm relieved Reena's recovering at the ranch. I think she's going to be fine."

"That's good to hear." Should he dig a little? Why not? Chance was stuck at the party like he was. What harm could she do? "I suppose it makes me glad that Lee Whitehorn left Paladin when he did."

Chance blinked rapidly. "Uh... I don't— Wait, Whitehorn? Is that the Paladin employee who left the company?"

"Yes, the one in Oklahoma City. Brigid talked to you about him, right?"

"Like I told her, I only knew Lee a little." She swallowed and kept her eyes on the dancers. "Just to say hi at parties and stuff, you know?"

Pretty sure you told Brigid you didn't know him at all. "Was Lee dating anyone?"

Visible tension in her neck. "No, I don't think so. But then, he's a very private person."

But you barely knew him, right?

"I mean..." She angled her shoulders toward him. "He seemed that way. One introvert can spot another, you know what I mean?"

"Absolutely."

Chance motioned toward the dancers. "We had a great time last night," she said. "It was really fun getting to know Brigid and Tenzin a little more. Who knew Tenzin would be so funny?"

He caught the tiny wind vampire gliding by on the dance floor, her partner trying to unobtrusively keep her from floating upward, and the look Tenzin shot at Chance when the other woman wasn't looking was murderous.

"Tenzin?" Carwyn smiled. "Yes, she's quite the character, isn't she?"

"And an extraordinary singing voice."

"I think you can thank the Corsican mafia for that." Carwyn snagged a couple of champagne glasses from a passing waiter's tray and shoved one toward Chance. "Champagne?"

"The Corsican—? Thanks." She took the glass. "It's a wedding, right?"

"Right." Carwyn lifted his glass and gulped the alcohol down. "To nights of celebration."

Chance clinked her glass to his. "To Gavin and Chloe."

"And to getting what you deserve."

Chance nearly choked on the swallow of champagne. "Wh-what?"

"For Gavin, I mean. He's lived a long time alone." Carwyn smiled. "I think he deserves all the happiness in the world, don't you?"

"Yes." Chance blinked. "Absolutely."

———

THE FARM in Saint Tammany Parish would more accurately be described as an estate. Brigid scanned the grounds from the air and had to agree with Tenzin. This wasn't European royalty, but it was American. The massive two-story ranch house had a wraparound porch, a grand front staircase, and numerous balconies on the second floor.

The barn was twice the size of the house with immaculate white siding and a slate-tiled roof. Rolling fields surrounded the house and barn, and an alley of oak trees led to the front gate, which was heavily guarded by both humans and vampires plus electronic surveillance.

"Two wind vamps on the eastern side," Ben said quietly. "We should land."

"Alonzo increased security for this place as soon as the girl we rescued came here."

"Yeah." His voice was grim. "That should keep her safe, but it keeps us out too."

She pointed to a small building that sat on the edge of the woods surrounding the property. "What is that?"

Ben flew in a little lower, heading toward the shelter of the trees. "Lots of lines running in and out of that place," he said. "Let's take a closer look."

Brigid closed her eyes as Ben dropped suddenly from the sky. Her stomach gave a great heave, but luckily nothing came up. "What was that?"

"They almost saw us." He patted Brigid's head as he set her on the ground. "Sorry about that."

"It's a good thing I trust you enough not to ignite." Brigid stretched her arms out, having been stuck in Ben's grip for a solid half hour. "This place is beautiful."

"It really is."

A gentle breeze soughed through the woods around the estate, touching the Spanish moss and making the canopy above them dance.

Brigid looked around at the rolling hills and verdant meadows. "Almost makes me want to leave California."

"And your giant redwoods?"

Brigid and Carwyn had been paid for a job the previous year with a massive old mountain house in the middle of the forest. It was stone and timber surrounded by foggy redwood forests and utter wilderness. Nothing at all like the soft gothic canopy of oaks that surrounded Chance's ranch.

"It's beautiful here, but there's something very..."

"It doesn't fit somehow," Ben said. "Does that make sense to you?"

"That's what I'm feeling too. This feels like a set on a movie."

Ben nodded at the outline of the building in the distance. "I think it's all new. Maybe built in the past thirty years or so? Not brand-new, but pretty new."

"That might explain it." There was still something unsettling about the place, though the smell of horses, hay, and fresh grass reminded her of Wicklow and the farm where she grew up. "I feel like I should like this more than I do."

"We're not on vacation." Ben started creeping through the woods, moving in the shadows with Brigid behind him. "We're looking for kidnapped computer programmers."

"I hav'ta ask, when Kit or Savi start talking about firewalls and throw around phrases like external software integration, does any of that make sense to you?"

He reached over and patted her head. "You're not that much older than me, you know."

"And yet I look younger." She batted his hand away. "I had a bleedin' social life instead of a computer, Benjamin."

"Ouch?" Ben crouched behind a dense hedge of bushes planted along the edge of the woods. "You seeing any security?"

Though the building on the edge of the woods was wired to the gills with dark lines branching from the corner of the building to the main line that ran through the woods, there was no one moving around the building.

"Let me feel." Ben closed his eyes and lifted his hands toward the building. "There are a bunch of electrical lines, some cables I can feel but they aren't as clear. Probably fiber-optic."

"You can feel the electricity?"

"Sometimes." His eyes opened and swept the grounds. "There isn't anyone in that building."

Brigid swept her hand out. "Shall we?"

"Definitely." He jogged toward the back door that faced the barn, taking a set of lockpicks from his pocket. "I gotta tell you, this is fun. I don't feel like I've had a nice, normal break-in for years."

She stood behind him, watching the grounds as he opened the door. "Well, you've been off chasing mythical artifacts instead of playing the petty thief."

"I know. So boring, right?"

"A bit." She smiled. "Please tell me you're in. That guard circling the barn is going to be making another round in just a minute."

"I'm almost..." The door cracked open, and Ben yanked her by the back of her shirt. "We're in."

A low beeping started in the corner, and Brigid knew they had a limited amount of time before they were found. "Alarm."

"I have an idea." He tapped on the alarm keypad until there was smoke rising behind the small box. "If I fry the system, they'll be as blind as we are."

There was a wall of monitors opposite the door, and Brigid watched as one by one, Ben fried the feeds to each and every one, eventually crushing the Wi-Fi router in one hand before he jogged toward the door, grabbing Brigid by the hand.

"Was that really necessary?" she hissed.

"It's a distraction." He grabbed her around the waist and jumped onto the roof of the next building over, lying down while he watched the guards come running.

Brigid lay next to him, glancing at the dark slate tiles that were still warm from the sun. "And this is why we wear black."

"Exactly." He pointed his lips toward the house. "Let's see which ones come running and which ones don't."

Anyone guarding people wouldn't move; they'd more likely spread out to assess the threat but keep an arm's length, at most two, from the body they were guarding.

"Main house is empty," Brigid said. "No one home."

"Two guesthouses." Ben pointed to the clutch of guards gathered between two houses. "I bet you anything that's where the girl and the doctor are."

"Does that mean that Nic and Bex aren't here?"

Ben didn't answer, but Brigid had a feeling she knew why. "Let's search the house," he said. "Take a quick look while the rest of them are scrambling to figure out why their system went offline."

She followed him when he dropped over the edge of the building and ran in the shadows toward the main house. There were two human guards on the front porch by the main door, but Brigid spotted a set of french doors on the second-story balcony.

She tugged Ben's arm, pointed toward the doors, and he grabbed her and flew them up to the balcony.

Amazingly, the doors weren't even locked. Brigid and Ben slipped into the dark house and were immediately assaulted by the scent of lemon oil and wax.

They were standing in a lushly furnished bedroom with a

bathroom attached and a sitting area included. No one was there.

"Let's find the main bedroom," Ben whispered. "I want a peek into Chance's brain."

They found the main bedroom two doors down the hallway to the left; they even found a locked day chamber built into the walk-in closet.

Something about the entire room set Brigid's hair on end.

"This looks like a magazine."

Ben shrugged. "It's very... neat."

"No, it's more than that." Brigid looked around at the catalog-perfect furnishings, the immaculately organized closet, and the generic art decorating the walls. "She doesn't live here."

Ben walked in the closet and looked at the shoes. "If she doesn't, then someone else does, and she really likes horses."

"No, I mean..." How to explain? "I think Chance uses this house." She poked through the dresser drawers, also immaculately organized. "Some of this is clean because she's an organized person. But look around you." She spun in a circle. "She's nearly one hundred years old," Brigid said. "Where are the pictures? Where are the memories? Even older vampires who don't take pictures at all will have objects they've collected, artwork they admire..." Brigid looked around at the stark white walls covered in tasteful landscapes. "This is nothing. Literally nothin' about this house is personal."

Ben frowned. "You're right. Even Tenzin, who is the ultimate minimalist, has her standing loom. A few books. Some jewelry. There's nothing here."

They crept through the house, avoiding the windows, and Brigid's instinct about the house was confirmed. It reminded her more of a rental house than a home. Beautiful, useful, and impersonal.

As they rose into the air from the balcony, Brigid saw the

guards spreading out to the buildings again and lights slowly flickering on. Two in the guesthouses, several in the barn, and one bright one spilling around the guardhouse where they'd broken in.

"We need to check." Brigid tapped Ben's hand. "We need to be sure."

"Agreed." He flew her back to the trees. "Let me. If I'm not carrying you, I can be fast."

"Okay." She trusted Ben not to miss anything.

He flew away in a blur, looking like nothing more than a gust of smoke streaking through the compound. He lingered by one window, then another. He paused near the barn and flew through a window in the hayloft, then shot out the other side in a matter of seconds.

Ben swooped in, grabbed her under the arms, and lifted them into the sky.

"Nothing," he said. "It's an efficient horse ranch. The employees who live here have personalized their rooms—even Reena's guesthouse looks personalized—but there's no sign of Chance, Nic, or Bex. If Chance has the two kids from Paladin, she's not keeping them here."

NIC V

They brought her into his room just to remind him they still had her under their power. That had to be the reason. It was the only one that made sense.

Bex was silently crying. "You need a hospital."

"They won't take me to one. They won't even bring a doctor." He wiggled his ten perfect fingers. "As long as they don't damage my hands, I can work."

She was gingerly trying to tend the bandage over his left cheek, but every time she moved, his nerves wanted to scream.

He said nothing. It was worth it as long as he could spend a few minutes with her.

"Monsters." She brushed her soft fingers over his face. "They're monsters."

"Have they touched you?" His voice was hard, but oddly enough, the more injured he became, the easier it was to look Bex in the eye. He examined her face, the light freckles over her nose and the tiny curls along her hairline. What had she called them once? Baby hairs. She and Savi had laughed about taming them.

He loved her curls and the wild disorganization of them. He

didn't want it tamed. One day her hair would curl one direction and the next, something completely different. He loved when she accidentally started speaking Spanish when she was angry. He loved that she was so fiercely protective of Savi and Kit.

"We need to get out of here before they hurt you," he said. "I'll have to—"

"Nic, you can barely move."

It was true, but he would have to. "We've seen their faces, Bex. They're not going to let us go."

"What if we could get a message out?" she asked. "I know their guy is watching your email and your online activity when you're working—"

"If I tried anything, they'd hurt you, Bex. They tell me every day. Every five minutes, they remind me you're in a room down the hall."

"I know that, but—"

"If you know that, why do you think I'd even take a chance trying to get a message out? I don't even know where we are. I'm guessing we're in Saint Tammany Parish maybe or Saint James, but I don't know that for certain, and there's no way—"

"Will you listen?" She put a finger over his mouth.

He resisted the urge to kiss it. That would be strange. Normal people didn't kiss fingers.

Did they?

"There is a landline in the kitchen."

Nic blinked. "A what?"

"A landline. Literally a phone attached to a wall. I saw it when they were bringing me in. All the internet connections have been routed through proxies, but—"

"A landline?"

Landlines could be traced. Landlines were tied to a distinct location, and it was entirely possible that their captors had overlooked it.

He muttered, "A landline might be worth the risk."

"We could distract the guards."

"How?"

"They want you alive, right?" She put her hands on his cheeks. "They're outside most of the day. What if you pretended to have a seizure or something? I could bang on the door, and whoever answered it would probably panic. I might be able to get out and run after them, keep them outside. They'll think you're out of commission, run to get help, and you can run downstairs and call?"

He frowned. "That seems needlessly convoluted."

"You know, just because a plan has multiple steps doesn't mean it's inherently disorganized. You said the same thing when I decided to—"

He put a hand over her mouth. "I'm not letting you get involved in this. They already beat me up daily. They leave you alone because you're leverage over me, so I'm not going to do anything to disrupt that balance. My having a seizure is a good idea and not improbable considering how many minor concussions I've probably suffered over the past two weeks, but I'll do it when French Creep is watching me, not when you're involved."

"Nic, I can help."

"I know you can, and I'm going to depend on you when we manage to break out of here, but for now?" The thought of Bex putting herself in danger terrified him. He shook his head slowly. "I won't be able to concentrate if I think something might happen to you. Please let me do this on my own. I think I have a plan."

———

THE SECOND BLOW landed harder than the first, and Nic felt his bruised rib crack.

"Did you think you were clever? They're never going to trace that call." The human who'd been watching him while he was working, French Creep, was far more vicious than any of the vampires, even the redheaded one.

"You piece of shit!" Another punch to the gut. "Do you want to get me killed?"

Nic had managed to leave a message with Savi, and he only prayed she wouldn't erase it, thinking it was junk. He said nothing to the Creep though. He said nothing when he'd been caught in the kitchen. He said nothing when they passed Bex's room at the top of the stairs. He said nothing.

He became the robot that so many had accused him of being over the years. If he even started to break, they might hurt Bex.

"Maybe you're not taking this seriously enough." The man picked Nic up off the ground and propped him against the wall. He leaned forward and spat in Nic's face. "Maybe I need to bring your little girlfriend in here and make her hurt so you—"

Nic roared and went for the man's throat, knocking him to the ground as the human screamed and vampires ran into the room. He pounded his fists in the man's belly, his ribs, under the jaw, and finally a blow to his face, every punch mirroring one of the dozens Nic had suffered himself. They tried to pull him off but only managed to bind his arms behind his back.

The vampires were arguing in French, trying to decide what to tell "the Russian" when the vampire they were frightened of swept into the room.

"What is this?" The Russian looked at Nic, who was still straddling the Creep with his arms wrestled behind him. They cocked their head as if examining a specimen under a microscope. "What did Mr. Cooper do? I thought he was supposed to be working tonight."

The Creep groaned, and Nic knew he wouldn't tell the

others. Wouldn't tell his masters that he'd allowed the captive to get to the phone.

"He pissed me off," the Creep muttered. "That's all."

The red-haired vampire shook his head sadly. "Why can't you cooperate, Mr. Cooper? Then we wouldn't have to hurt your friend."

Nic tried to get to his feet, but two vampires held him down.

"Let me see his hands."

They wrestled his hands from behind his back. His fingers were bruised and his knuckles bleeding from hitting the Creep, but Nic's hands weren't broken.

"Good." The Russian bent and looked into Nic's eyes. "You need all ten fingers to type." They put a hand on Nic's face and pressed a thumb under his bruised left eye. "But you don't need two eyes."

TWENTY-SIX

Carwyn listened to Brigid, Ben, and Tenzin debating as he removed layers of formalwear in their walk-in closet. Off with the formal jacket. Away with the uncomfortable shoes.

"They weren't at the ranch." Brigid said. "I think at this point, we need to talk to Gavin."

"What do we actually know though?" Ben asked. "All we found at Chance's ranch was exactly what we knew was already there. There is no evidence she's holding anyone there against their will."

"Wouldn't your trip imply that Chance is *not* the traitor?" Tenzin asked. "Should we turn our attention to Gaines? No one has had as much access to the humans as him, Nic trusted him, and he has every motive to betray Marie-Hélène."

"Why do you say that?" Brigid asked. "Gaines has been nothing but helpful."

Carwyn finally unknotted his tie and flung it across the closet. He pulled on a worn T-shirt and juggled the twin knots of realization and resolve that were lodged in his gut.

"Gaines is new," Tenzin said. "He has no loyalty to Marie-Hélène; Chance does."

He walked out of the closet and leaned against the door-jamb. "It's Chance."

Every eye turned to him.

"Why are you so sure?" Ben asked.

"I talked to her tonight. Mentioned Lee Whitehorn, and she said she knew him a little but only in passing, brushed it off." He shrugged. "She was lying. I think she's lying about everything."

Brigid sat up straight. "When I asked her, she acted like she didn't recognize the name. Said she remembered someone with that description, but she never mentioned knowing him personally."

"She knew him, and I think they were far closer than we imagined." Carwyn thought back to their visit in Oklahoma City the week before. "Remember what Lee said? He didn't have anything to do with vampires anymore. Didn't work for them. Didn't socialize with them. Didn't—"

"*Date* them." Brigid's eyes went wide. "You think Chance and Whitehorn had a relationship?"

"I got a very... familiar feeling when Chance mentioned Lee tonight. I can't say for certain, but I think we need to call Lee Whitehorn again and see if there's anything he left out of his statement to us."

"We can do that," Ben said. "But just a familiar mention doesn't seem like enough to—"

"It's her." Carwyn bit out the words, tasting the bitter honesty of them as they left his mouth. "I don't know how I know, but I do. And I feel sick—" He clutched a fist to his stomach. "I feel sick about it. I don't understand it, and I have a strong suspicion that she got caught up in something she didn't quite understand, but Chance is in this." He looked up and met Brigid's eyes. "I know you like her."

"That doesn't mean she's innocent," Brigid said. "If you say it's her, I believe ya."

Ben looked skeptical, but Tenzin's eyes were narrowed on Carwyn. "If you believe that, Priest, then I believe you. We should tell Gavin what we think."

"I know," he said. "But let's call Lee first. It's late, but he might be awake."

———

LEE WAS awake and he answered their video call when Brigid dialed him.

"I haven't gotten any more letters," he said. "Haven't seen anyone else hanging around. My elder put a bunch more guards around my family's houses though, so we may have scared them off."

"That's good." Brigid sat in front of the camera with Carwyn looking over her shoulder so Lee could see him there. "We have another question for you, and I hope you'll be able to help. We don't want to pry, but Bex was taken too."

Lee looked stricken. "Shit."

Ben and Tenzin had left for the lofts, eager to get back to the Paladin employees and make sure they were safe.

Carwyn was the one to ask it. "Lee, I was at one of Marie-Hélène's parties tonight, and I spoke to Chance."

A flicker in Lee's eyes. "Oh yeah?"

"You know her." It wasn't a question.

Lee looked away. Embarrassment. A hint of anger. "It was dumb, but it wasn't really a..." He huffed out a breath. "She doesn't have anything to do with this."

"Did you date?" Brigid asked. "Obviously you know her, and you mentioned dating vampires, so we have to—"

"Date?" He curled his lip slightly. "I wouldn't call it dating when you're someone's dirty secret."

Carwyn frowned. "What do you mean?"

"I met Chance..." He took a breath. "We met when she and Marie-Hélène were touring Paladin months ago, and we... I guess you could say we hooked up. Is that what the kids say? I saw her again, we hooked up again. She sought me out, okay? And I don't make a habit of getting involved that way with immortals, but I thought she was different. She seemed different. Wasn't in the party crowd. She seemed... I don't know. She likes horses, the outdoors, stuff I like."

Brigid nodded. "I've met her. That fits. Makes sense."

"So after we'd hooked up a couple of times, I started to call her. She called me too, and we talked, but I could tell... I don't know. She didn't want to go places together. Not even out for a drink at a non-vamp bar. If any of Marie-Hélène's people came around when we were hanging out, she acted like she barely knew me. It was strange."

"Was this before or after you started having gaps in your memory?"

"Before," he said quickly. "Weeks before. That's why I didn't bring it up. We hadn't seen each other for over a month when I went to that party." He frowned. "She was there though. I think she was there."

"Do you *remember* her being there or—?"

"I don't remember much, okay? I tried not to. I hadn't seen her for weeks, and she acted like she didn't know me, so I acted like I didn't know her. It wasn't a long-term thing or anything like that."

Carwyn leaned forward. "Did Chance ever show any interest in what you were doing at Paladin?"

"I mean, that's where we met, so yeah, a little. Just kind of polite interest. What are you guys working on? How is it different from Nocht? That kind of thing. She's not a technical person, so it was just polite questions. I didn't think anything of it." He rubbed a hand over his jaw. "Did I misread that?" He rolled his eyes. "Fuck, I probably did. I misread everything with her."

"Is there anything else that jumps out at you in retrospect?" Brigid asked. "Anything that struck you as off about her? Any dodgy feelings or intuitions?"

Lee looked off to the side, frowned, then glanced back at the camera. "I don't think it has anything to do with any of this but... I guess I'd say that she's not the dutiful daughter she seems to be."

Carwyn asked, "Why do you say that?"

"I don't know." He frowned. "I just got this feeling whenever she talked about Marie-Hélène. Like... I don't know, it was like a love-hate thing, I think. Maybe that's common with vampires and their sires. I don't know."

"Marie-Hélène is not Chance's sire," Brigid said. "She takes care of her, but she's not Marie-Hélène's blood daughter."

"Huh." Lee nodded. "Well, that's actually kind of a relief."

"Why do you say that?" Carwyn asked.

The human looked directly at the screen. "Because when I think about the way she talked about her, it reminded me of the way people talk about their exes sometimes. It was pretty weird. Like, there are all these mixed feelings. Love, familiarity, but also resentment. Does that make sense?"

Carwyn's heart sank even further. "Yes. I think that makes a lot of sense."

———

"WE NEED to find Chance's human name." Brigid was whispering in the back of their car while they drove to Paladin's lofts. "We need to do a property search."

"Why?"

"It was a feeling I got when I was in her house." She

drummed her fingers on the car door. A spark leaped up and arced to her fingertips, and she smelled the scent of burning wires. "Shit, I think I broke the window again."

"Don't worry about the car. What was the feeling you had in the house?"

"Just that she didn't live there. I mean, she did, but it wasn't her place."

Carwyn frowned. "What do you mean?"

"There was nothing personal. No pictures, no mementos, no evidence of her personality at all." She shook her head. "Every vampire has mementos. Every person does, even if it's just a few yokes, but there was nothin' there. Nothing."

"Like a hotel?"

"Yes, it felt like a hotel."

"Then you're right; she has somewhere else. Probably some place related to her human life."

Brigid looked up at him. "We hav'ta tell Gavin. He might know her human name."

"I know, but will he be at Paladin tonight?"

"He will be if you call him."

"I'll text." Her husband looked as grim as she'd ever seen him. "Everything about this is shit."

"I know." She reached for his hand. "I know."

They pulled into the parking lot at Paladin and saw Ben and Savi standing in the parking lot, waiting for the car. She could see some kind of news nearly bursting from Savi's face. Brigid had the door open before they came to a stop.

"What's up?"

Savi was bouncing up and down. "I got a voice mail! Nic called me! It was hours ago during the day, but no one ever calls me except my parents and I didn't recognize the number, so I didn't think anything of it, it was just a junk call I thought, and I almost deleted it, but then I didn't and I started listening and it was Nic!"

"Fuck a duck." Brigid breathed out a sigh of relief. "Where are they?"

"He doesn't know."

Her heart sank to her toes. "Are you feckin' kidding me?"

"He said it's out in the country somewhere and he's pretty sure it's north of the city and something about birds? He only had a few seconds before the guards came back, he said. But he's okay! They both are, but he apologized because he has to really try to hack the system now because they took Bex. I'm not sure, it was really confusing, but I saved the message." She held up the phone. "You can hear it for yourself."

They walked inside the building, and she saw Carwyn speaking quietly into his phone. Calling Gavin? Possibly. Even if they didn't need information about Chance, Gavin would want to know about this message from Nic.

They hurried upstairs to see Tenzin, Miguel, Kit, and Gaines huddled around an open laptop.

"I loaded it onto my laptop so everyone could hear it," Savi said. "I was so afraid I'd delete it accidentally if I left it on my phone."

Brigid patted the girl's shoulder. "Good thinking. Have you been monitoring the firewalls?"

"I have the whole team on guard right now. I don't know what he's talking about, but we'll be watching."

"Good girl," Carwyn said. "Let's listen to that message."

"You're here." Kit looked up from the laptop. "It's definitely Nic, and I don't think he was coerced or anything, but it's kind of hard to make sense of this message."

"Play it," Brigid said. "From the beginning, full volume."

Miguel bent over, turned the volume on high, and pushed a button.

"Of course it's your voice mail." Nic sounded frustrated. "Okay, maybe this is better. Save this, Oliver! I don't have much time. Bex and I are safe right now, but I've seen their faces and I know what they did to that girl, so they're not going to let me go. They don't know I speak French, but I can understand enough to know what they're trying to do. I'm pretty sure we're still in Louisiana because it smells like it and I know how long I was in the car when we left the farm, but I can't tell what direction. North though, I think from the trees. We're in an old house, two-story with six-paned windows on the ground floor. The trim looks grey and I can see a pond and a big stand of water hickory out my window. There's a pair of scarlet tanagers who've been hanging around. Fuck!" The words tumbled out, his accent getting stronger as he spoke. "The, uh, the wiring for this place is really new and thrown together. Uh..." He paused. "I had this all planned and now I'm forgetting."

Brigid glanced to her right and saw Savi holding back tears.

"I was handling it until they took Bex." Nic's voice cracked. "Tell Gavin I'm sorry, but she's more important than money, so I have to do it. Oliver, I'm gonna do what they want for real now, so I'm going to have to break in. I can't tell what the program is, but I don't think it's going to hurt anyone for now. If I can get me and Bex out of this, I'll fix it."

He paused again, and Brigid heard doors slamming in the background.

Nic continued, his voice growing more panicked. "I don't have much time; try to trace this number; it's a landline. Uh... shit! Sorry. Dammit, none of this should have happened. I got in the car and I shouldn't have, but... I don't know what to tell you, Oliver. It was chance. It was just chance."

The line cut off, and Brigid put her arm around Savi's shoulders.

"I don't know what he means." Savi had started to cry. "I

guess it could have been anyone? He had bad luck? I don't know what he means."

"It was Chance."

Brigid heard a voice behind her and turned to see Gavin standing in the common area, staring at the computer. His face was a careful mask, and fury flashed in his eyes.

He turned his head and met Brigid's gaze. "It was Chance."

TWENTY-SEVEN

The old house in Saint Tammany Parish wasn't accessible except by a single dirt road that led to a two-story farmhouse surrounded by woods. There was a pond behind the house, a broken-down barn, and two horses under a small paddock shelter.

From the woods, the farmhouse appeared like something out of a horror movie. The moon was full, and the ancient trees cast deep shadows onto the pale grey structure. Twin windows like empty eye sockets stared out from the second floor, and the railing that wrapped around the porch was cracked and leaning with age.

Gavin, Brigid, Carwyn, Tenzin, and Ben watched the house, keeping their distance from the guards patrolling outside. There were no lights on in the house, and the silver moonlight illuminated the tall grass and brush that had taken over the yard. Lightning bugs danced in the darkness, sparking as they zoomed between the trees, the long grasses, and the overgrown shrubs around the yard.

"She was human here," Gavin said. "This is the farm where she was born. The farm where she should have died." His face was a blank mask. "Marie-Hélène sent me a telegram that Chantelle was dying. Her favorite. 'My light,' she called her. She was in Europe; she never would have arrived in time. She asked me..."

Carwyn put a hand on his shoulder. "Chance is your child."

His voice was bitter. "I turned her, but she was never mine. She was always Marie-Hélène's. Maybe that was a mistake."

"She's still in New Orleans," Brigid said. "We're only here to get Nic and Bex."

He nodded, but she could see the devastation behind his eyes. "She's fast. If she hears—"

"We can take the house and everyone in it within minutes." Tenzin had already drawn the long, curved knives she fought with from the air. "They are no match for us. If they were, they would have already sensed us."

Ben said, "I spotted six outside when we flew in."

Gavin nodded. "I counted the same, but Tenzin is right. If their amnis was strong, we wouldn't be able to get this close. These are young vampires."

Ben added, "We flew to the woods before I could get anything from inside the house. When we get closer, I'll be able to tell which rooms have electric lines."

Brigid shook her head. "I don't know that we'll have time." She turned to Carwyn. "Can you go underneath?"

He nodded. "The ground here is soft. I can tunnel under the house within a few minutes. Breaking through the floor shouldn't be difficult; the house has a raised foundation."

Brigid stood on her toes and pressed her lips to his in a fast kiss. "Go now. We need to secure Nic and Bex before the guards get a chance to react."

Gavin looked at Tenzin and Ben. "Do you want us from the air?"

"Yes, but wait. I'll distract them in the front. There's dry grass there. I think I can start a fire without it getting out of control if I do a back burn. That will draw them to the front of the property."

"We don't know who these soldiers belong to," Gavin said. "We need some of them alive if we're going to find out who Chance is working with."

Tenzin narrowed her eyes. "We'll try."

Ben put a hand on her shoulder. "We can take some of them alive, Tiny."

"And if Chance shows up," Gavin said. "She's off-limits. She goes to Marie-Hélène; I promised."

Brigid turned to him. "When?"

"Days ago, Brigid." Gavin's voice was clipped. "I haven't tipped her off. Alonzo promised whoever had taken Nic would be brought to Marie-Hélène, and I'm not going to overrule her authority. If Chance is here, we take her alive."

"Fine." Brigid could feel Carwyn beneath her feet, moving under the earth toward the old farmhouse. She crouched down and pressed her hands into the earth.

Ben frowned. "What are you doing?"

She might have been born to fire, but her sire was an earth vampire, and there was a dark energy in this ground that unsettled her. "What is this place?"

"Just an old farm," Gavin said. "Probably around two hundred years old, something like that. It was Chance's family property."

There was a restless energy here, a thread of death and anger that crept beneath her skin. It made her doubly hungry to call the fire.

"I'm going to the front." She stood, keeping the soil beneath her fingernails, rubbing the grit between the pads of her thumb and her fingertips. "They'll pour out like ants from a flood when it starts. Go then. Take 'em out, but like Gavin said, we need a few alive."

"Understood," Ben said. "We'll wait for them to move."

Brigid ran along the edge of the woods that surrounded the house, bending to hide in the tall grass as she reached the front of the property.

There was something else in the ground here, some familiar amnis that pricked at her memory. Was it Chance? It didn't feel like wind energy—it felt like something older.

Brigid bent down and took off her boots to ground her feet in the earth, then flicked her lighter to start a ball of flame. She tossed it back and forth in the humid air, waiting for the moment that felt right.

Two shadows emerged from behind the house, guards patrolling the perimeter.

She tossed the fire into the grass, coiled and ready for the smoke to trigger them. It only took a moment for the flames to grab the thick underbrush and spread.

Brigid stood back, curled her arms around the growing flames, and pushed them toward the house.

———

CARWYN COULD HEAR the shouts and smell the acrid tinge of smoke threading through the air. He was under the house, waiting to hear footsteps, waiting to break through.

Thuds of running feet overhead, clipped orders shouted in a language he couldn't decipher. He waited until the pounding footsteps reached the porch, then lifted himself, pressing his shoulders to the floorboards between the joists.

Crack.

The first floorboard broke, and he paused.

Silence from inside the house.

Carwyn pressed up again, unwilling to wait any longer. He forced the old pine planks up, and thin strips of oak splintered into his face, neck, and shoulders. Shaking his head, he flung the scraps of wood away and launched himself into a dark, silent room where nothing moved but the swing of an old grandfather clock in the corner.

Tick, tick, tick.

He could hear the growing hubbub outside and the shouts that grew more panicked the thicker the smoke became. He reached out with his senses and felt the distinct energy of three humans in the house, two above him and one on the far end of the hallway.

He went with his gut and ran to the entryway and the wide staircase leading to the second floor. There was no way to hide the thundering footsteps, and he prayed that Brigid's distraction worked. He hated taking any life, but in defense of the innocent, he wouldn't hesitate.

The room at the top of the stairs was locked; he shoved his shoulder into the door and it popped open like the top of a tin can. At first he saw nothing, and then a scuffling in the corner drew his attention.

Wide eyes behind horn-rimmed glasses and a mop of curly hair.

Carwyn grinned and ran to Bex, who was already struggling with her bindings.

"There we are, my girl." He snapped the zip ties around her wrists and gently pulled the tape that covered her mouth.

"Nic is here." The words poured out of her mouth. "They brought me to this place, shoved me into his room, and said they'd kill me if he didn't break into Paladin's servers to plant their program."

"Shhh." He rubbed her wrists to get the color back into her hands. "Let's go find him, shall we?"

"He yelled." Bex had tears pouring down her face. "I think they were hurting him. He yelled so loud."

"Come on." Carwyn took the girl by the hand, walked to the door, and paused at the top of the stairs. The smoke was thicker, but there was no activity in the house, and the human on the first floor was gone. "Which way, Bex?" There had to be half a dozen rooms on the second floor.

She turned and headed down a hallway, yelling Nic's name.

"Roland!" She banged on the door next to the one where she'd been kept, but it was locked tight.

Carwyn broke down the door but saw nothing inside. "Not here."

"Roland?" Bex ran to the room across the hall. "Nic?"

Carwyn punched through the door and wrenched it open only to see a massive wall of computer equipment, wires trailing out windows, and a chair with traces of blood on the armrest.

"Oh God." Bex covered her mouth. "Is it Nic's?"

The room was empty save for the monitors and processors humming in the background.

"Find him," Bex said. "I'm going steal the hard drive."

"Will fire destroy it?"

"Yes."

"Then don't bother." Carwyn knew that the fire was heading toward the house. He needed to get the kids out and into the tunnel that led to the woods, but Nic wasn't in this room either.

He followed his nose until he smelled blood. He put a hand on Bex's shoulder. "Stay right here."

Carwyn broke through the door and saw a huddled figure in the corner of the room, leaning against the wall and holding a shoe in his hand. He flung the shoe at Carwyn before the vampire could say a word.

"Nic, it's me!" Carwyn stepped into a shaft of light shining through a high window. "It's Carwyn. I'm here to get you."

The young man crawled from the shadows, and Carwyn immediately saw that Bex had been right. They'd more than hurt him, they'd slashed his face, bloodied his lip, and there was a rough bandage over one eye.

"Bex?" he croaked.

"Oh God!" She was at the door, running to him and throwing her arms around his neck. "What did they do to you?"

He held up both hands, not a scratch on them, and gently wrapped them around her back. "They didn't hurt my hands."

She pulled away. "What—?"

"I only needed one eye to hack though." The tips of his fingers delicately touched the arch of his cheekbone, right below the bandage. "I'll be okay. Just get us out of here."

Animals. Carwyn wanted to rip someone's head from their body, but that wasn't his job right now.

"Let's go." Carwyn crossed the hallway and saw the flames barreling toward the house. Something or someone had taken control of the fire, and it wasn't his mate. "Down to the first floor, you two. There's a tunnel in the salon that will take us to the woods."

Bex helped Nic to his feet and he immediately took her hand, leading her out the door with Carwyn at their backs.

They rushed down the hallway, but Carwyn nearly ran them over when they froze at the top of the stairs. "What are you—?"

"Naughty humans." The vampire curled his lip, baring the fangs that already dripped with blood. "Such a shame we weren't able to finish our game." He raised a gun and pointed it at Bex. "Oh well."

"No!" Nic flung himself in front of Bex just as the gun went off.

TWENTY-EIGHT

The fire wasn't obeying her; it was moving much too fast. While Tenzin, Ben, and Gavin swooped from the sky, picking off one guard after another, Brigid struggled to regain control of the flames.

What was going on? What the hell was happening?

Brigid pulled with all her might, grasping her amnis and wrenching control of the fast-moving flames. Without an intervention of some kind, the fire would sweep toward the house and consume everything between the road and the pond, including the house where Carwyn was searching for Bex and Nic.

She felt it from her feet first, a slithering kind of energy that crept from the ground, up and over her ankles, raising every hair on her body.

There was another fire starter here. A familiar one.

Pieces from the previous weeks fell into place.

He was White. Or she? Maybe it was a she. They had... glow in the dark. Glow-in-the-dark red...

The voice of a traumatized girl in her mind.

"What kind of accent?"

"Maybe... I think it was Russian..."

"Sokholov!" Brigid screamed into the smoky darkness.

Walking through an alley of burning trees, Brigid saw Zasha Sokholov, arms out and hands holding twin flames. The vampire's gold-red hair and luminous face made them look as if they weren't a separate entity at all but that they *were* the fire. They were devastation in immortal form.

This is bad, this is bad, this is bad.

There weren't a massive number of fire vampires in the world, but after meeting this one last year, Brigid had done some research.

Zasha Sokholov had managed to live somewhere between rumor and mystery for hundreds of years. Living mainly in remote parts of Siberia, the immortal was considered an odd and scarcely regarded offshoot of a powerful immortal gang. Until Brigid had met them the year before, she'd had no idea who Zasha was.

No idea the chaos they reveled in.

"Why are you here?" she shouted. "What does any of this—?"

"Not even a hello, dear Brigid?" Zasha shook their head. "It's been over a year, and not even a hello?"

"Hello, Zasha." Ash coated Brigid's face, hopefully hiding her expression. "Did you call Chance or did Chance call you?"

They flicked a hand as if brushing off something distasteful. "Is Chance a person? A vampire? You speak of things beneath my notice."

Brigid was confused. If Zasha wasn't working with Chance, why were they at the farm? What reason could the Sokholovs have to interfere with Marie-Hélène or Gavin?

Zasha looked her up and down. "I see you haven't learned much in the past year. Your amnis isn't going to train itself,

Brigid." They shook their head. "So much potential, and I don't want to have to kill you."

"So leave."

"Leave now?" Zasha stomped their foot a little. "After doing so much to get your attention?"

She stood her ground, unbending to the older vampire's far more powerful presence. That was the problem with Zasha Sokholov: as powerful as Brigid might have been as a fire vampire, Zasha was older, stronger, and seemingly immune to fire. In a direct confrontation, Brigid had no chance.

"What do you want?" Brigid yelled over the dull roar of flames that surrounded them.

"Finally a good question!" Zasha smiled and revealed their sharp, curving fangs that reminded Brigid so much of Tenzin. "I am curious about you, Brigid Connor."

She saw the fire growing, sweeping toward the trees where they had landed. "How did you know I would come?"

"Gavin Wallace is your friend," Zasha said. "And you are married to a man who would save the world. Who else would they call when children go missing?"

"Think you're clever, do ya?"

Zasha began walking toward her again. "Do you think he knows, Brigid?"

"What are you talking about?"

"Do you think your mate knows you don't want to be saved?" Zasha smiled at her, their eyes wide and staring. "You never did."

———

BEX CRADLED Nic on the landing where he'd fallen, blood from the wound in his shoulder soaking her front and dripping down the stairs as Carwyn flung himself at the vampire, knocking the gun from his hand. They tumbled down the stairs, bashing through the railing that splintered like toothpicks snapping between fingers.

Carwyn landed with the vampire on top of him, but he knew the fight would be short. He was young and untrained, probably a water vampire.

The vampire muttered curses in French, but Carwyn simply reached up, took the man's head between his hands, and twisted.

His neck snapped like a twig and he went still. That didn't stop his mouth though.

"Fuck you!"

Carwyn kept to his feet and ran to Bex and Nic. "Get his shirt off!"

Bex looked up with tear-filled eyes. "Don't make him a vampire. He didn't want that."

"I'm not going to turn him, my dear." Carwyn almost laughed. The bullet appeared lodged in Nic's shoulder since it hadn't gone through Bex too. "But my blood can help with the bleeding."

The young man was paler than usual and not speaking. He was clearly in agony.

Bex struggled to find a way to get Nic's shirt off, and then in desperation, she took the torn edges where the bullet had entered and ripped, exposing Nic's torn flesh.

This had to be quick. Carwyn didn't know what had happened to Brigid's plan, but the fire was coming toward the house far faster than he'd anticipated.

"Hold him still."

Carwyn did his best to ignore Nic's grunts of pain as he wiped the wound as clear as possible; then he bit his own wrist, slashing open a vein to let his blood drip into the open wound.

He could see the edges of the wound react to the amnis in

his blood. He looked at Nic, held his gaze steady. "You're not going to die, but this is going to hurt very badly."

Nic clenched his jaw. "Am-amnis."

He raised an eyebrow. "You want me to put you under?"

"You need to be fast. If I struggle—"

"Understood." The young man was smart; he knew that sometimes human instincts didn't understand who was a rescuer and who was a threat. He put a hand on Nic's neck and let his amnis flood the boy's mind.

Nic slumped in Bex's arms immediately.

"Nic!"

"He's fine." Carwyn stood, hoisted the boy over his shoulder, and headed down the stairs. "Let's get you to the woods, then I'll come back for this one." He nudged the shooter with his foot. "He's alive."

Carwyn dropped under the floorboards, helping Bex down with his hand, and directed her toward the tunnel he'd dug beneath the house.

"You did this?"

"I'm an earth vampire, dear." He grunted when he banged his head on a floor joist. "It's one of our favorite pastimes."

Bex shimmied herself into the hole. "Who knew that vampires were really just kids who liked to dig holes for fun?"

"Me." Carwyn felt a tug in his amnis from Brigid. His mate was facing a challenge and she needed him. "Once you get to the bottom, the tunnel should be tall enough for you to stand," he said. "It's dark, but it's clear. If you can run, do it."

He held Nic securely as he dropped to the bottom of the passageway, then followed Bex, wishing with every step he took that the girl had immortal vision because even though the ground was smooth, she was hesitant to go faster than a rapid walk.

He felt the tug from his mate again and resisted the urge to shout.

————

BRIGID FELT naked under their stare, and fury curled her lip. "You don't have any rule but chaos, do you?"

"I have no sire." A muscle in their jaw twitched. "I have no clan. The last child of my line was killed by a little girl in California." Zasha pointed at Brigid. "And your mate helped."

Brigid heard more shouting in the distance and knew that Ben, Tenzin, and Gavin would have taken care of the guards at the house. She hoped beyond hope that Carwyn had gotten the children out. Hoped they were safe in the ground or away from the house.

There was no stopping the fire now; the wind had picked it up and tossed it toward the house, the air above the burning earth a churning mass of ash, smoke, and sparks.

"I'm torn, Brigid." Zasha looked up and sighed, the alley of trees behind them beginning to collapse in on itself. "I want to kill you, but I am also fascinated by you."

"Luck of the Irish, huh?" Brigid looked up, hoping that the wind vampire she saw hovering above the clouds and smoke was a friend. "What do we do now? If you really don't want to kill me, you should leave. Whatever this little game is that you were playing is over."

"It wasn't just me!" Zasha put their hands on their hips. "You act like it was just me. The Ankers are neck-deep in this."

Well, at least they had confirmation about that.

"We know about Chance," Brigid continued. "We know about *you*. We're taking Gavin's people, and all of this is going to burn."

Zasha simply watched her.

"What do you want?" Brigid screamed.

"You never answered my question." They stepped forward, and Brigid backed into the road. "Does Carwyn ap Bryn know the darkness in his mate? He has so many lines he would never cross—does he know yours are a little more... flexible?"

It was as if they'd poked a bleeding wound. "I don't know what you're talking about."

Zasha's eyes gleamed. "You've come close, haven't you? You dabble at human morality—resisting the urge to use power that is rightfully yours—"

"How do you know that?" Brigid felt naked again. Who was this vampire? How did they know her so well?

"—and yet you tiptoe along the edge of control." Zasha stopped walking, and their expression was almost soft. "You love it. Fire, temptation, bloodlust... They're the only things that make you feel alive."

"I'm no monster," she yelled. "I am nothing like you!"

"I never said you were." Zasha smiled. "But you said it. Because deep down, you believe it." They lowered their voice to a snaking whisper that slithered into Brigid's ears. "In your heart, you know what you are."

The shadow swooped down, the curved blade a blurry silhouette in the smoke.

Was it Brigid's eyes that gave her away? Or did Zasha feel the approaching amnis? A second before Tenzin struck, Zasha turned, flinging a spear of flame toward the wind vampire as they ducked and rolled on the blackened ground. Tenzin escaped to the air, disappearing behind billowing black smoke.

Brigid sent a tendril of flame snaking along the ground to grab the fire vampire by the ankles, but Zasha reached out and the flames pulled Brigid's fire and swallowed it whole.

Zasha grinned and threw their head into the sky. "The blood of Temur remembers who you were!"

A pause and the air around them grew utterly still.

What on earth was that?

Then a torrent of wind picked up the flames and swirled them into a churning spear pointing directly at Zasha Sokholov's heart.

The vampire batted the attack away with another burst of fire and a wild laugh, dancing through the burning meadow as if the inferno were nothing more than a spring shower.

The ground beneath Brigid rumbled and she knew Carwyn was coming.

Zasha felt it too. They turned, glared at Brigid, and curled their lip. "Not playing fair inviting friends, Brigid."

The fire vampire turned, ran deeper into the flames, and disappeared as the ground beside Brigid opened up and her mate emerged from the earth.

"Get to the woods!" he shouted at Tenzin. "I'll take Brigid from here."

She closed her eyes, felt the cool earth envelope her like her mate's embrace, and everything went dark.

TWENTY-NINE

Carwyn watched a black sedan pull up to the front of the charred meadow the following night, the smoking farmhouse in the distance. He stood in front with Brigid and Gavin. Tenzin had decided to stay at the ranch, guarding the girl, while Ben stayed in the city, watching over Nic and Bex as Gavin's private doctor treated them at the clinic.

Alonzo exited the vehicle first, quickly walking around to open the door for Marie-Hélène.

Carwyn wasn't surprised to see Chance crawl out of the car behind her.

The play of emotions on the vampire's face was a tapestry of shock, fear, panic, and cunning. "What on earth?" She looked at Marie-Hélène immediately. "What is going on?"

Marie-Hélène's face was a carefully composed mask of caution. "Alonzo, what are we doing at this old house?"

Gavin stepped forward. "I asked him to bring you, and I'm sorry for the secrecy." He made no attempt to hide his emotion when he looked at Chance. "We found them—Nic and Bex."

Chance's eyes locked with Gavin's, but she didn't say a word.

"Oh thank God!" Marie-Hélène burst out. "Where are they? Are they safe? Were they in this fire? What...?" She caught Gavin's eyes staring at Chance. She looked at the woman she loved like a daughter, then back at her old friend. "Why are we here, cher? What is this place?"

Chance's smile was bitter when she looked at the ruins of the house. "You don't even remember, do you?"

"Chantelle, what are you talking about?"

Gavin spoke when Chance didn't answer. "This is Chance's old house, Marie. The house I turned her in. The house she's continued to own, and the place she took Nic and Bex after she discovered we were going to raid the other farmhouse where she'd been keeping them."

Marie-Hélène burst into laughter. "That is the most preposterous thing I've ever heard." She turned to Chance. "Chantelle —" The vampire froze when she saw Chance's expression. "No."

Carwyn could actually feel it in the air when Marie-Hélène's disbelief turned to shock.

And then fury.

"My own daughter?" Marie-Hélène raised her hand and slapped the back of it across Chance's face before Carwyn could blink. Her rings scraped deep cuts into Chance's cheek, and the scent of blood filled the air.

The tension went from simmering to electric.

"Marie." Gavin rushed to Marie-Hélène and grabbed her arm. "Don't—"

Chance cut him off with a burst of laughter. "Oh, now you're interested?" She laughed and she couldn't seem to stop, holding her stomach as blood and tears mingled on her cheeks. "Now you care?"

Marie-Hélène shoved Gavin away. "She is *my* daughter. I told you when you turned her—"

"I am not your daughter!" Chance screamed, and the air whipped around her. "I am not your daughter." She stepped forward and shoved her face in front of Marie-Hélène's. "I. Am not. Your daughter."

Marie-Hélène shook her head. "What are you talking about? Of course you are. Just because I didn't turn you—"

"Oh God." Chance dissolved into bitter laughter that mingled with cries of pain, anger, and shame. She shook her head. "This wasn't supposed to happen. I didn't want any of this to happen. I didn't know anything about the girl. I felt terrible when I..." She grimaced. "I didn't want any of this to happen."

Marie-Hélène's face was a cold mask. "What, exactly, *did* you want to happen, Chantelle?"

Gavin was the one who spoke. "The vampires holding Nic and Bex were hired by the Ankers. We confirmed it late last night and informed Alonzo this morning. He agreed to keep silent about the matter until I could bring you and Chance here." Gavin kept his eyes on Chance. "He agreed that it was better dealt with privately. Out of the city."

"Privately?" Chance couldn't seem to stop laughing. "Oh of course!" She waved a hand at Alonzo, Carwyn, and Brigid. "This is so private, isn't it?"

Brigid stepped forward. "Why did you do it? It was the one thing that never made sense. I didn't want to believe it, Chance. I didn't..." Brigid stopped, overwhelmed by emotion. "I thought we were becoming friends."

"I guess we can break any rule if it means getting our freedom," Chance said. The tears were drying on her face as she looked at Brigid, then at Carwyn. "You two have everything, do you know that?" She looked at Gavin. "And so do you."

"Why, Chance?" Gavin said. "Make me understand."

"I needed the money." The woman's tall figure seemed to

droop like a wilted flower. "Isn't that boring? I needed money. Otto offered a way that seemed to be..." She shrugged. "Easy. No one was supposed to get hurt."

Marie-Hélène scoffed. "What could you possibly have needed money for? You are my daughter. If you needed anything, all you had to do—"

"I'm not your daughter!" Chance laughed again. "Oh God, I love you, but you're so clueless." She turned her eyes to Marie-Hélène. "God, Marie, you are so blind."

Marie-Hélène's eyes widened. "What are you talking about?"

"I loved you. I *love* you. So much. I never wanted to be your daughter. God, maybe if you'd turned me, I would feel that for you." She rubbed a hand over her eyes. "But that's not the way I love you, Marie."

Marie-Hélène stood frozen and speechless, shock evident on her face.

"Do you know what it's like to love someone for so long and have them feel something... *totally* different." Pain radiated from Chance. "To have them always want you nearby but never in the way you need? You would never let me leave you, but I couldn't have you either."

Marie-Hélène frowned with confusion. "Chantelle, you were only ever a daughter to me."

"I know." Chance's voice was bitter. "You think I don't know?" She looked at Gavin. "I wish you'd let me die."

"It would have been better." Gavin's voice was cold. "You could have come to me, Chance. I've always told you if you needed anything—"

"You turned me and then gave me to *her*!" She flung her arm toward Marie-Hélène. "Like a servant. Like a... a *thing*!"

Gavin frowned and shook his head. "You know that's not how it was."

"I gave you everything." Marie-Hélène walked toward her.

"You spoiled child. I gave you *anything* you wanted. A ranch of your own? It's yours. A life away from me? All yours. I never demanded your attention, Chantelle. Never."

"But you leaned on it, didn't you?" Chance swallowed hard. "And I would take the scraps of your affection instead of the alternative."

Carwyn couldn't take any more.

"This is all very tragic." He stepped forward. "But you just said you did this for *money*. I'm assuming so you could be independent of Marie-Hélène and the New Orleans court. Is that right?"

Chance nodded and looked toward the burned house.

"Well, isn't that precious?" Carwyn felt burning anger in his chest. "Only three human girls had to die at the old farm for you to get what you wanted."

Brigid walked to his side. "Lee only had to be blackmailed and his mind violated. Reena was just terrorized and abused. Nic and Bex had to be broken, but after all, Nic only lost *one* eye, didn't he?"

Chance went pale. "Nic lost—"

"All because Otto Anker told you... what?" Carwyn shrugged. "Some kind of business deal?"

"It was a back door into Paladin," Chance muttered. "His programmers had built it, but they needed someone to plant it."

Gavin curled his lip. "My God, Chance."

"All it would have done was scrape a dollar or two from the payment platform for transactions! I just... I needed an income. Something I could depend on, not charity."

"Oh no, not *charity*. How horrible to accept help from willing friends instead of lying and scheming to take what isn't yours!" Carwyn rarely resorted to violence against the weak, but he wanted to hurt Chance. Hurt the selfish creature who had ended and destroyed lives for her own enrichment.

"So much death," he spat out. "For what? Nothing."

Chance's eyes were dead. "Says the priest who's richer than Midas."

"Amadán Mór! You fool," Brigid said. "Did you really think Otto Anker would be content with a few dollars?" She crossed her arms over her chest. "Are you that naive?"

"He could have used that back door for anything," Gavin said. "To spy on Marie and me. To spy on our customers and gain inside information. To track people he wanted to kill. He wouldn't have stopped at a little theft, Chance. That's not how he works."

"I didn't know."

"You should have!" Gavin yelled. "Dammit, Chance, ask the questions! I wish I'd let you die in that house."

"But you didn't." Chance stepped toward him and got in his face. "What now, *Father*? What happens to your only child?"

Gavin's face went cold. "You are not my child. It was a mistake to turn you and a mistake to leave you with Marie. I thought I was doing a kindness."

Chance's eyes shone. "So what now?"

Gavin turned to Marie-Hélène. "Marie-Hélène Charmont, regent of New Orleans, you demanded that when we found the person responsible for Nicolas Cooper's abduction, we give them to you and your judgment." He turned back to Chance. "She is before you."

Marie-Hélène's gaze was impassive. "I will need time to determine your fate. Perhaps a lot of time. Luckily, we have a dungeon that will keep you."

Alonzo stepped forward and took Chance by the arm. He spoke gently, though his expression was grim. "Listen, Chance—"

"No!" Chance flung herself toward Marie-Hélène, a small knife suddenly in her hand.

The vampire queen stood in shock, her eyes wide. Carwyn felt the immediate pull of amnis, but Marie-Hélène was a water vampire, and the air and ground around them was parched from fire.

A flat-tipped machete caught the attacker by the neck, the hand that wielded it moving even faster than a vampire could run. Carwyn blinked and Alonzo stood in front of his mistress, the blade in his hand bloody and his hand holding Chance's arm as her body jerked, then crumpled to the ground.

"God." Gavin clutched a hand to his chest, nearly staggering from the severed amnis linking his and Chance's immortal lives.

Carwyn put an arm around Gavin's shoulders and held him up. "Not here."

"I know."

Brigid ran to Marie-Hélène and stood at the ready. "Madame Charmont?" Her eyes darted from Alonzo to Marie-Hélène, who stood staring at the ground where Chance's eyes looked up at the night sky, lifeless and unseeing.

Alonzo had done what was necessary to protect his queen, but would Marie-Hélène see it the same way?

She reached out, and Alonzo took her hand. "Thank you, my faithful Alonzo."

"My lady." His voice was rough. "I am sorry."

Her eyes closed.

"I had no choice."

"I know." She squeezed his hand. "I know."

––––––––

"SO IT WAS HER?" Reena looked confused. "It was Chance the whole time?"

"She's not the one who took you or held you, but she was

working with the people who did." Brigid sat in a chair opposite the injured girl, playing a game of checkers with her.

"I did not see that one coming." Reena's color was better and the bruises were fading, but her eyes were still wary, and she hadn't met Brigid's gaze the entire time they'd been talking. "Maybe she was the one they hid me from."

"Maybe." Brigid had her own theory about that. Chance had claimed she didn't know about the house, but there was no way she could have visited that house and not smelled the dead bodies. Brigid was fairly sure that the one they'd hid Reena from had been Zasha Sokholov.

But since no one knew where Zasha was, Brigid didn't want to share that news with Reena and worry her needlessly. Zasha didn't know Reena had survived; for now, the vampire was no threat to the girl.

Brigid, on the other hand...

She didn't want to think about that right now, not when Reena was beating her at checkers, Nic and Bex were recovering, and Brigid was attending a fancy society wedding the following night.

"What do you think you want to do when you leave here?" Brigid asked. "Did Marie-Hélène's secretary talk to you?"

Reena frowned. "I don't know. I mean, yeah she did, but she mentioned some scholarship and mentoring program, and I don't know about that. I'm not sure I want one of... them as a mentor." Her hand froze. "No offense."

"None taken." Brigid brushed off the girl's embarrassment. "If I were you, I'd be cautious too. But I'd take the scholarship. The offer is sincere."

"You think?"

"You know Dr. Kaur?"

"Uh, she's basically my roommate here, so yeah."

"She was one of Marie-Hélène's girls."

Reena finally looked up. "Really?"

Brigid nodded. "Her family is hardworkin' but not rich. Dr. Kaur excelled in school and was also a promising classical musician. Someone mentioned her talent to Marie-Hélène, and she offered her a scholarship to school and took an interest in her schooling and career."

"And now Jauna works for vampires."

"Is that her first name? Jauna? That's lovely." Brigid made another move and immediately realized Reena could take two of her pieces.

Dammit. This game was impossible.

Reena immediately removed those two pieces from the board. "You're avoiding the question."

"Yes, you might end up working for Marie-Hélène, but lots of people do." Brigid sat back. "That's the secret of vampires, you know? We need humans far more than humans need us."

"Uh yeah. Like for food."

"For everything." Brigid kept her eyes on the girl, hoping she'd look up. "Blood is the least important thing humanity offers us, Reena. You keep us honest about our weaknesses. You keep us humble." She remembered Zasha's taunts. "Without connection to humanity, any one of us could become pretty monstrous."

Reena looked up and frowned a little. "Didn't you want to be a vampire?"

"No, but that's life, isn't it? You never know what it might throw at you."

Reena looked up. "Yeah."

Their eyes met in a moment of understanding before Reena looked at the board again.

"I may not have wanted this life," Brigid continued, "but I'm making the best of it." She leaned forward and made another move. "Give me another hundred years and I might even be able to play a decent game of checkers."

"Mmmm." The corner of Reena's mouth inched up. "You're immortal, right?"

"Brat!" Brigid laughed. "Okay, maybe two hundred."

THIRTY

Brigid stared at the brilliant blue cloak hanging from the wardrobe in the corner of their room. "What is it?"

"God, your education." Carwyn pursed his lips. "Damn the British. It's a *brat*, darling girl." The word was pronounced more *brot* than *brat*. "Have you truly never seen one before?"

"It's a cloak?" She frowned and held out the fabric to examine it. "A fancy one. Is this what I'm wearing? It's very nice."

"Nice?" He stood and walked over to the wardrobe. "The brat was the cloak of cloaks, outlawed by the queen! An item of clothing so dangerous it was spoken of in hushed tones and songs were written about it."

She pursed her lips and tried to hold back the smile. "It's a cloak."

"It's... Oh here, just put it over your shoulders and be glad I decided on Irish clothing and not Welsh for tonight."

"I don't even know what traditional Welsh dress looks like. Jumpers and wellies, all in bright red?"

"Stovepipe hats. Are you grateful yet?"

"Stovepipe whats?"

It was the night of Gavin and Chloe's wedding, and their

clothing had arrived by courier from Dublin two nights before. Carwyn had been starting to worry, but the brats he'd ordered were as magnificent as he'd imagined.

His own was a deep forest green with a red plaid fringe over the right shoulder that made his chest look even broader than it already did. Brigid's was a deep blue with a saffron lining, scalloped edges, and a fringe of shaggy black trim that draped over her right shoulder like some mythical pelt.

Both brats were fastened with heavy pewter brooches, Carwyn's with a Welsh dragon and Brigid's with a silver harp.

Under the brat, Brigid wore a pair of dark blue fitted breeches, a loose léine shirt in saffron yellow to match the trim of her cloak, and a belt to keep the léine snug around her waist. He'd considered ordering a traditional dress for her but knew his wife would much prefer the flexibility of men's dress.

He watched her fix her cloak with the broach, then turn to the long mirror in the corner. Her chin lifted as she examined herself.

"There is something about it, isn't there?" Her eyes gleamed. "I feel like I need a short sword and a club to hang from my belt."

"Sadly, not allowed at the wedding, but I do have one more thing to add." He reached into his top drawer and retrieved the box he'd ordered from a jeweler in Galway. "What Irish warrior doesn't have a torque to strike fear into the hearts of vile invaders?"

He stood behind her and slowly bent the silver torque into shape around her slender neck. It was twisted wire in fine silver, the terminals made of cast silver serpents with green emerald eyes.

Her lips parted, and she touched the tips of her fingers to the serpent heads. "Carwyn, mo ghrá. This is too much."

"No." He ran his fingers over the shining silver. "Someone

reminded me recently that I have more money than Midas, and I wanted to spend some on my wife. This is perfect."

"I look..." Her eyes couldn't seem to leave her reflection in the mirror.

Stunning, Carwyn thought. Gorgeous. Powerful. Dangerous. "So you don't mind the old-fashioned clothes?"

"I look like a complete badass."

"You really feckin' do." He grinned and lifted her by the waist to set her on the edge of their bed. "Do you know one of the reasons that the brat was banned by the English invaders?"

She turned and ran her hands over his wool-covered shoulders. "Why?"

He parted her mantle and ran his hands up the inside of her thighs. "Apparently a couple could hide any number of lurid acts behind a good cloak."

"I hadn't even thought about that." Brigid gasped and arched her back when his hands reached the juncture of her thighs. "Do you suppose we should test the quality of this cloak? We wouldn't want to wear defective garments to such an important event."

"I think a quality test is absolutely essential before an event such as a society wedding." He hooked his fingers under the waistband of her breeches and tugged them down. "Just stay standing there, my lovely bride. Let me try this cloak out."

Brigid stood on the edge of the bed and braced her hand on Carwyn's shoulder, her right hand clutching his hair. "I must demand a very thorough test, you know. I take quality control very seriously."

He licked up the sweetness gathering between her thighs and savored the tug of her fingers in his hair. "As do I."

She smiled down at him, her lips already swollen with desire. "Dangerous garments, these cloaks."

"You have no idea." Carwyn turned his mouth back to her

sex and feasted.

———

STUNNING. The whole ceremony was stunning but especially the bride and groom.

Gavin and Chloe's wedding of the century was held in a breathtaking cathedral in the center of New Orleans.

The priest was an old friend of Carwyn's and had been flown in from the special office in Rome that liaised very unofficially with immortal persons in the church. The bride and groom had arrived by carriage as the moon rode over the cool New Orleans night.

The guests were clad in every formal attire imaginable, from the Italian Renaissance finery of Beatrice and Giovanni to the elegant Chinese imperial dress Ben wore as a nod to his mate and sire.

Marie-Hélène herself appeared as royalty, escorted by two of her human attendants and adorned in jewels and a diamond-studded tiara, watching the wedding mass from the front row next to the bride's closest friends.

Orange, plum, and toffee-brown flower arrangements surrounded the altar as Chloe Reardon and Gavin Wallace exchanged vows in front of four hundred of their close friends, family, business associates, and very large numbers of vampire security.

The bride was dressed in a custom gown with intricate lace that covered her arms, shoulders, and neck. The groom was resplendent, wearing a dress kilt in Wallace plaid of hunter green and black.

The wedding mass had come to its end, and Gavin and Chloe's hands were clasped together as Gavin solemnly wrapped a green-and-black-plaid ribbon around their wrists.

The priest read out in a broad Scottish brogue: "Let this binding remain for as long as love endures. Let the vows you have spoken never grow bitter in your mouths. Hold one to the other through good times and bad, and may this company bear witness as your strength and unity grow ever greater through the passage of time, however long that time may be. In the joining of hands and the fasting of this knot, so are your lives and souls now bound, one to the other."

Chloe looked up and her smile was brilliant.

Gavin couldn't seem to look away.

Brigid was having a hard time relaxing in a confined space with so much amnis bouncing around. She'd be grateful when the ceremony was over and they could retreat en masse to Marie-Hélène's Bonnevue estate.

She looked over and saw her own husband's eyes glistening with unshed tears.

Oh, how she adored this giant sap of a man.

"I remember when she was in school," he whispered.

Brigid reached over and clasped his hand in her own.

"...so are your lives and souls now bound."

Yes, and yes again. Every night unto eternity.

"Amen," said the priest.

Amen.

———

SHE COULDN'T STOP TRACKING Alonzo, who appeared to be more stressed than ebullient. Then again, juggling a gathering of this many immortals without anyone resorting to violence on a private estate in the middle of New Orleans was a feat for the ages.

Brigid sipped a glass of red wine. "Poor Alonzo needs a holiday after this."

Carwyn smiled. "He'll never take one unless Marie-Hélène does."

"You'd never know from looking at them."

He shook his head. "She is the consummate politician."

While Chance's absence was conspicuous to those who knew what had happened, she wasn't missed by many outside Marie-Hélène's inner circle. The vampire had been the private sort, so the lack of her presence wasn't noted that night.

It would be. Eventually questions would be asked, but by then, Marie-Hélène would have a likely story that couldn't be tied to infiltration by the Anker clan or the mysterious presence of a Sokholov enforcer.

Brigid was still trying to put things together with Nic and Bex. Raj and Alonzo had confirmed that the vampires hired to hold Nic and Bex were contractors associated with the Ankers, but the human hacker who had been staying at the farm had disappeared with Zasha Sokholov, leaving Gavin on the defensive with Paladin and Nic scouring their servers to see what damage had been done.

"Stop." Carwyn squeezed her shoulders. "I can see your mind racing, but tonight is for celebrating."

"I know." She looked up and stood on her tiptoes to press a kiss to his cheek. "But cheers for the reminder."

Ben and Tenzin looked as distracted as Brigid felt. The two vampires had been busy taking care of the human employees at Paladin, ensuring that Gaines was brought up to speed, checking the server security, and seeing to Bex's and Nic's medical needs.

They both looked uncomfortable in their formalwear, but Tenzin was the only one pulling at her collar.

"It itches."

"It's silk." Ben batted her hand away. "Stop messing with it. Do you want Arthur to have to measure you again?"

The look she shot her mate promised death, but she stopped tugging.

The grounds outside Bonnevue were a fairy-tale landscape of lights in the trees, succulent feasts the vampire guests would only sample, and music and dancing until dawn. Security details circled the estate to ensure privacy as a temporary reprieve from conflict led to a surprisingly relaxed environment.

"I think Bonnevue is as bad as Penglai," Tenzin muttered. "Only with more feather hats and less formality."

Carwyn nodded. "I do love a good feather hat."

Ben smirked. "And the political theater is just as amusing."

Brigid saw more than one discreet handshake and knew that business was being conducted during the general festivity surrounded by opulence. Perhaps that had been the intention all along.

"Chloe's going to be shattered." Brigid caught a glimpse of her through the paned windows of the mansion. "Do you think she knows half of what's happening in there?"

The bride and groom were holding court in the front salon, and a river of immortals presented themselves as well-wishers, all offering gifts and vying to outdo each other in their generosity to Gavin Wallace and his lovely human bride.

"She knows enough now." Carwyn watched the goings-on with interest, ever the protective uncle. "And she's good at faking it when she doesn't. Gavin will fill her in. She's part of this world now."

"She has been for a long time," Tenzin said.

Ben's eyes were a little sorrowful. "Sometimes I still wonder—"

"Don't." Tenzin touched his arm and motioned to the window. "Look how happy she is."

Ben narrowed his eyes. "Did that vampire just give her a crown?"

Tenzin's eyes lit up. "A crown?"

"No." Ben grabbed her hand. "Absolutely not. Don't even think about it."

Tenzin whispered, "Too late."

Carwyn was still watching Chloe with worried eyes.

"She'll be fine." Brigid squeezed his hand again. "None of this has touched her, Carwyn. Not even a hint."

Though Brigid was sure Gavin would be grateful when the both of them were back in New York in more familiar territory.

Alonzo walked into the salon and bent to Marie-Hélène's ear. The vampire queen of New Orleans gave him a nod that told Brigid nothing. The lieutenant might have been reporting a security breach, informing on a problem guest, or telling his mistress she looked stunning in purple.

Marie-Hélène's face gave nothing away.

"Do you think it was a good idea?" Ben asked. "To loop Paladin's security into Marie-Hélène's organization?"

"I think as good as Gaines is, he's human." Brigid sipped her wine again. "And when you're mortal, there are certain threats you simply don't anticipate."

Carwyn muttered, "No one expects betrayal from those they love the most."

"True." Brigid nodded. "I suppose that's what makes trust the most precious commodity in our world."

"To be trusted is a greater compliment than being loved." Ben smiled at Tenzin. "Someone very wise told me that once."

"Me," Tenzin said. "I told him that."

"Really?" Carwyn glanced at Tenzin. "I never would have guessed."

Brigid smiled and looked back at Chloe and Gavin. What had Chloe said? As long as she was married by the end of the night, she'd consider the whole event a success?

Mission accomplished.

THIRTY-ONE

Two days later...

Brigid leaned on the table, standing next to Gavin and as far away from the computers as she could while still seeing the screen. Nic was still pale, but his cheeks weren't hollow, and he'd swapped the ratty bandage over his eye for a fitted patch that made him look more like a pirate than a crime victim.

Savi was next to him, murmuring in the foreign language of code that was still incomprehensible to Brigid, but with Bex at Nic's left-hand side, Miguel and Kit hovering around them, she at least felt like she'd brought this small family of friends back together.

Nic turned and spoke to Brigid and Gavin. "Savi and I have found the breach and patched it, but they still got far enough into the firewalls to understand their structure."

Savi continued, "I can start over again, but it will push the project back. On the other hand, we can accept that at some point, whoever the Ankers hired would have hacked far enough into the firewalls to understand their structure anyway. We were always going to face this threat."

Gavin's stare was intent. "And there's no way of remaking them?"

"Yes," Savi said. "By starting over. It will be a long delay."

Gavin didn't look pleased with either option.

"Computers are a dynamic battleground," Kit said softly. "There will never *not* be a threat on the horizon." They shrugged. "At least we know what they were after."

"You think it was just the payment scrape?" Gavin asked.

Savi bit her lip. "That's all we're seeing at the moment, but..."

"No." Nic was blunt. He turned and met Gavin's examining gaze with his one remaining eye. "What is money to a vampire? From what you've said about the Ankers, I think the real motivation would have to be data."

Information was more valuable than gold in their world.

Brigid nodded. "I agree. The way you described this secret door, they could have returned and altered other parts of the operating system or the..." She motioned toward the computers. "...the memory banks—"

"Servers." All five humans corrected her.

"Yes, those." She looked at Gavin. "What's more valuable? Money or the combined information from your clients that you and Marie-Hélène will eventually hold in trust?"

Brigid was starting to be more and more convinced that the device she tucked in her pocket was not worth the convenience it offered, and she should probably toss it in the Mississippi on the way back to California. She trusted Murphy and Nocht, but did she trust his security and his ability to hold back the insatiable vampire appetite for secrets?

Bex turned to look at them, and Brigid could see the shadows of her captivity in her eyes. "These people, they're not going to stop, and they've already proven they're willing to do nearly anything to get Paladin's secrets." Her hand shook, and

Nic reached over and took it in his. "I don't even know if I want to work here anymore. No offense, Gavin."

"None taken." He stared at the girl. "You were my responsibility, and I didn't take care of you. I will carry that guilt for the rest of my life, but I will learn from it. I promise."

Nic squeezed his right hand into a fist. "Hey." He looked at Gavin. "I think Alonzo is a giant asshole, but making Gaines work with him is a good idea. I'm here. I won't speak for Bex, but I'm here. And I promise you we can make this work, and we can make it even more secure than Nocht."

If anything, Brigid thought the young man looked even more determined than when she'd met him.

"If you're still in, so am I," Bex said. "If you're sure."

"I'm sure." Nic turned back to the computers. "I'll get back to work now. When you talk to Lee, tell him we could use him back on the project if he wants."

The paladins turned back to their digital battleground, Kit and Miguel pulling out their own laptops while Savi and Nic collaborated over one screen. Brigid turned toward the stairs and started walking out. Her job was done, and she'd be billing the hell out of Gavin Wallace when she got back to California.

"Hey, Brigid!"

She turned and saw Bex walking toward her.

"How are ya feelin'?" Brigid waited for the young woman to reach her at the top of the stairs. "Your color is better."

"Physically? Better. The other stuff..." She shrugged.

"It takes time. Don't be shy about seeking trauma therapy. It really does help." She sensed there was something else the girl wanted to talk about. "How's Nic? Other than the eyes, any permanent damage?"

"Not according to the doctors." She looked at the ground and frowned.

"What's on your mind?"

"Nic jumped in front of a bullet for me." Bex looked at the heavily bandaged young man on the other side of the loft, then crossed her arms over her chest. "How am I supposed to process that?"

"You don't process it," Brigid said. "You accept that someone exists in the world who cares more about your safety than his own life."

Bex looked to the side. "And then what?"

"Then you're grateful that person exists," Brigid said. "And that they love you in such a tangible and powerful way."

Bex bit her lip. "Even if they don't say it?"

Poor thing. Brigid looked at Nic, then back to Bex.

"Sometimes," she started, "love doesn't come to us the way we expect it. That doesn't mean it's not real."

Nic kept glancing over his shoulder at Bex and Brigid, clearly unhappy that Bex was so far away from him.

Brigid smiled. "You think I dreamed of a redheaded giant with a jackhammer voice and an extensive Hawaiian shirt collection?"

Bex returned the smile. "Probably not, but I think he's pretty great."

"Aye, he's the best man in the world. Even if he is Welsh and a vampire." She nodded toward Nic. "He wants you back. You're making him nervous being so far away."

She glanced at Nic, and the corner of her mouth turned up. "Yeah?"

"Yeah. Put him out of his misery soon, will ya? Even if he has trouble saying the words, I think you know how he feels. He just needs to hear it from you."

"Yeah." Bex loosened her arms and her tense stance. "Thanks for everything. Thanks for finding us."

"I'm glad I could help. So you're staying?"

"Yeah," Bex said. "For now, yeah."

Brigid stuck out her hand. "Best of luck. Don't go shaking hands with strange vampires, all right?"

"Does that get me out of shaking hands with your husband?"

"Ha!" It felt foreign to laugh, but it was good.

It was good.

Brigid pointed at Bex. "I'm going to tell him you said that."

"Good." Bex's eyes were a little bit lighter. "See you around, Brigid."

Brigid gave her a small salute. "See ya round."

———

THEY TOOK the freeway to Baton Rouge, then headed north into rural Louisiana and Arkansas to camp in some beautiful, untouched places where no one could reach them. They visited caves that Carwyn had been itching to explore. They played in mountain streams and relaxed under moonlit swimming holes that teemed with life. Brigid lit numerous campfires that didn't burn out of control.

The solitude fed Brigid's soul, so by the time they returned to Oklahoma City to visit Lee Whitehorn and give him an update, she was feeling rested, easy, and didn't want to snap anyone's neck. She also had a much clearer memory of the night the farmhouse burned.

"Carwyn?"

"Hmm?" He glanced across the cab of their camping van. "No, you can't drive. I just managed to fix the instrument panel from the last time."

"I don't want to drive." They were only an hour outside Oklahoma City. Could she really break their van in an hour's time?

Probably.

"Do you know what 'the blood of Temur' means?"

Carwyn frowned. "In what context?"

"Zasha Sokholov shouting it at Tenzin, I think."

"I don't know, love. Giovanni might."

"It's probably not important."

The frown didn't leave his face. "We live in a world of long memory, Brigid, and Tenzin has made more than her share of enemies."

"I know." She turned her eyes back to the road. "Not our concern."

"Not our concern." He pursed his lips. "Zasha Sokholov, on the other hand..."

"Yes."

"That vampire is obsessed with you."

"*Obsessed* seems like a strong word."

"I don't think it is."

She looked at him. "I don't know why they would be."

"Don't you?" He glanced at her. "There aren't many of your kind, but somehow this vampire feels a tie to you. I want to know why."

"We'll be on the lookout," Brigid said. "That's all we can do right now. I have no desire to entangle myself with the Sokholovs any more than we already have."

"Like I said, darlin' girl. We live in a world of long memories." He reached over and took her hand. "I have a feeling we'll see Zasha again."

———

Oklahoma City

"SO IT'S OVER?" Lee sat in his kitchen again, still looking as uncomfortable as the first time they'd met. "I can tell my elder it's over?"

"The threat from Chance is over. Marie-Hélène's people

304

examined Chance's computers and found the pictures she'd taken of you," Brigid said. "They're all destroyed; it appears she was the one blackmailing you."

Carwyn added, "The people she was directly working with have been eliminated, but their bosses are still active in Europe. However, we don't think they have any interest in you or your family."

Lee shook his head. "I never would have thought..." He stared at the table. "I guess you never really know people."

"She fooled everyone," Brigid said. "Even the humans and vampires closest to her. It's no reflection on you. If it's any consolation, I don't think she ever expected things to get so out of control. She pushed herself into a corner by teaming up with the Ankers. They used her like she used you."

"It doesn't make me feel any better, but I guess I feel a little sorry for her." He glanced up. "Thanks for letting me know. I'm glad it's over."

"How are you?" Brigid asked. "How are ya feeling now?"

The lines of worry on the man's face had only grown deeper, and Brigid could see silver along the edge of his hairline. This ordeal had aged Lee Whitehorn faster than Brigid would have expected, and she could see he was still recovering from the loss of control.

"I'm dealing with it," Lee said. "Can't say I'm real happy with work. After the initial relief of not working with any vampires, it's pretty damn boring. Being back here?" He shrugged. "It's fine, but I left for a reason, you know? Wanted to strike out on my own if that makes sense."

Carwyn was quick to say, "Of course that makes sense."

Brigid could tell he was an independent person; it probably irritated him to feel like he was being watched over all the time. There were still guards outside his house, and she could feel the amnis surrounding them.

"I can tell you the crew at Paladin would love to have you back," Carwyn added. "Nic said so. They have a lot of work to do."

Lee shook his head. "I don't want to go back to New Orleans. Not ever. No offense to Nic or anyone on that team, but it's not for me. I want..." He huffed. "I want something new, but I have no idea what." He smiled a little. "Not your problem. I'll figure it out. I appreciate the in-person visit."

An idea struck Brigid, and she probably should have asked Carwyn first, but she went with her gut. "Have you ever been to California?"

Lee looked up. "No. What... I mean, why do you ask? I'm familiar with Silicon Valley, obviously, but I don't know much about the place otherwise."

Carwyn jumped in, picking up her cue immediately. "Do you like forests, Lee? Isolated houses in the woods where there's not much nightlife but there are very adorable bear cubs you're not allowed to play with?"

Brigid looked at him. "Don't bring up the bears."

"I'm just letting him know the general atmosphere." Carwyn looked back at Lee. "It's quiet, there's solitude, and you could buy whatever equipment you wanted."

Lee was still confused. "Do you have a software company or something?"

"Jaysus no," Brigid said. "But the work we do... It's recently come to my attention that every device we have, every time we make a call or do a search on a tablet, that can all be traced, can't it?"

"On a mobile device, even one running Nocht, which is pretty secure, sure. A determined hacker could get into your phone."

"But we need to find information," she said. "We need to be

able to search government databases, find property ownership, look through court records, things like that."

"Are you saying you need a tech guy to hack into private and government servers?"

Carwyn pursed his lips. "*Hacked* is a complicated word. Think of yourself as an information-retrieval specialist."

Brigid added, "For the good guys."

"And" —Lee looked between them— "*you're* the good guys?"

"Obviously."

"Lee, I'll be honest. We have no idea how most of the computer world works," Carwyn said. "When we need to look something up, we mostly use the voice assistance on our phones."

"Oh my God." Lee looked horrified. "You know that can all be traced, right?"

"I don't know what tracing our phones would mean or how one would go about doing it," Carwyn said. "I'm a thousand years old."

"And I was shite in school," Brigid said. "I used to be computer literate, but that was about ten years ago."

Lee was watching them with wide eyes. "What do you guys actually do?"

Brigid said, "We help people."

Carwyn leaned forward on the table. "Brigid and I don't owe our allegiance to anyone but ourselves, so when humans or vampires need help, we do our best."

Lee's eyes jumped between Carwyn and Brigid. "So you used to be a priest." He pointed to Carwyn.

"Yes." He nodded toward Brigid. "And she has an overdeveloped sense of justice and a hatred for bullies."

Lee nodded. "I can respect that."

"What do you say?" Brigid asked him. "Big trees, lots of fog, and not many vampires."

Carwyn whispered, "And fat, adorable bear cubs."

She didn't say a word, but she smacked her husband's thigh with the back of her hand.

Lee sat back in his chair and the corner of his mouth turned up. "Yeah." He nodded a little bit. "I might be willing to give that a try."

"Excellent." Brigid smiled. "When can you start?"

———

Still hungry for the Elemental Universe?
Catch up with Ben and Tenzin in their all-new story, PEARL SKY, coming December 2022.

———

And return for Brigid and Carwyn's next adventure in BISHOP'S FLIGHT, an all-new Elemental Covenant novel coming summer of 2023.

ACKNOWLEDGMENTS

Every time I do this I think: I don't know how I can keep thanking the same people over and over again. Then I think, I'd be kind of a cruddy person NOT to thank them, so I better figure out how to do it.

I'm eternally grateful to my readers who make all this worth the time, mental stress, and effort. Seeing you at signings, interacting with you online, and seeing your lovely notes and emails is extraordinarily inspiring and has really gotten me through more than one hard day.

I'm grateful to my sister who acts as my assistant, sounding board, and often the more responsible adult in the room. At least, that's what I tell myself when we decide that working some afternoons just isn't a good use of our time and we really need to watch Ted Lasso again for our mental health.

Thanks, Ted Lasso.

And thanks to all the regular crew that make the books happen. Thanks to Bee Whelan and Amy Cissell, who make my stories better. Thanks to Damonza who gives me gorgeous covers. Thanks to Anne and Linda at Victory Editing who make sure I don't embarrass my English degree. And thanks to everyone at Dystel, Goderich, and Burrell, and all those at Valentine PR who get my work out to the world.

And really, thanks, Ted Lasso.

LOOKING FOR MORE?

Whether you're a fan of contemporary fantasy, fantasy romance, or paranormal women's fiction, Elizabeth Hunter has a series for you!

THE ELEMENTAL MYSTERIES

Discover the series that has millions of vampire fans raving! Immortal book dealer Giovanni Vecchio thought he'd left the bloody world of vampire politics behind when he retired as an assassin, but a chance meeting at a university pulls student librarian Beatrice De Novo into his orbit. Now temptation lurks behind every dark corner as Vecchio's growing attachment to Beatrice competes with a series of clues that could lead to a library lost in time, and a powerful secret that could reshape the immortal world.

Ebook/Audiobook/Paperback

THE CAMBIO SPRINGS MYSTERIES

Welcome to the desert town of Cambio Springs where the water is cool, the summers sizzle, and all the residents wear fur, feathers, or snakeskin on full moon nights. In a world of cookie-cutter shifter romance, discover a series that has reviewers raving. Five friends find themselves at a crossroads in life; will the tangled ties of community and shared secrets be their salvation or their end?

Ebook/Audiobook/Paperback

THE IRIN CHRONICLES

"A brilliant and addictive romantic fantasy series." Hidden at the crossroads of the world, an ancient race battles to protect humanity, even as it dies from within. A photojournalist tumbles into a world of supernatural guardians protecting humanity from the predatory sons of fallen angels, but will Ava and Malachi's attraction to each other be their salvation or their undoing?

Ebook/Audiobook/Paperback

GLIMMER LAKE

Delightfully different paranormal women's fiction! Robin, Val, and Monica were average forty-something moms when a sudden accident leaves all three of them with psychic abilities they never could have predicted! Now all three are seeing things that belong in a fantasy novel, not their small mountain town. Ghosts, visions, omens of doom. These friends need to stick together if they're going to solve the mystery at the heart of Glimmer Lake.

Ebook/Audiobook/Paperback

And there's more! Please visit ElizabethHunterWrites.com to sign up for her newsletter or read more about her work.

ABOUT THE AUTHOR

ELIZABETH HUNTER is a nine-time *USA Today* and international best-selling author of romance, contemporary fantasy, and paranormal mystery. Based in Central California and Addis Ababa, she travels extensively to write fantasy fiction exploring world mythologies, history, and the universal bonds of love, friendship, and family. She has published over forty works of fiction and sold over a million books worldwide. She is the author of the Glimmer Lake series, Love Stories on 7th and Main, the Elemental Legacy series, the Irin Chronicles, the Cambio Springs Mysteries, and other works of fiction.

ELIZABETHHUNTERWRITES.COM

ALSO BY ELIZABETH HUNTER

The Devil and the Dancer

Night's Reckoning

Dawn Caravan

The Bone Scroll

Pearl Sky (December 2022)

The Elemental Covenant

Saint's Passage

Martyr's Promise

Paladin's Kiss

The Irin Chronicles

The Scribe

The Singer

The Secret

The Staff and the Blade

The Silent

The Storm

The Seeker

Glimmer Lake

Suddenly Psychic

Semi-Psychic Life

Psychic Dreams

Moonstone Cove

Runaway Fate

Fate Actually

Fate Interrupted

Vista de Lirio

Double Vision

Mirror Obscure

Trouble Play

The Cambio Springs Series

Long Ride Home

Shifting Dreams

Five Mornings

Desert Bound

Waking Hearts

Linx & Bogie Mysteries

A Ghost in the Glamour

A Bogie in the Boat

Contemporary Romance

The Genius and the Muse

7th and Main

Ink

Hooked

Grit

Sweet

Made in the USA
Middletown, DE
09 November 2022